完全剖熙
新制多益

聽力、閱讀、口說高效應考指南

申芷熙 Dr. Estella Chen ——著
Judd Piggott ——審訂

自序

在這些年來，我有幸與許多準備多益考試的考生交流，並見證了他們的努力與挑戰。多益作爲一項國際化的英語能力測試，不僅是求職者的利器，也是不少人進修與提升英語能力的重要目標。

這本書的特色在於三個關鍵點：

1. 深入剖析試題結構

書中針對多益的聽力、閱讀、口說與寫作四大部分，逐一拆解各種題型與其背後的考察重點。我們不僅提供解題技巧，還會引導讀者了解試題設計的邏輯，幫助你站在命題者的角度思考，從而更有把握地應對考試挑戰。

2. 強調實戰應用

理論固然重要，但實戰經驗更是高分的關鍵。書中提供了大量模擬試題與練習，並附上詳細解析，讓讀者能夠在練習中逐步提升應考能力。此外，書中還收錄如何利用加強口說策略增進聽力技巧，更提供英國澳洲腔的範例，爲讀者提供多項的學習資源。

3. 打造高效學習計劃

時間有限是每位考生的共同難題。因此，我在書中設計了一套靈活的多益高頻單字背誦計畫，無論是全職學生還是在職人士，都能根據自身時間安排，有效完成備考目標。

最後，送給所有努力中的考生一句話：學習的道路或許崎嶇，但每一步的堅持都會成爲你未來成功的基石。讓我們一起踏上這段挑戰與成長的旅程，向著多益高分的目標邁進！

祝各位考生旗開得勝，前程似錦！

申芷熙老師
Dr. Estella Chen
Estella Chen

完全剖熙新制多益：
聽力、閱讀、口說高效應考指南

Contents

自序	002
音檔使用說明	004
本書使用說明	005

第 1 章
了解多益考試 006
1-1　TOEIC 考試簡介　008
1-2　TOEIC 準備技巧　014
1-3　TOEIC 作答技巧　015

第 2 章
詞彙擴展 018
2-1　多益考試的基本詞彙　020
2-2　學習並記住新詞彙的技巧　028
2-3　字根、字首和字尾　031

第 3 章
文法基礎知識 040
3-1　多益試題的關鍵語法規則　042
　　　新制多益模擬試題　062
3-2　改善句子結構和清晰度的技巧　078

第 4 章
口說和發音 080
4-1　用口說練出聽懂的能力　082
4-2　英澳腔的基礎加強版　085
4-3　辦公室常見句型練習　088

第 5 章
聽力部分解題攻略 096
5-1　Part 1 照片描述　098
　　　新制多益模擬試題　106
5-2　Part 2 應答問題　114
　　　新制多益模擬試題　117
5-3　Part 3 簡短對話　126
　　　新制多益模擬試題　132
5-4　Part 4 簡短獨白　142
　　　新制多益模擬試題　147

第 6 章
閱讀部分解題攻略 156
6-1　Part 5 句子填空　158
　　　新制多益模擬試題　162
6-2　Part 6 段落填空　170
　　　新制多益模擬試題　174
6-3　Part 7 閱讀測驗　188
　　　新制多益模擬試題　197

第 7 章
新制多益模擬試題一回 214
新制多益模擬試題一回解答、翻譯和解說　263

音檔
使用說明

STEP 1

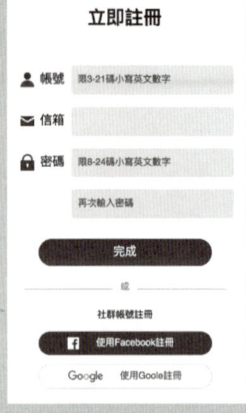

掃描書中 QRCode

STEP 2

快速註冊或登入 EZCourse

STEP 3

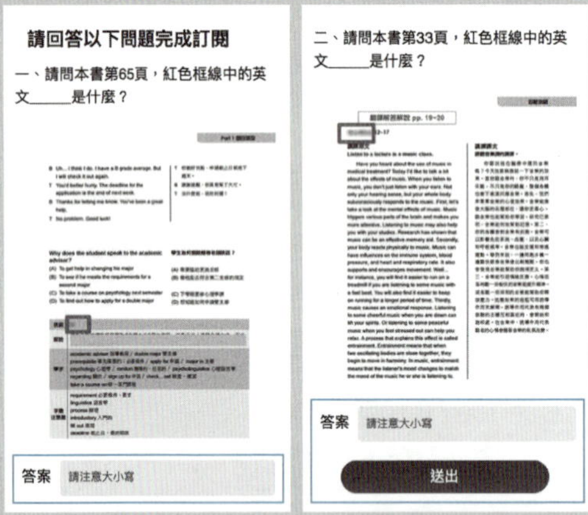

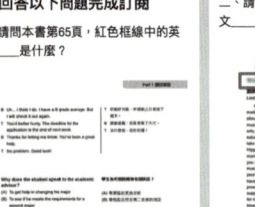

一、請問本書第65頁，紅色框線中的英文＿＿＿＿是什麼？

回答問題按送出

答案就在書中（帶注意空格與大小寫）。

STEP 4

二、請問本書第33頁，紅色框線中的英文＿＿＿＿是什麼？

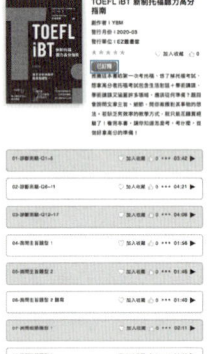

完成訂閱

該書右側會顯示「已訂閱」，
表示已成功訂閱。
即可點選播放本書音檔。

STEP 5

點選個人檔案

查看「我的訂閱紀錄」
會顯示已訂閱本書，
點選封面可到本書線上聆聽。

本書使用說明

STEP 1 先快速**掌握題型**與解題技巧說明。

STEP 2 解題技巧教學提供**範例與解析**，學習具體答題技巧。

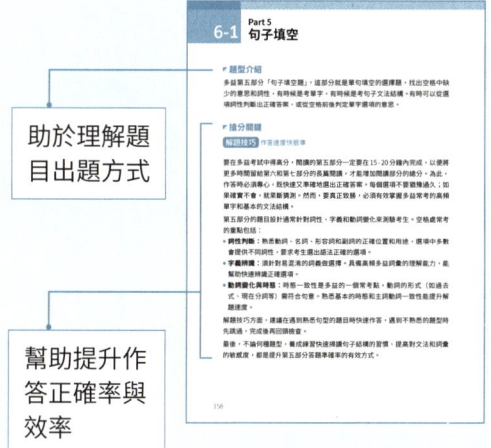

- 助於理解題目出題方式
- 幫助提升作答正確率與效率

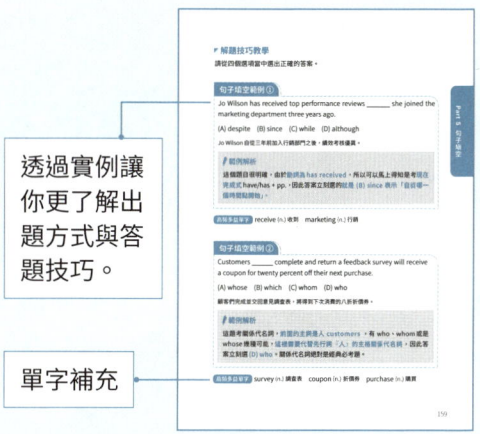

- 透過實例讓你更了解出題方式與答題技巧。
- 單字補充

STEP 3 **新制多益模擬試題**驗收實力，並提供**詳細解題**說明。

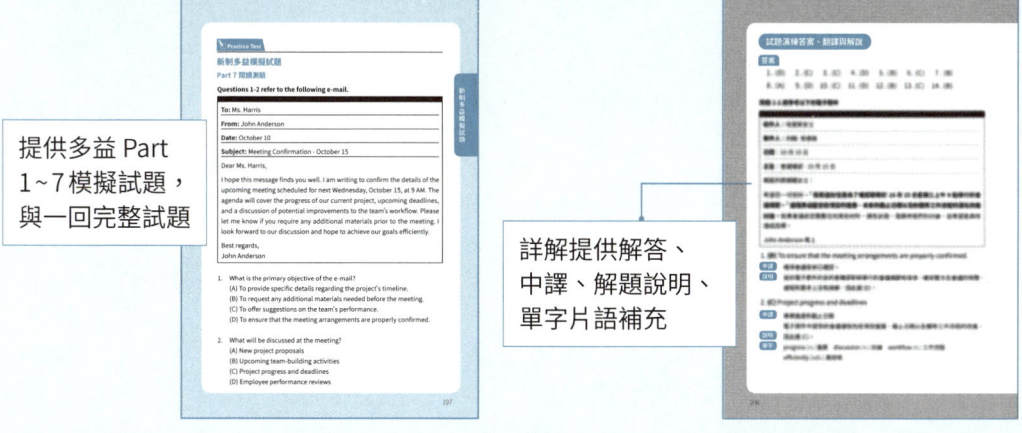

- 提供多益 Part 1~7 模擬試題，與一回完整試題
- 詳解提供解答、中譯、解題說明、單字片語補充

第1章

了解多益考試

1-1 TOEIC 考試簡介
1-2 TOEIC 準備技巧
1-3 TOEIC 作答技巧

本章節會清楚介紹多益考試有哪些項目與準備方式，搭配老師獨家的解題技巧，讓你在考試前能更有效率的準備。

1-1 TOEIC 考試簡介

考試由來

多益 (TOEIC - Test of English for International Communication) 是由美國教育測驗服務社 (ETS - Educational Testing Service) 所策劃製作的英文程度檢定測驗。最早是由日本人請 ETS 幫他們研發可以檢測專業人士在職場上英文運用程度的測試。行之有年之後，亞洲各國也開始實施多益測驗，多益測驗在台灣也成為公司行號及學校畢業的英文能力參考指標。

考試介紹

多益測驗分為聽力與閱讀測驗和口說與寫作測驗。

聽力與閱讀測驗 (TOEIC Listening and Reading Test)：

時間約 2 小時30 分鐘，總共有 200 題，全部為單選題。聽力與閱讀兩者分開計時。

聽力測驗 (Listening Test)

聽力測驗包含 4 大題，共有 100 題。聽力問題將包含以下形式：直述句、問句、短對話，以及短獨白，考生須根據所聽到的內容回答問題。

聽力測驗時間大約為 45 分鐘，題型如下。

聽力測驗題型	
Part 1	照片描述 6 題（選項 4 選 1）
Part 2	應答問題 25 題（選項 3 選 1）
Part 3	簡短對話 39 題（選項 4 選 1）
Part 4	簡短獨白 30 題（選項 4 選 1）

閱讀測驗 (Reading Test)

閱讀測驗包含3大題，共有 100 題，題目及選項都印在題本上。考生須閱讀多種題材的文章，並回答相關問題。

閱讀測驗時間為 75 分鐘，考生可在時限內依自己的能力調配閱讀及答題速度，題型如下。

	閱讀測驗題型
Part 5	單句填空 30 題（選項 4 選 1）
Part 6	短文填空 16 題（選項 4 選 1）
Part 7	單篇文章理解 29 題（選項 4 選 1）；多篇文章理解 25 題（選項 4 選 1）

作答方式：考生選好答案後，需在與題目卷分開的答案卷上畫卡。雖然答題時間約為 2 小時，但考生尚須在答案卷上填寫個人資料，並簡短的回答關於個人背景資料的問卷，因此在考場內的時間會較長。

多益分數換算方式

聽力測驗答對題數	聽力測驗對應分數	閱讀測驗答對題數	閱讀測驗對應分數
96 - 100	480-495	96-100	460-495
91 - 95	435-490	91-95	410-475
86 - 90	395-450	86-90	380-430
81 - 85	355-415	81-85	355-400
76 - 80	325-375	76-80	325-375
71 - 75	295-340	71-75	295-345
66 - 70	265-315	66-70	265-315
61 - 65	240-285	61-65	235-285
56 - 60	215-260	56-60	205-255

聽力測驗答對題數	聽力測驗對應分數	閱讀測驗答對題數	閱讀測驗對應分數
51-55	190-235	51-55	175-225
46-50	160-210	46-50	150-195
41-45	135-180	41-45	120-170
36-40	110-155	36-40	100-140
31-35	85-130	31-35	75-120
26-30	70-105	26-30	55-100
21-25	50-90	21-25	40-80
16-20	35-75	16-20	30-65
11-15	20-55	11-15	20-50
6-10	15-40	6-10	15-35
1-5	5-20	1-5	5-20
0	5	0	5

口說與寫作測驗 (TOEIC Speaking and Writing Test)：

TOEIC測試的口說和寫作部分，主要是評估考生在職場環境中的英語溝通能力。這部分測試考生能否精準的以口語交流和書面表達，對於需要用英語進行工作互動的專業人士尤為重要。TOEIC口說和寫作測試的評分範圍是0到200分，以下是各部分的介紹及題型說明。

口說測驗 (Speaking Test)

TOEIC口說測驗包含11題，考試時間約20分鐘。這部分主要測試考生的表達流暢度、語調準確性以及語言結構和邏輯性，具體題型如下：

口說測驗題型	
文章朗讀（2題）	考生需朗讀指定的英文短文，重點在於發音、語調和流暢度的自然程度。

圖片描述（2題）	考生將看到一張圖片，並需要描述其細節，這部分主要評估語言描述能力和細節表達的準確性。
回答問題（3題）	考生需根據題目設定的情境回答問題，測試其反應速度和交談能力。
依據題目資料應答（3題）	考生需依據題目設定的情境與提供的資料做出恰當的回應，測試其在不同情境中的閱讀與即興表達能力。
陳述意見（1題）	考生需對指定的議題發表看法，並清晰地陳述支持的理由，此項目強調邏輯思維、條理性以及觀點組織能力。

寫作測驗 (Writing Test)

TOEIC 寫作測驗包含 8 題，考試時間約 60 分鐘。這部分重點檢視考生在溝通中的書面語言使用準確性、清晰度和結構組織能力。寫作部分的題型如下：

寫作測驗題型	
描述照片（5題）	考生根據照片寫出符合情境的句子，重點在於語法準確性和基本語言運用能力。
回覆書面要求（2題）	考生需針對情境要求撰寫回應，測試考生信件格式、正式用語及回答的得體性。
陳述意見（1題）	考生需針對指定議題撰寫短文，須展示邏輯推理和說理能力，並通過語言組織和內容連貫性來陳述立場。

評分標準

TOEIC 口說和寫作測驗的評分標準涵蓋多個方面，包括語言的流暢度、語法和詞彙的準確性、語調和語速是否適當，以及對情境能否應對得體和邏輯等。透過不同的題型設計，這項測試能準確評估考生在職場英語溝通中的實際應用能力。

作答方式：口說與寫作測驗為電腦測驗，考生須藉由麥克風進行口說測驗，透過鍵盤進行寫作測驗。

新制多益

所謂的新制多益是從 2018 年 3 月改制後實施的多益，聽力和閱讀大致有以下的改制方向：

聽力測驗改制方向

1. **簡短對話及簡短獨白增加圖表**：除了仔細聽以外，考生也需要加強閱讀圖表的能力與整合能力。

2. **新增「三人以上」的對話**：簡短對話從二人增加為三人對話，更符合實際的職場情況。

3. **新增「口語化」的說法**：為符合實際生活對話情景，對話內容也更口語化，如：You bet! 意思是「當然啊！一點也沒錯！」

閱讀測驗改制方向

1. **新增短文填空，類似托福「句子插入題」**：考生須將正確的句子插入文章的位置中，須對上、下文文意理解的更清楚、文章脈絡更熟悉，才有辦法正確作答。

2. **新增多篇閱讀**：從原本的雙篇閱讀，增加「多篇閱讀」。考生必須閱讀最多 3 篇文章，並從中擷取重點並理解相關的訊息。

3. **新增「即時通訊軟體的對話內容」**：閱讀內容包含即時通訊軟體的對話內容，更貼近現代人的溝通模式。

考試題型變更綜合分析

英文能力須更紮實：

1. 新制多益難度提升，出題方式更靈活，英文的掌握度須更高。

2. 聽力測驗優化出題模式與細節

3. 更強調考生整合能力,及重要訊息的掌握。

4. 閱讀測驗兩種新題型:

   I. **句子插入**:要將一句話插入文章中最適當的地方,考生需對全文內容更加理解,上下文邏輯鋪陳更加清楚。

   II. **多篇閱讀**:文章長度與訊息量增加,但考試時間一樣,因此閱讀速度需大幅提升,且閱讀技巧也是關鍵。

目前 TOEIC 官方尚未宣布具體的口說改制計劃,但下列方向可能會成為未來改進的重點。

口說測驗可能的改制方向

1. **情境的真實性提升**:未來的考試可能會更加強調職場場景的真實模擬,例如引入多樣化的對話主題,讓考生在回答問題時能有更多即興表達的機會。

2. **跨文化交流測試**:考試中可能會增加不同英語口音的對話題型,以更真實的反映國際工作環境中的多元文化情境。考生需要適應各種發音差異,以便更能與來自不同國家的客戶或同事交流。

3. **評分標準的精細化**:在語言流暢度、語法準確度、語音和語調等方面,評分標準可能會進一步細化,以更準確地區分不同層次的表達能力。

4. **增強即興應對能力**:若未來進行改制,口說測試可能會加強考生的即興反應和邏輯思維能力,特別是在表達意見和回答問題的題型中,讓考生有更多機會展示個人觀點。

1-2 TOEIC 準備技巧

關鍵字彙

準備多益考試的第一個關鍵元素是字彙。由於這個考試大多和商務相關，所以單字也都非常實用，建議平常就用有聲音的字卡，用聽力朗讀的方式，背誦常出現的高頻率單字。這部分我有一個社群和專門的 YouTube 頻道，每週會固定提供不同類別的多益高頻率字卡，也建議考生可以自行建立單字本。

申老師的 Instagram

聽力秘訣

準備 TOEIC 聽力測試時，掌握一些訣竅能顯著提升你的技巧。

1. **熟悉聽力部分題型**：這些題型包括問題、對話和獨白，了解題型進行方式能幫助你考試進行得更順暢。
2. **多多撰寫模擬考題和分析錯誤**：能幫助你找出聽力上的盲點，並針對問題進行訓練。
3. **建立每天練習聽力的習慣**：例如聽英語廣播或觀看英文電影，都是非常有效的方法。

這些技巧將幫助你在 TOEIC 聽力測試中取得高分。加油！

文法考點

文法一直是各種考試必備的基礎，在閱讀部分的第五大題，除了單字詞彙以外，文法規則就是另一個重頭戲，因此必須熟悉基礎時態、被動語態、連接詞等。唯有能把各種文法題目如反射方式作答，才能有效節省答題時間，能夠更充裕的完成第七大題的閱讀篇章。

▎閱讀效率

閱讀速度的練習是需要積年累月培養出來的，不過在考場上確實能夠藉由上下文，或者是從題目及選項，找出原文當中的答案，這就是我所謂的考場上的閱讀效率。後續的章節我就會教大家怎麼樣在考場上「有效率的閱讀」，並找到正確的答案。

1-3 TOEIC作答技巧

聽力部分

在撰寫聽力部分時，**保持專注是關鍵**，考生需要全神貫注聆聽講者的語氣和重點，這樣才能避免分心。此外，**要記下關鍵詞和重要資訊**，這樣在回答問題時，才能幫助你快速作答。

另外**在題目播放前，要迅速閱讀試題本上的問題，並預測可能的答案**。可以讓你的聽力過程更加順利。由於考試中會出現各種口音，建議你多聽聽不同地區的英語，這樣可以提升你的聽力理解能力。

第一大題 照片描述：

在播放題目時，快速觀察圖片，看清楚題目究竟在問圖片中的什麼重點。人物圖片題通常會問的是**動作**、**穿著**、**場景**、**職業**等等，大多是「現在進行式」。事物圖片題則考場景細節描述、物品位置、狀態等，因此以「現在簡單式」或「現在完成式」居多，表示位置關係的介系詞也是重點。此外，注意避開相似字發音的陷阱。

第二大題 應答問題：

常見題目類型有：WH- 疑問句、Yes/ No 疑問句、附加疑問句、陳述式疑問句、間接疑問句、選擇疑問句等等。不過台灣考生要注意，不熟悉的英國澳洲腔在這裡很容易讓你混淆，讓你聽到疑問詞就卡住。

第三大題 簡短對話：

請務必確認中心主旨為何，第一句話往往就是關鍵，並且要習慣多人的對話以及各國腔調和口音。至於搭配圖表的題型，在聽對話內容之餘，也必須對照表格及圖表中的資訊。

第四大題 簡短獨白：

這一大題是整個聽力測驗中內容最長、資訊量最大的部分，請耐著性子，邊聽邊作答。通常問題順序會按照聽力內容所提供的訊息依序排列，考生需要透過聽力內容做出推論。

閱讀部分

閱讀部分重點如下：

第五大題 句子填空：

考生須找出空格中缺少的意思和詞性，可以從詞性或是從空格的前後來判斷出正確答案。這部分「文法」和「字彙」的出題比例相近，考生除了要增加字彙量以外，對單字型態變化、介系詞、片語搭配等也都要掌握，才可在這部分得到較高分數。

第六大題 段落填空：

這一大題就是短文填空，由於有「句子插入題」，因此要根據上下文語意選出合適且不影響文意的句子放在相對位置。本大題測試考生對於字義、文法、時態以及文章內容、目的、態度等的理解力。

第七大題 閱讀測驗：

新制多益從原本的「雙篇閱讀」增加為「多篇閱讀」，文章型態包含：廣告、信件、電子郵件、公告、新聞、問卷，還有通訊軟體介面呈現的對話內容等等。在有限的作答時間內，考生須運用「略讀」快速瀏覽文章，掌握文章的大意和主要概念，須特別注意標題、副標題、首段、尾段與關鍵詞。另外也須使用「掃讀」技巧快速搜尋特定資訊，掌握關鍵訊息作答。常見的資訊包括：數字、日期、名字或關鍵詞。運用略讀和掃讀的技巧，考生能在閱讀測驗中更有效率地找到關鍵資訊和並解題，進而提升多益成績。

口說部分

在準備 TOEIC 口說測驗時，掌握一些有效的作答技巧可以幫助你提升作答表現。以下是幾個簡單的**口說部分作答技巧**：

1. **清晰發音與自然語速**：保持發音清晰，語速適中，這樣考官才能聽懂你的回答。

2. **組織思路**：在回答問題之前，快速思考回答的結構，使用「First（首先…），Next（其次…），Finally / Last（最後…）」等連接詞來組織你的觀點。

3. **使用具體例子**：用你自身或友人的具體例子和經歷來支持你的觀點，讓你的回答更具說服力。

4. **保持自信**：在口說時自信地表達，遇到表達卡關時保持冷靜，以自己會說的字詞取代，這會讓你的表達更為流利。

第 2 章

詞彙擴展

2-1 多益考試的基本詞彙
2-2 學習並記住新詞彙的技巧
2-3 字根、字首和字尾

> 本章節依據官方13種情境,提供多益必考單字,接著分享獨門多益單字記憶法,讓你輕鬆記憶!

2-1 多益考試的基本詞彙

基本詞彙介紹

在多益考試中，熟悉基本詞彙意思是取得高分的關鍵。這些詞彙包括日常商務溝通中的常見用語，諸如辦公室交流、電話會議、電子郵件溝通、旅遊安排等相關內容。學習這些詞彙時，要著重於其實際應用，並且可以透過閱讀和做模擬考題來加強理解和記憶。

根據多益官方所提供的資料，多益中出現的單字是從以下 13 種情境中所出的：

類別	細項
企業發展	研究、產品研發
外食	商務／非正式午餐、宴會、招待會、餐廳訂位
娛樂	電影、劇場、音樂、藝術、展覽、博物館、媒體
金融／預算	銀行業務、投資、稅務、會計、帳單
一般商務	契約、談判、併購、行銷、銷售、商業企劃、會議、勞動關係
保健	醫療保險、看醫生、牙醫、診所、醫院
房屋／公司地產	建築、規格、購買租賃、電力瓦斯服務
製造業	工廠管理、生產線、品管
辦公室	董事會、委員會、信件、備忘錄、電話、傳真、電子郵件、辦公室器材與家具、辦公室流程
人事	招考、雇用、退休、薪資、升遷、應徵與廣告、津貼、獎勵
採購	購物、訂購物資、送貨、發票
技術層面	電子、科技、電腦、實驗室與相關器材
旅遊	火車、飛機、計程車、巴士、船隻、渡輪、票務、時刻表、車站、機場廣播、租車、飯店、預定、交通工具延誤與取消

13 類必考多益單字表

1 企業發展　美🎧001

單字	字義
innovation	(n.) 創新
strategy	(n.) 策略
market research	(phr.) 市場研究
product development	(phr.) 產品開發
patent	(n.) 專利
competitive advantage	(phr.) 競爭優勢
market share	(phr.) 市占率
research and development	(phr.) 研究與開發

2 用餐　英🎧002

單字	字義
dine-in	(adj.) 內用
takeout	(adj.) 外帶
menu	(n.) 菜單
reservation	(n.) 預約
waiter/waitress	(n.) 服務人員
chef	(n.) 主廚
tip	(n.) 小費
special	(n.) 特別菜色或優惠餐
appetizer	(n.) 開胃菜
bill/check	(n.) 帳單

多益考試的基本詞彙

3 娛樂 澳 🎧 003

單字	字義
entertainment	(n.) 娛樂
performer	(n.) 表演者
concert	(n.) 音樂會、演唱會
theater	(n.) 戲劇院
audience	(n.) 觀眾
ticket	(n.) 票
film	(n.) 電影
popularity	(n.) 受歡迎程度
gaming	(n.) 遊戲
leisure	(n.) 休閒時間

4 金融 / 預算 美 🎧 004

單字	字義
budget	(n.) 預算
revenue	(n.) 收入
expense	(n.) 費用
profit	(n.) 利潤
loss	(n.) 損失
allocation	(n.) 分配
cost-cutting	(n.) 削減成本
forecast	(n.) 預測
financial statement	(n.) 財務報表
balance	(n.) 餘額

5 一般商務　英 🎧 005

單字	字義
negotiate	(v.) 協商
collaborate	(v.) 合作
delegate	(v.) 分派
agenda	(n.) 議程
minutes	(n.) 會議記錄
presentation	(n.) 簡報
proposal	(n.) 提案
deadline	(n.) 截止日期
correspondence	(n.) 信函
report	(n.) 報告

6 保健　澳 🎧 006

單字	字義
insurance	(n.) 保險
hospital	(n.) 醫院
doctor	(n.) 醫生
patient	(n.) 病人
appointment	(n.) 預約
prescription	(n.) 處方

7 房屋 / 公司地產　英 🎧 007

單字	字義
property	(n.) 房地產
real estate	(phr.) 不動產
mortgage	(n.) 抵押貸款
lease	(n.) 租約
tenant	(n.) 房客
landlord	(n.) 房東
property manager	(phr.) 房產經理
commercial property	(phr.) 商業地產
residential property	(phr.) 住宅地產
rental	(n.) 租金、出租

8 製造業　澳 🎧 008

單字	字義
production	(n.) 生產
assembly line	(phr.) 生產線
quality control	(phr.) 品管
inventory	(n.) 庫存
logistics	(n.) 物流
supply chain	(phr.) 供應鏈
machinery	(n.) 機械設備
automation	(n.) 自動化
raw materials	(phr.) 原材料
efficiency	(n.) 效率

9 辦公室 [美] 🎧 009

單字	字義
conference room	(phr.) 會議室
photocopier	(n.) 影印機
file cabinet	(phr.) 文件櫃
manager	(n.) 經理、主管
office supplies	(phr.) 辦公用品
fax machine	(phr.) 傳真機
whiteboard	(n.) 白板
office hours	(phr.) 辦公時間、營業時間

10 人事 [美] 🎧 010

單字	字義
recruitment	(n.) 招聘
résumé	(n.) 履歷
interview	(v./n.) 面試
candidate	(n.) 應徵者、候選人
hiring	(n.) 雇用
training	(n.) 培訓
performance appraisal	(phr.) 績效評估
benefits	(n.) 福利
promotion	(n.) 晉升
resignation	(n.) 辭職

11 採購 澳 🎧 011

單字	字義
purchase	(v./n.) 採購
supplier	(n.) 供應商
contract	(n.) 合約
price quote	(phr.) 價格報價
vendor	(n.) 賣方、供應商、小販
delivery	(n.) 交貨、運送

12 技術層面 美 🎧 012

單字	字義
database	(n.) 資料庫
software	(n.) 軟體
hardware	(n.) 硬體
network	(n.) 網路
firewall	(n.) 防火牆
encryption	(n.) 加密
virus	(n.) 病毒
troubleshooting	(n.) 疑難排解
operating system	(phr.) 作業系統
cybersecurity	(n.) 資訊安全

13 旅遊　英 🎧 013

單字	字義
accommodation	(n.) 住宿、特殊安排
reservation	(n.) 預訂
itinerary	(n.) 行程表
sightseeing	(n.) 觀光
tourist attraction	(phr.) 觀光景點
transportation	(n.) 交通工具
passport	(n.) 護照
visa	(n.) 簽證
currency exchange	(phr.) 貨幣兌換
guidebook	(n.) 旅遊指南

2-2 學習並記住新詞彙的技巧

學習新詞彙的最佳方法是將其應用於真實情境中。例如，嘗試使用新學到的詞彙來寫句子或參與對話。同時，定期複習也是記住新詞彙的關鍵，可以使用單字卡、詞彙應用程式 (app)，或進行詞彙測驗來加強記憶。此外，將新詞彙與熟悉的概念連結起來，可以有效地加深印象。

語境學習 (Contextual Learning)

提供與詞彙相關的真實語境，例如閱讀文章、對話或情境劇本，讓自己能夠在實際場景中理解詞彙的含義。

舉例來說，在學習「**efficient** (adj.) 有效率的」這個字時，閱讀描述工廠如何藉由新技術提升生產效率的文章，來增進對這個單字的全面理解。

重複練習範例 ①：填空練習

The new product launch attracted a lot of attention in the _____. (market)

Understanding the needs and preferences of our _____ is crucial for business success. (customers)

The company conducted extensive research to identify potential _____ for their new line of products. (markets)

We need to explore new _____ to expand our customer base. (markets)

The company's success is attributed to its ability to meet the changing demands of its _____. (customers)

重複練習範例 ②：情境對話

A: Have you seen the latest trends in the fashion _____ (market)?

B: Yes, I've been keeping an eye on them. The _____ (market) demand for sustainable clothing seems to be on the rise.

A: That's interesting. Our company might consider tapping into that _____ (market).

B: Definitely. Meeting the demands of eco-conscious _____ (customers) could be a smart move for us.

多角度學習 (Multi-Perspective Learning)

從不同的角度閱讀特定詞彙，以幫助自己更全面的理解和加深印象。
舉例來說，從企業角度和個人角度討論「**innovate** (v.) 創新」，便能更了解創新在不同情境下的意義和重要性。

企業角度：

1. To stay competitive, companies must continually **innovate** their products and services.
   （為了保持競爭力，公司必須持改革他們的產品和服務。）

2. The tech giant invested heavily in research and development to **innovate** new technologies for the market.
   （這家科技巨頭在研發上投入了大量資金，以改革市場上的新技術。）

3. Successful startups often thrive by **innovating** in ways that challenge existing industry norms.
   （成功的新創公司通常藉由挑戰現有行業規範的方式，進行改革而蓬勃發展。）

4. The company's ability to **innovate** has allowed it to lead the market with cutting-edge solutions.
   （公司創新的能力使其能夠以領先的解決方案引領市場。）

個人角度：

1. To stand out in your career, you should look for ways to **innovate** in your approach to solving problems.
（為了在職業生涯中脫穎而出，你應該尋找創新解決問題的方法。）

2. **Innovating** your daily routines can help you increase productivity and maintain a fresh perspective.
（改革你的日常例行工作可以幫助你提高生產力，並保持新鮮的視角。）

3. As a creative individual, she constantly seeks to **innovate** her art by experimenting with new techniques and materials.
（作為一位創意型人士，她不斷透過嘗試新技術和材料使她的藝術創新。）

4. He believes that personal growth comes from the ability to **innovate** and adapt to new challenges.
（他相信個人成長來自於創新和適應新挑戰的能力。）

2-3 字根、字首和字尾

藉由認識字根、字首及字尾，可讓推斷出不熟悉詞彙的含義更為容易。例如，字首 "un-" 通常表示否定或相反的意思，字尾 "-tion" 通常指名詞形式。掌握字根和字首能讓自己擴展詞彙量，掌握**字尾的詞性**有助於在閱讀測驗 Part 5 中選出正確答案。

常見字根 (Roots)

字根 (Roots) 指的是某一組單字中具有相同字根的部分及其代表的意義。以下是一些常見的字根及其在單字中的意義：

1 "graph" 意思是「寫」或「記錄」

單字	字義
photo**graph**	(n.) 照片
graphic	(adj.) 圖像的、生動的
tele**graph**	(n.) 電報
para**graph**	(n.) 段落
auto**graph**	(n.) 親筆簽名
calli**graphy**	(n.) 書法

2 "cent" 意思是「百」

單字	字義
cent	(n.) 分 (貨幣單位)
per**cent**	(n.) 百分比
centennial	(adj.) 百年一次的
centipede	(n.) 蜈蚣
centenary	(n.) 百年紀念

031

3 "dict-" 意思是「說」

單字	字義
pre**dict**	(v.) 預測
dictionary	(n.) 字典
ver**dict**	(n.) 裁決
contra**dict**	(v.) 反駁、相矛盾
dictate	(v.) 口述
bene**dict**ion	(n.) 祝福
male**dict**ion	(n.) 詛咒

4 "port-" - 意思是「運送」、「攜帶」和「移動」

單字	字義
trans**port**	(v.) 運輸、運送
im**port**	(v.) 進口
ex**port**	(v.) 出口
porter	(n.) 搬運工
de**port**	(v.) 驅逐
re**port**	(v.) 報告

5 "struct-" - 意思是「建造」

單字	字義
in**struct**	(v.) 指導
structure	(n.) 結構
de**struct**	(v.) 毀壞
re**struct**ure	(v.) 重組
con**struct**	(v.) 建造

6 "spect-" 意思是「看」、「觀察」

單字	字義
spectacle	(n.) 景象、壯觀的演出
in**spect**	(v.) 檢查
re**spect**	(v.) 尊敬
su**spect**	(v.) 懷疑
pro**spect**	(n.) 展望
retro**spect**	(n.) 回顧
spectator	(n.) 觀眾

字根、字首和字尾

7 "path-" 意思是「感情」、「疾病」

單字	字義
sym**path**y	(n.) 同情
em**path**y	(n.) 同理心
pathology	(n.) 病理學
a**path**etic	(adj.) 漠不關心的
pathogen	(n.) 病原體
tele**path**y	(n.) 心靈感應
psycho**path**	(n.) 精神病患者

8 "nov-" 意思是「新」

單字	字義
novel	(n.) 小說
novelty	(n.) 新奇（事物）
novice	(n.) 新手
in**nov**ation	(n.) 創新
re**nov**ate	(v.) 翻新
in**nov**ator	(n.) 創新者

9 "vid-/vis-" 意思是「看」

單字	字義
video	(n.) 影片
tele**vis**ion	(n.) 電視
vision	(n.) 視覺、願景
vista	(n.) 遠景
visible	(adj.) 可見的
en**vis**ion	(v.) 想像、預見
re**vis**e	(v.) 修改、校訂
super**vis**e	(v.) 監督、指導

10 "mot-/mov-" 意思是「移動」

單字	字義
motion	(n.) 動作、移動
motor	(n.) 馬達
pro**mot**e	(v.) 促進
re**mov**e	(v.) 移除
de**mot**e	(v.) 降級
movement	(n.) 移動、運動
com**mot**ion	(n.) 騷動

字根、字首和字尾

常見字首 (Prefixes)

代表意思	字首	範例
…之後	after–	**after**noon (n.) 下午、**after**ward (adv.) 之後、**after**math (n.) 後果
在…後面	post–	**post**pone (v.) 延遲、**post**script (n.) 附錄
…先前	ante–	**ante**date (v.) 填上更早的日期、**ante**chamber (n.) 前廳、**ante**cedent (n.) 前情
在…前面	pre–	**pre**fix (v.) 放在前頭、**pre**fer (v.) 寧可、寧願（選擇）、**pre**historic (adj.) 史前的
先前、代理	pro–	**pro**logue (n.) 開場白、**pro**cedure (n.) 程序、手續、**pro**noun (n.) 代名詞
反…	anti–	**anti**social (adj.) 反社會的、**anti**biotic (n.) 抗生素、**anti**dote (n.) 解藥
不、無	dis–	**dis**agree (v.) 不同意、**dis**grace (n.) 丟臉、**dis**honest (adj.) 不誠實
不、無	il–	**il**legal (adj.) 非法的、**il**logical (adj.) 不合邏輯的、**il**legible (adj.) 難辨識的
不、無	in–	**in**ability (n.) 無能、**in**correct (adj.) 不正確的、**in**humane (adj.) 不人道的
不、無	ir–	**ir**regular (adj.) 不規則的、**ir**responsible (adj.) 不負責任的、**ir**relevant (adj.) 不相關的
相反	contra–	**contra**dict (v.) 與…矛盾、**contra**ry (adj.) 相反的、**contra**st (n.) 對比
對立	counter–	**counter**act (v.) 對抗、**counter**feit (adj.) 假冒的、**counter**part (n.) 對應的人（或物）、對等物
好	bene– beni–	**bene**fit (n.) 利益、**beni**gn (adj.) 有利的、良性的
不當、不良	mal–	**mal**function (n.) 故障、**mal**practice (n.) 瀆職、**mal**nourished (adj.) 營養不良的
不當、不良	mis–	**mis**take (n.) 錯誤、**mis**fortune (n.) 不幸、**mis**place (v.) 誤置

代表意思	字首	範例
環繞	circu-	**circu**late (v.) 循環、**circu**lar (adj.) 環形的、**circu**s (n.) 馬戲團
一起	co-, col-	**co**operate (v.) 合作、**co**worker (n.) 同事、**col**lect (v.) 收集
互相、之間	inter-	**inter**national (adj.) 國際的、**inter**action (n.) 互動、**inter**fere (v.) 干涉
兩個	bi-, bin-	**bi**cycle (n.) 腳踏車、**bi**lingual (adj.) 雙語的、**bi**focal (adj.) 雙焦點的、**bin**oculars (n.) 雙筒望遠鏡
多元、多樣	multi-	**multi**ple (adj.) 多樣的、**multi**cultural (adj.) 多元文化的、**multi**lingual (adj.) 多語言的、**multi**national (adj.) 多國的
多數	poly-	**poly**glot (adj.) 包含多種語言的、**poly**gon (n.) 多邊形、**poly**technic (adj.) 綜合技術的
全、總	omni-	**omni**scient (adj.) 全知的、**omni**vorous (adj.) 雜食性的、**omni**potent (adj.) 全能的
過度…	over-	**over**active (adj.) 過於活耀的、**over**flow (v.) 氾濫、**over**draw (v.) 透支、誇張
過度…	hyper-	**hyper**critical (adj.) 吹毛求疵的、**hyper**bole (n.) 誇飾法、**hyper**sensitive (adj.) 過度敏感的
低於…	hypo-	**hypo**dermic (adj.) 皮下的、**hypo**glycemia (n.) 低血糖症
自動	auto-	**auto**matic (adj.) 自動的、**auto**mobile (n.) 汽車、**auto**biography (n.) 自傳
重新、再次	re-	**re**write (v.) 重寫、**re**peat (v.) 重複、**re**place (v.) 取代、**re**fill (v.) 再填滿

字根、字首和字尾

常見字尾 (Suffixes)

代表意思	字尾	詞性	範例
使…/ 進行某種行為	–ate	動詞	activ**ate** (v.) 使活動起來、使活化 reciproc**ate** (v.) 報答 elev**ate** (v.) 使上升、提高
使…/ 進行某種行為	–fy	動詞	beauti**fy** (v.) 美化、clari**fy** (v.) 澄清 speci**fy** (v.) 具體指出
使…/ 進行某種行為	–ize	動詞	computer**ize** (v.) 使電腦化 modern**ize** (v.) 使現代化 legal**ize** (v.) 使合法化
變成…	–en	動詞	short**en** (v.) 變短 length**en** (v.) 變長 fatt**en** (v.) 使變胖
狀態、性質	–ance	名詞	resist**ance** (n.) 反抗 accept**ance** (n.) 接受 extravag**ance** (n.) 奢侈
狀態、性質	–ancy	名詞	vac**ancy** (n.) 空缺 pregn**ancy** (n.) 懷孕 redund**ancy** (n.) 多餘
狀態、性質	–ency	名詞	expedi**ency** (n.) 適宜 leni**ency** (n.) 寬大 lat**ency** (n.) 潛伏
狀態、性質	–ity	名詞	authentic**ity** (n.) 真實性 public**ity** (n.) 宣傳 civil**ity** (n.) 禮貌
狀態、性質	–ment	名詞	enjoy**ment** (n.) 樂趣 procure**ment** (n.) 採購 employ**ment** (n.) 受雇
狀態、性質	–ness	名詞	kind**ness** (n.) 仁慈 dark**ness** (n.) 黑暗 like**ness** (n.) 相像

代表意思	字尾	詞性	範例
狀態、性質	-ship	名詞	endship (n.) 友情 relationship (n.) 人際關係 kinship (n.) 親屬關係
…狀態	-tion, -ation	名詞	inspiration (n.) 靈感 separation (n.) 分離 deviation (n.) 偏差
…狀態	-hood	名詞	childhood (n.) 幼年時期 adulthood (n.) 成人時期 manhood (n.) 男性成年期
…的	-al	形容詞	influential (adj.) 有影響力的 provincial (adj.) 地方性的 financial (adj.) 財務的、金融的
…的	-ary	形容詞	primary (adj.) 首要的 secondary (adj.) 次要的 fiduciary (adj.) 信託的
…的	-ic	形容詞	economic (adj.) 經濟的 scientific (adj.) 科學的 scenic (adj.) 風景的
…的狀態	-ous	形容詞	nervous (adj.) 緊張的 anxious (adj.) 焦慮的 jealous (adj.) 忌妒的
…地	-ly	副詞	clearly (adv.) 清楚地 yearly (adv.) 每年地 ordinarily (adv.) 通常地

字根、字首和字尾

第 3 章

文法基礎知識

3-1 多益試題的關鍵語法規則
3-2 改善句子結構和清晰度的技巧

在多益考試中，文法是提升閱讀理解的關鍵要素。透過紮實的文法基礎，考生不僅能快速理解文章重點，還能更清晰地理解句子結構，進一步提升答題效率。本章將帶領大家深入掌握多益考試中的核心語法規則，解析常見的錯誤，並提供改善句子結構的小技巧，幫助考生在聽力和閱讀中穩健得分。

3-1 多益試題的關鍵語法規則

▎TOEIC 關鍵語法規則整理

在 TOEIC Part 5 考試中，考生需要特別注意動詞在句中的變化。在以下部分，將著重介紹動詞時態、動詞的分詞用法和動詞在句中的變化，並提供範例進行解析。

考點 1　動詞時態

請熟記十二時態公式表及常搭配的時間副詞

時態	句型	常搭配的時間副詞
現在簡單式	S + V (present tense)	every..., always, usually 等頻率副詞
過去簡單式	S + V (past tense)	...ago, last..., yesterday, this morning, then, just now
未來簡單式	S + will + V	next..., tomorrow, in...
現在進行式	S + be (am, are, is) + V-ing	now, at present
過去進行式	S + be (was, were) + V-ing	
未來進行式	S + will + be + V-ing	
現在完成式	S + have / has + pp.	since, for..., so far, until now, up to now, already, yet, recently, lately, once, twice, ...times
過去完成式	S + had + pp.	
未來完成式	S + will + have + pp.	by the time
現在完成進行式	S + have / has + been + V-ing	
過去完成進行式	S + had + been + V-ing	
未來完成進行式	S + will have + been + V-ing	

根據句子的時間選擇合適的時態。多益考試中常見的時態包括現在式、過去式和未來式。

說明

- **現在式**：She work**s** at a bank.（她在銀行工作。）
- **過去式**：He completed the report **yesterday**.（他昨天完成了報告。）
- **未來式**：They **will** attend the conference **next week**.（他們下週將參加會議。）

語法規則範例 ①

By the time the report is presented at the annual meeting, the research team _____ all the necessary data from various sources and _____ it into a comprehensive analysis.

(A) collected / organizes
(B) will have collected / organized
(C) has collected / organizing
(D) will collect / organizes

中譯 在年度會議上發表報告時，研究團隊將已從多個來源收集到所有必要數據，並將其組織成一份完整的分析報告。

範例解析

本句描述一個**未來情境，因為看到 by the time**：在報告發表前，研究團隊將完成數據的收集與整理，因此**主要子句需要使用未來完成式**（will have + 過去分詞）來表示動作在未來某一時間點之前已經完成。

(A) "collected / organizes" 是過去式和現在式的混用，語法和時態不符。
(C) "has collected / organizing" 使用了現在完成式和現在分詞，與未來情境不符。
(D) "will collect / organizes" 的第一部分是未來式，第二部分是現在式，結構不一致且不合語意。**所以正確答案是 (B)**。

高頻多益單字 present (v.) 發表　necessary (adj.) 必要的　data (n.) 資料
various (adj.) 多元的　source (n.) 來源
comprehensive (adj.) 完整的　analysis (n.) 分析

考點 2　動詞的分詞用法

分詞構句是由子句簡化而來的句構，這是個各種英文考試檢定都非常愛考的文法。簡化的口訣如下：

現在分詞 (V-ing) 做形容詞用　→　表主動或進行
過去分詞 (PP) 做形容詞用　→　表被動或完成

範例

形容詞子句與分詞片語的互換

The girl **who is talking** with our teacher is Elsa.
= The girl **talking** with our teacher is Elsa.
（跟我們老師說話的那個女孩是艾爾莎。）
▶ 形容詞子句內的關係代名詞 + be 動詞 **(who is)** 一起**省略後**就能**簡化成分詞片語**。

The window **that was broken** by Kevin is very expensive.
= The window **broken** by Kevin is very expensive.
（凱文打破的那扇窗戶很貴。）
▶ 可以**把關係代名詞和 be 動詞省略**，剩下過去分詞 broken，修飾前面的 window，因為窗戶是「被打破的」。

分詞構句

副詞子句改為分詞構句

簡單來說，就是只有**在副詞子句和主要子句主詞相同的情況下**，把副詞子句改為以**分詞片語形容主詞**的形式呈現。

When **Leanne** found out the truth, **she** became extremely sad.
= Finding out the truth, Leanne became extremely sad.
（當莉安發現事實時，她極度傷心。）
▶ 由於副詞子句和主要子句的主詞相同，都是 Leanne，所以把副詞子句的主詞刪掉，由於 Leanne 是主動發現，所以可以把 found 改為 finding。

語法規則範例 ②

_____ the details of the contract thoroughly, the lawyer suggested a few modifications to ensure clarity and fairness.
(A) Reviewed
(B) Reviewing
(C) Having been reviewed
(D) Being reviewing

中譯 仔細審查合約細節後，律師建議做幾處修改，以確保清晰和公平。

範例解析

由於本句前面的附屬子句中沒有主詞，可推測原本是副詞子句，**由於主詞和主要子句一樣，所以被省略。**

(A) Reviewed 是過去分詞，通常用於被動或補充說明，主詞律師應該是主動檢查，reviewed 和語意不符。

(B) 本句主詞要去後面的主要子句尋找，主詞 lawyer 是主動檢查，要用代表主動的現在分詞 Reviewing，表示律師正在主動檢查，為正解。

(C) "Having been reviewed" 表示動作已被完成，且是被動語態，不符合語意。

(D) "Being reviewing" 是不正確的結構，因為分詞構句中不使用 Being 與現在分詞的組合。

高頻多益單字 detail (n.) 細節　contract (n.) 合約　thoroughly (adv.) 徹底地　suggest (v.) 建議　modification (n.) 修改　ensure (v.) 確保　clarity (n.) 清楚　fairness (n.) 公平

考點 3　被動語態

被動語態 (passive) 的構成，就是把主動語態動詞的受詞，變成被動語態動詞的主詞。主動語態動詞的主詞在被動語態中接在 by 之後，後面所接的名詞稱為「行為者」，就是做動作的那一方。**被動語態用於強調動作的接受者，常用於正式或商業的書寫中。**

範例

主動語態　**The manager** submitted **the report**.

被動語態　= **The report** was submitted by **the manager**.
（報告由經理提交。）

主動語態　**The government** will implement **the new law** next month.

被動語態　= **The new law** will be implemented by **the government** next month.（新政策將於下個月實施。）

但如果是一般不需要再去額外說明的資訊，因為**行為者在句中不是重點**，那就不用把「by + 名詞」也就是這個行為者，置於被動語態後方。像是以下的範例：

Big Ben **was built** in London.
（大笨鐘被建造在倫敦。）

The construction of Taipei 101 **was completed** in 2004.
（台北101的建造工程於2004年完成。）

請牢記被動語態的基本句型：be + pp.

下表為**搭配時態一起使用的被動語態公式**

	簡單式	進行式	完成式
現在	am, are, is + pp.	am, are, is being + pp.	have, has been + pp.
過去	was, were + pp.	was, were being + pp.	had been + pp.
未來	will be + pp.		will have been + pp.

最後與被動語態相關的常考使役動詞展示如下：

1. 強迫	make	+O.	+V.	}	主動
	want / force / order / cause	+O.	+to V.		
	make / want / force / order / cause	+O.	+pp.	}	被動
2. 要求	have	+O.(人)	+V.	}	主動
	have	+O.(物)	+pp.	}	被動
3. 說服	get	+O.(人)	+to V.	}	主動
	get	+O.(物)	+pp.	}	被動
4. 允許	let	+O.	+V.		主動
5. 幫助	help	+O.(人)	+V./to V.		主動

多益試題的關鍵語法規則

語法規則範例 ③

A security check _____ at the entrance every morning.
(A) conducts
(B) conducted
(C) is conducting
(D) is conducted

中譯 每天早晨在入口處進行安全檢查。

範例解析

(A) conducts 是現在簡單式主動語態，句子中的 "every morning" 提示了這是每天反覆的動作，但是 security check（安檢）須由人來操作，因此需使用被動語態的情境。
(B) conducted 是過去簡單式主動語態，不符合被動語態的語境。
(C) "is conducting" 是現在進行式主動語態，表示正在進行的動作，但根據語境，安檢是被動，所以不適用。
(D) "is conducted" 是現在式的被動語態，表示 security check（安檢）每天早上都在入口處進行，**符合被動語態的語境，為正解**。

解析重點

- 句子中提到 **"every morning"**，**顯示事件是每天都常態發生**，因此**應選擇現在簡單式**的被動語態 "is conducted"。
- 被動語態強調的是 安檢 無法主動執行，將會被執行，因此必須 使用被動語態。

高頻多益單字 security check (n.) 安檢　　conduct (v.) 執行

語法規則範例 ④

The conference details _____ to all participants by the end of the week.
(A) have sent
(B) were sent
(C) will be sent
(D) be sending

中譯 會議的詳細資訊將於本週末前發送給所有參與者。

範例解析

這題考被動語態搭配時態的使用。句子的關鍵在於**主詞「研討會細節」會在這星期之前** (by the end of the week) **被提供給參與者**，因此這是一個**被動語態**的情境。

(A) "have sent" 是現在完成式，表示某事從過去到現在的某個時間點已經完成，與句子的語境不符。
(B) "were sent" 是過去式的被動語態，但題目中要使用未來的時間去配合 by the end of the week（在這星期之前），因此不適用。
(C) "will be sent" 是未來式的被動語態，符合句子中提到的「在這星期之前」發生的事件，此為正解。
(D) "be sending" 完全不是被動語態的形式，故不可以選。

解析重點

- 句子中的時間是 by the end of the week（這星期之前），因此需要選擇未來式被動語態 "will be sent"。
- 被動語態強調的是「研討會細節」將會被發送給參與者。

高頻多益單字 conference (n.) 會議　participant (n.) 參加者

考點 4　連接詞的使用

連接詞用來連接句子或詞語，幫助表達更複雜的概念，常見的連接詞如下：

範例

- **and**：I like tea **and** coffee.（我喜歡茶和咖啡。）
- **but**：He wanted to go, **but** he was too busy.（他想去，但他太忙了。）
- **because**：She stayed home **because** it was raining.（她因為下雨而待在家裡。）

底下將所有的連接詞分成兩大類，由老師自創的**連接詞家族一覽表**搭配範例來說明：

這些**連接詞**的共同特點是它們總是成對出現好比麻吉（好朋友的概念），並用來**連接**兩個**相似、有關係或對立的句型**。它們不僅使句子結構更具層次感，還能強調選擇、強化或對比的關係。

名稱	記憶方式	
對等連接詞 (Coordinating Conjunctions)	粉絲男孩家族 FANBOYS	**F**OR, **A**ND, **N**OR, **B**UT, **O**R, **Y**ET, **S**O
相關連接詞 (Correlative Conjunctions)	麻吉家族	both...and; not only... but also; neither... nor; either... or

對等連接詞【粉絲男孩家族】：

對等連接詞 (Coordinating Conjunctions)

AND
We will offer a discount on all products **and** provide free shipping for orders over $50.
（我們將對所有產品提供折扣，並且對超過50美元的訂單提供免費運送。）

說明　AND 用來**連接**兩個**相似的**項目或動作，這是 FANBOYS 中最常見的用法。

BUT
The meeting was scheduled for 10 AM, **but** it was delayed due to technical difficulties.
（會議訂於上午10點召開，但由於技術問題，會議被延遲了。）

說明 BUT 用來連接兩個對立或相反的情況，這表達了一種轉折或反差。

OR
The training session will take place on Wednesday, **or** it will be rescheduled for next month.
（培訓課程將於星期三舉行，或是將重新安排到下個月。）

說明 OR 用於提供選擇或替代方案，表示兩者之間的選擇。

SO
The company has seen significant growth in recent years, **so** it plans to expand its operations.
（該公司近年來經歷了顯著的增長，因此計劃擴充業務。）

說明 SO 用來表達因果關係，顯示前一個事件或情況是後續行動的原因。

FOR
She loves to paint, **for** it allows her to express her creativity.
（她熱愛作畫，因為這讓她展現創意。）

說明 FOR 用來表示原因，解釋為何某個行動或情況發生。

YET
The movie received bad reviews, **yet** it became a box office success.
（那部電影的評價很差，然而票房卻很好。）

說明 YET 用來新增非預期或令人驚訝的後續結果。

NOR
He doesn't like coffee, **nor** does he enjoy tea.
（他不喜歡咖啡，也不喜歡茶。）

說明 NOR 用來連接兩個否定的情況，通常出現在否定句中，表達兩者都不成立。

相關連接詞【麻吉家族】：

相關連接詞 (Correlative Conjunctions)

both... and
Both the manager **and** the assistant attended the conference.
（經理和助理都參加了會議。）

> 說明　both...and 用來連接兩個詞性相同的單字、成對的片語，或結構類似的子句，強調這兩者都有某種共同特徵或動作。

---

not only... but also
The company has **not only** expanded its operations **but also** introduced new products.
（公司不僅擴展了業務，還推出了新產品。）

> 說明　not only...but also 用來強調兩個相關的事實或動作，並表達出「並且更強」或「更進一步」的語氣。

---

neither... nor
Neither the sales manager **nor** the marketing director could attend the meeting.
（銷售經理和市場部總監都無法參加會議。）

> 說明　neither...nor 用來表示兩者皆否定，強調兩者都不發生某個動作或情況。

---

either... or
The project will be completed **either** by the end of this month **or** early next month.
（這個專案將於本月底或下月初完成。）

> 說明　either...or 用來表達選擇或替代，指出兩個可能的選項或結果。

語法規則範例 ⑤

The company plans to expand its operations in Europe _____ improve its supply chain efficiency globally.
(A) but
(B) or
(C) and
(D) so

中譯 該公司計劃在歐洲擴展業務，並在全球提高供應鏈效率。

範例解析

句子中**需要一個對等連接詞**來連結兩個具有並列關係的動詞短語 "expand its operations" 和 "improve its supply chain efficiency"。**and 表示「以及」，連接相似或相等的動作**。
(A) but 表示轉折，語意不符。
(B) or 表示選擇，不符合句子的意圖。
(D) so 表示結果，但這裡的兩個短語並非因果關係。正解為 (C)。

高頻多益單字　expand (v.) 擴張　operation (n.) 營運　improve (v.) 改善
supply chain (n.) 供應鏈　efficiency (n.) 效率
globally (adv.) 全球地

從屬連接詞：

引導名詞子句的連接詞家族一覽表		
…之事	名詞子句引導詞	是否…
that	who　when what　which where　why　how	whether / if

引導形容詞子句的連接詞家族一覽表	
關係代名詞	
人	事／物
who whom whose that	which whose that

引導副詞子句的連接詞家族一覽表			
原因 because since now that as	**目的** so that (in order) that	**意外結果** though although even though	**直接對比** while whereas
時間 after before when while as as soon as since until whenever	**頻率、距離和程度** as once as adverb as every time (that / when) the next time (that / when) by the time (that / when) as if / as though	**條件** if whether or not unless / if . . . not only if even if in case in the event that	

語法規則範例 ⑥

The marketing team decided to postpone the product launch _____ they could gather more customer feedback.
(A) in case
(B) so that
(C) because of
(D) even though

中譯 行銷團隊決定延後產品發表，以便他們可以收集更多的顧客意見。

範例解析

句子中需要一個連接詞來引導目的子句，表示「為了能夠…」。(B) "so that" 正確表達了這種因果關係，表明延後產品發佈的目的是收集更多客戶的意見。
(A) "in case" 表示「以防」，不符合語意。
(C) "because of" 是介詞短語，後面應接名詞，而非完整子句。
(D) "even though" 表示讓步關係，這裡的主要子句並沒有讓人感到意外，所以也不符合語意。

高頻多益單字
marketing team (n.) 行銷團隊　decide (v.) 決定
postpone (v.) 延緩　product launch (n.) 產品發表
gather (v.) 收集　customer feedback (n.) 顧客意見

考點 5　關係子句（也稱形容詞子句）的使用

關係子句（形容詞子句）為從屬子句，作用和形容詞相同，用來修飾名詞或代名詞。首先我們先來了解什麼是獨立子句和從屬子句。

獨立子句 (Independent Clause)：完整的（＝主要子句）

獨立子句是完整的句子，能夠表達完整的意思，並且**可以單獨存在**。

範例

- She works at a bank.
  （她在銀行工作。）
  ▶ 這是一個獨立子句，因為它的語義完整，本身就是一個完整的句子。

- The manager will attend the meeting tomorrow.
  （經理明天將參加會議。）
  ▶ 這也是獨立子句，也是一個完整的句子。

從屬子句 (Dependent Clause)：不完整，必須與主要子句相連

從屬子句雖然有主語和動詞，但**無法單獨表達完整的意思**，必須與獨立子句結合才能構成完整句子。從屬子句**通常由從屬連接詞引導**，如：because, although, if, when 等。

範例

- **Although** she was tired, she continued working.
  （儘管她很累，但她繼續工作。）
  ▶ "Although she was tired" 是從屬子句，不能獨立存在，必須依賴 "she continued working" 來表達整句完整的語義。

- **If** it rains tomorrow, the event will be postponed.
  （如果明天下雨，活動將被延後。）
  ▶ "If it rains tomorrow" 是從屬子句，需要與 "the event will be postponed" 這個獨立子句結合，才能完整表達句義。

形容詞子句是由**關係代名詞引導的從屬子句**，功能就是用來**修飾前面的先行詞**。要根據**先行詞是人或事物、是限定或非限定、是主格、受格或所有格**來判斷要使用哪一種關係代名詞。

先行詞 \ 格	主格	受格	所有格
人	who/that	whom/that	whose
事物（非限定）	which	which	whose
事物（限定）	that	that	

關係代名詞

who / whom

當前面的先行詞為人時，要使用 who 或 whom 引導的從屬子句來修飾。
who 用來指代主詞，**whom** 是用來指代受詞，為正式用法，當形容詞子句的動詞為及物動詞時，必須和介系詞連用。

範例

- **The man who is standing over there is my boss.**
  （那位站在那裡的男子是我的老闆。）
  ▶ 形容詞子句 "who is standing over there" 用來描述 "the man"，關係代名詞 who 指代主詞 the man。

- **The person whom you spoke to is our director.**
  （你剛才和他說話的人是我們的主管。）
  ▶ 形容詞子句 "whom you spoke to" 用來描述剛剛和你說話的那個人 "the person" 和我們的關係，由於關係代名詞是這個附屬子句的受詞，所以要用 whom，並且要加介系詞 to，因為「和某人談話」會用 speak to 這個片語。

whose

whose 用來表示所有格關係，可**指代人或物的所有格關係**。

> 範例

- **The woman** whose car was parked outside is the manager.
  （那個車停在外面的女子是經理。）
  ▸ 形容詞子句 "whose car was parked outside" 用來描述 "the woman"，關係代名詞 whose 表示 the woman's。

which

which 用來指代事物或動物，也可以用來指代整個句子。which 只能用在非限定的情況，這代表 **which 子句的內容只是用來補充先行詞的資訊**，但**並非句子裡的重點訊息**，重要性不高。

範例：

- **The movie**, which was released last month, became a big hit.
  （那部上個月上映的電影票房很好。）
  ▸ 形容詞子句 "which was released last month" 用來描述 "the movie"，先行詞為 "the movie"，"which was released last month" 是補充訊息，若省略對句易影響不大。

- I bought **a new phone**, which has a large screen.
  （我買了一支新手機，這支手機的螢幕很大。）
  ▸ 形容詞子句 "which has a large screen" 用來描述 "a new phone"，"which has a large screen" 只是額外補充。

that

that 可用來指代人或物，常見於口語和書面語中，也經常省略，特別是在非正式或簡化語句中。**that 只能用在限定的情況**，這時，**that 子句的內容重要性高**，是必須讓對方知道的，**不可省略**。

範例

- This is **the book** <u>that</u> I recommended to you.
  （這是我推薦給你的書。）
  - ▶ 形容詞子句 "that I recommended to you" 用來描述 "the book"，為句子的重點，非額外補充。

- **The team** <u>that</u> won the game is celebrating.
  （贏得比賽的隊伍正在慶祝。）
  - ▶ 形容詞子句 "that won the game" 用來描述 "the team"，為句子的重點，非額外補充，所以關係代名詞要用 that。

範例

- **The manager** <u>who</u> <u>is new</u> will join us for lunch.（新來的經理將和我們共進午餐。）
  - ▶ 本句為主格關代，關代為子句中的主格。本句為限定修飾，因為 "who is new" 是重要訊息，但不管是限定或非限定，皆可以用 who 來連接。

- The book **that** I borrowed is interesting.（我借的書很有趣。）
  - ▶ 本句為受格關代，關代為子句的受詞。由於 "that I borrowed" 為重要資訊，若刪掉就不知道哪本書很有趣了，所以是限定用法，要用 that 連接或省略。

語法規則範例 ⑦

The new policy will benefit employees _____ the company has identified as high performers.

(A) where
(B) whom
(C) whose
(D) although

中譯 新政策將有利於被公司認定為高績效的員工。

範例解析

由於空格後面的子句看起來像是在形容 employees（員工），這個空格需要填入引導形容詞子句 " the company has identified as high performers" 的關係代名詞。**而先行詞 employees 是人，所以可能的選項只有 (B) whom**。
(A) where 為關係副詞，指代地點，不符合句子結構。
(C) whose 用來指代所有格，不適合這裡的語意。
(D) although 為連接詞，語意為「然而」，並不正確。

高頻多益單字 policy (n.) 政策　benefit (v.) 有利於　employee (n.) 員工
identify (v.) 認定　high performer (n.) 高績效者

語法規則範例 ⑧

The research paper, _____ in several leading scientific journals, has gained international recognition.
(A) was published
(B) published
(C) having been published
(D) that was published

中譯 這篇研究論文已在幾本領先的科學期刊上發表，並獲得國際認可。

範例解析

題目中的句子，最初應該是 "The research paper, which was **published** in several leading scientific journals, has gained international recognition." 可以簡化為 "The research paper, **published** in several leading scientific journals, has gained international recognition."
(A) "was published" 不正確，這個句子已有動詞，不會再出現一個動詞。
(C) "having been published" 是完成式的被動語態分詞構句，通常表示一個完成的動作，語意上不完全適合這裡的情境。
(D) "that published" 由於句中有加逗點，為非限定用法，前面先行詞為物，後面只能用 which，所以後面接 that 不正確。正確答案是 (B)。

高頻多益單字 publish (v.) 發表　leading (adj.) 領先的　scientific (adj.) 科學的　journal (n.) 期刊　gain (v.) 獲得　international (adj.) 國際的　recognition (n.) 認可

Practice Test

新制多益模擬試題

1. The CEO was unsure whether the project _____ completed on time.
   (A) had been
   (B) will be
   (C) has been
   (D) would have been

2. _____ the data collected from multiple sources, the team was able to form a comprehensive report.
   (A) Analyzing
   (B) Analyzed
   (C) Having analyzed
   (D) To analyze

3. _____ to a number of clients, the new product features were mostly met with approval.
   (A) Explaining
   (B) Explained
   (C) Having explained
   (D) To explain

4. We cannot proceed with the project _____ all necessary permissions are granted by the local authorities.
   (A) in case
   (B) so that
   (C) because
   (D) unless

5. The new product line _____ launched successfully by the end of the month, making the company the market leader.
   (A) is
   (B) will have
   (C) was
   (D) will

6. The new software is quite efficient, _____ some employees are finding it a little difficult to use.
   (A) since
   (B) although
   (C) because
   (D) despite

7. The new system _____ successfully by the IT department, and it is now fully operational.
   (A) has been implemented
   (B) had been implemented
   (C) will be implemented
   (D) is being implemented

8. The new employee, _____ work experience includes both project management and customer relations, was hired last week.
   (A) who
   (B) whose
   (C) whom
   (D) that

9. _____ a new overtime policy is necessary to comply with national labor laws.
   (A) Implementing
   (B) Implement
   (C) Implementation
   (D) Implemented

10. By the time the project manager arrived at the office, the team _____ their individual tasks.
    (A) completed
    (B) had completed
    (C) has completed
    (D) will complete

11. She accepted the job offer in the end, _____ the salary was lower than she expected and the commute was long.
    (A) as soon as
    (B) now that
    (C) in order that
    (D) even though

12. When she checked her e-mail, she saw that the invitation _____ the previous week.
    (A) had sent
    (B) had been sent
    (C) has sent
    (D) has been sent

13. The new system, _____ was designed to increase efficiency, will be launched next week.
    (A) that
    (B) who
    (C) which
    (D) it

14. When we reach the end of the fiscal year, the annual budget _____ fully spent.
    (A) will be
    (B) will have been
    (C) has been
    (D) had been

15. _____, he is now responsible for leading a larger team and managing more complex projects.
    (A) To be promoted
    (B) Was promoted
    (C) Having been promoted
    (D) Has been promoted

16. You can choose to attend the morning session _____ the afternoon one, depending on your schedule.
    (A) or
    (B) and
    (C) nor
    (D) for

17. They reported that they _____ the financial analysis and were prepared to present it at the meeting.
    (A) will complete
    (B) completed
    (C) have completed
    (D) had completed

18. _____ a survey to gather customer feedback, the marketing department aimed to identify key areas for improvement.
    (A) To conduct
    (B) Conduct
    (C) Conducting
    (D) Conducted

19. After several months of negotiation, the final contract _____ by both parties, ensuring all terms were agreed upon.
    (A) signed
    (B) was signed
    (C) sign
    (D) signing

20. The project _____ was completed by our research team will be presented at the conference next month.
    (A) when
    (B) what
    (C) which
    (D) that

21. _____ she had little experience in the field, her enthusiasm and willingness to learn impressed the hiring manager during the interview.
    (A) Because
    (B) Although
    (C) Even if
    (D) Unless

22. By the time the manager arrives, the team _____ already completed the task.
    (A) had
    (B) has
    (C) will have
    (D) will be

23. _____ the report, she felt a sense of accomplishment and was eager to present her findings to the board.
    (A) Finishing
    (B) Finished
    (C) Has completed
    (D) Had completed

24. The team needs to submit the plan by Friday _____ they will have sufficient time to review it before the meeting.
    (A) even if
    (B) in case
    (C) now that
    (D) so that

試題演練答案、翻譯與解說

答案

1. (A)	2. (C)	3. (B)	4. (D)	5. (B)	6. (B)	7. (A)	8. (B)
9. (A)	10. (B)	11. (D)	12. (B)	13. (C)	14. (B)	15. (C)	16. (A)
17. (D)	18. (C)	19. (B)	20. (D)	21. (B)	22. (C)	23. (A)	24. (D)

1. **(A)** The CEO was unsure whether the project <u>had been</u> completed on time.

   中譯 執行長不確定該專案是否已經準時完成。

   說明 主要子句 "The CEO was unsure" 是過去式，因此**從屬子句的動詞時態應與之保持一致**，根據語意與時態，正確答案是 **(A) had been**（過去完成式），表示在過去某個時間點之前，CEO 不確定專案是否已完成。

   其他選項：
   - **(B) will be**：未來式，與過去式的主句 "was unsure" 不一致，不符合語境。
   - **(C) has been**：現在完成式，表示與現在相關的動作，與主要子句的過去式不符合。
   - **(D) would have been**：完成條件式，通常用於與假設情況相關的語境，但題目中沒有假設條件，因此不適合。

   單字 unsure (adj.) 不確定的　project (n.) 專案

   片語 on time (phr.) 準時

2. **(C)** <u>Having analyzed</u> the data collected from multiple sources, the team was able to form a comprehensive report.

   中譯 分析了從多個來源收集的數據後，團隊得以完成一份全面的報告。

   說明 選項 **(C) Having analyzed** 是完成式分詞，表示**主要子句動作發生前，先完成了「分析數據」這個動作**，符合句子邏輯順序。

   其他選項：
   - **(A) Analyzing**：表示正在分析，但與主句「形成報告」的完成態不符。
   - **(B) Analyzed**：過去分詞，但缺乏完成動作的明確性。
   - **(D) To analyze**：不定式，不表示動作已完成。

   單字 collect (v.) 收集　multiple (adj.) 多重的　form (v.) 製作　comprehensive (adj.) 全面的

3. **(B)** Explained to a number of clients, the new product features were mostly met with approval.

中譯 向多位客戶解釋後，這項新產品的功能大致上受到肯定。

說明 選項 **(B) Explained** 是過去分詞，**作為分詞片語，表示被動語態**，指「新產品功能被解釋給客戶」。這與句子主語 "the new product features" 的被動關係相符。

其他選項：
- **(A) Explaining**：表示主動進行中，不符合邏輯。
- **(C) Having explained**：表示主動完成動作，不適合被動語態的主語。
- **(D) To explain**：不定式，不符合句子語意與結構。

單字 explain (v.) 解釋　client (n.) 客戶　feature (n.) 功能　approval (n.) 贊同

4. **(D)** We cannot proceed with the project unless all necessary permissions are granted by the local authorities.

中譯 除非當地政府批准所有必要的許可，否則我們無法繼續進行此專案。

說明 選項 **(D) unless** 表示「除非」，符合句子語意，指出專案必須在取得所有必要許可後才能進行，形成條件句的結構。

其他選項：
- **(A) in case**：表示「以防萬一」，不符合句意。
- **(B) so that**：表示「以便」，用於表示目的，不適合此處條件關係。
- **(C) because**：表示「因為」，與句子邏輯不符。

單字 proceed (v.) 繼續進行　permission (n.) 許可　grant (v.) 准予
local authorities (n.) 當地政府

5. **(B)** The new product line will have launched successfully by the end of the month, making the company the market leader.

中譯 新的產品線將在本月底之前成功推出，使該公司成為市場領導者。

說明 **未來完成式 (will have + 過去分詞)** 表示某個動作在未來特定時間之前完成，"will have launched" 是未來完成式，表示動作會在未來某一時間點之前完成，**(B) will have** 符合 "by the end of the month" 的語意，因此正確。

其他選項：
- **(A) is**："is launched" 是現在式被動語態，無法表示未來某個時間點之前完成的動作，因此不正確。

069

- **(C) was**：“was launched" 是過去式，表示動作已經在過去完成，與題目中的未來時間點不符，因此不正確。
- **(D) will**：“will launched" 語法錯誤，因為助動詞 will 後必須接動詞原形，launch 而非過去分詞形式，因此不正確。

單字 launch (v.) 發表

6. **(B)** The new software is quite efficient, although some employees are finding it a little difficult to use.
    (A) since
    (B) although
    (C) because
    (D) despite

中譯 這套新軟體效率很高，儘管有些員工覺得使用起來有些困難。

說明 選項 **(B) although** 表示「雖然」，用來引導**讓步子句**，說明即使新軟體很有效率，但有些員工仍覺得難用，**符合句子邏輯**。

其他選項：
- **(A) since**：表示「因為」，不符合句子邏輯。
- **(C) because**：表示「因為」，同樣不符合句子邏輯。
- **(D) despite**：應接名詞或動名詞，不能直接接完整子句，語法錯誤。

單字 efficient (adj.) 有效率的

7. **(A)** The new system has been implemented successfully by the IT department, and it is now fully operational.

中譯 新系統已由資訊部門成功實施，現在已全面運作。

說明 選項 **(A) has been implemented** 使用現在完成式，表示「新系統已經成功實施」，強調完成的動作與現在的結果（系統已完全運作）有直接關聯，符合句子語意。

其他選項：
- **(B) had been implemented**：過去完成式，表示動作在過去另一事件之前完成，但句中沒有提到相關的過去參照點，不符合語境。
- **(C) will be implemented**：未來式，不符合句子描述已完成的動作。
- **(D) is being implemented**：現在進行式，被動語態，表示動作正在進行中，但與「已完全運作」的語意不符。

單字 implement (v.) 實施　operational (adj.) 運作的

8. **(B)** The new employee, <u>whose</u> work experience includes both project management and customer relations, was hired last week.

中譯 這位新員工的工作經驗包括專案管理和客戶關係，於上週被錄用。

說明 選項 **(B) whose** 是正確答案，指代 "the new employee"，用於引導關係子句，語意通順且符合語法。

其他選項：
- **(A) who**：作主詞用來指代人，但後面不能直接接名詞 "work experience"。
- **(C) whom**：作受詞用來指代人，結構不符此處需修飾名詞的需求。
- **(D) that**：不能用來引導表示「所有格」的關係子句。

單字 project management (n.) 專案管理　customer relations (n.) 客戶關係

9. **(A)** <u>Implementing</u> a new overtime policy is necessary to comply with national labor laws.

中譯 實施新的加班政策是符合國家勞動法的必要措施。

說明 這是一個完整句子，**主語必須為動名詞（表示動作的名詞形式）**，因為句子描述的是「實施一項新加班政策」這個行為的必要性。**(A) Implementing**：動名詞，表示「實施」這個行為，適合作為主語，句子結構完整。

其他選項：
- **(B) Implement**：為動詞原形，無法直接當主詞。
- **(C) Implementation**：為名詞，表示「實施這個行為的結果」，語義上不如動名詞貼切。
- **(D) Implemented**：為過去分詞，通常作為被動語態的一部分或修飾語，無法作為主詞使用。

單字 labor law (n.) 勞工法
片語 comply with (phr.) 遵守

10. **(B)** By the time the project manager arrived at the office, the team <u>had completed</u> their individual tasks.

中譯 當專案經理抵達辦公室時，團隊已經完成了各自的任務。

說明 句子中有關鍵詞 **"By the time"**，表示「到…的時候」。這通常表示過去某一時間之前，某個動作已經完成。句子中的時態暗示："**the project manager arrived**" 是過去的某個時間點發生的事件，因此**前面的動作（完成任務）應該發生在此之前，空格內應填入過去完成式 (B) had completed**。

其他選項：
- **(A) completed**：這是過去式，表示動作與「到達辦公室」同時發生，但這不符合「先完成任務，後到辦公室」的時間順序。
- **(C) has completed**：這是現在完成式，表示動作與現在有關，與句中的過去時間點「到達辦公室」不符。
- **(D) will complete**：這是未來式，與句中的過去時間點不符。

單字　individual (adj.) 個人的　task (n.) 任務

11. **(D)** She accepted the job offer in the end, <u>even though</u> the salary was lower than she expected and the commute was long.

中譯　儘管薪水低於她的預期且通勤時間較長，她最終還是接受了工作邀請。

說明　前後兩個子句之間的關係為「意外結果」，表示儘管存在某些較差的條件（薪水低、通勤長），她仍然接受了工作。**(D) even though**：表示「儘管」，符合句子的邏輯和語意。

其他選項：
- **(A) as soon as**：表示「一…就…」，用於時間關係，與句意不符。
- **(B) now that**：表示「既然」，用於表示原因，與句意不符。
- **(C) in order that**：表示「以便於」，用來表示目的，與句意不符。

單字　job offer (n.) 工作邀請　salary (n.) 薪資

12. **(B)** When she checked her e-mail, she saw that the invitation <u>had been sent</u> the previous week.

中譯　當她查看電子郵件時，她發現邀請函已在前一週寄出。

說明　副詞子句是 "she checked her e-mail"，發生在過去。「邀請函被寄出」這一動作發生在她檢查郵件之前，因此需要使用**過去完成式**（表示「過去的過去」）。邀請是「被寄出」，因此需要使用被動語態。故選 **(B) had been sent**。

其他選項：
- **(A) had sent**：過去完成式的主動語態，表示主詞寄出了邀請函，與句意不符（邀請函是被寄出的）。
- **(C) has sent**：現在完成式的主動語態，與句中過去的背景不符，且語態錯誤。
- **(D) has been sent**：現在完成式的被動語態，與句中的過去背景不符。

單字　invitation (n.) 邀請　previous (adj.) 先前的

13. **(C)** The new system, which was designed to increase efficiency, will be launched next week.

中譯 這套旨在提高效率的新系統將於下週啟用。

說明 形容詞子句或關係子句 "which was designed to increase efficiency" 是用來補充說明 "the new system" 的主詞，由於這裡有逗點為非限定用法，所以主詞的關係代名詞不可以用 (A) that，只能用 (C) which 來補充說明主詞 "the new system"。

其他選項：
- **(B) who**：用於人，這裡主詞是 "the new system"（物），不適用。
- **(D) it**：不是關係代名詞，無法引導關係子句。

單字 increase (v.) 增加

14. **(B)** When we reach the end of the fiscal year, the annual budget will have been fully spent.

中譯 當我們到達會計年度的末尾時，年度預算將已完全用盡。

說明 句子開頭的 "When we reach the end of the fiscal year" 表示未來的某一時間點。「年度預算被完全花掉」是這一時間點之前完成的動作，因此需要用**未來完成式**來表達。**(B) will have been** 未來完成式的被動語態，正確表示在未來某一時刻之前已經完成的被動動作。

其他選項：
- **(A) will be**：未來簡單式，表示未來的狀態，但無法表達在未來某一時刻之前完成的動作，不符合句意。
- **(C) has been**：現在完成式，描述與現在相關的完成動作，與未來的背景不符。
- **(D) had been**：過去完成式，表示過去某一時刻之前完成的動作，與未來的背景不符。

單字 fiscal year (n.) 會計年度　annual budget (n.) 年度預算　fully (adv.) 全部地

15. **(C)** Having been promoted, he is now responsible for leading a larger team and managing more complex projects.

中譯 因為被升職，他現在負責領導一個更大的團隊並管理更複雜的專案。

說明 分詞構句 **Having been**「因為他被升職」來描述主要子句 **he is now responsible...** (C) Having been promoted 正確表示「因為已經被升職」這個已完成的動作，結構完整。

073

其他選項：
- **(A) To be promoted**：不定詞表目的，為不正確的句子結構。
- **(B) Was promoted**：直接使用過去式，不符合分詞構句的語句。
- **(D) Has been promoted**：現在完成式的被動語態，為不正確的句子結構。

單字 complex (adj.) 複雜的
片語 be responsible for (phr.) 負責

16. **(A)** You can choose to attend the morning session <u>or</u> the afternoon one, depending on your schedule.

中譯 你可以選擇參加上午場或下午場，取決於你的時間安排。
說明 句子表達的是「選擇」的關係，應使用 **(A) or**：表示「或」，用於連接兩個選項，正確表達選擇關係。

其他選項：
- **(B) and**：表示「和」，用於連接兩個同時成立的條件，但此處須做出選擇，不適合。
- **(C) nor**：表示「也不」，通常與 **neither** 搭配，用於否定，與句意不符。
- **(D) for**：表示「因為」，用於解釋原因，與句子需表達的選擇關係不符。

單字 attend (v.) 參加
片語 depend on (phr.) 取決於

17. **(D)** They reported that they <u>had completed</u> the financial analysis and were prepared to present it at the meeting.

中譯 他們報告說，已完成財務分析並準備在會議上進行報告。
說明 主要子句 **"They reported"** 是過去式，表示這個動作發生在過去。從屬子句 **"they ＿＿＿ the financial analysis"** 的動作發生在「報告」之前，因此需要使用**過去完成式**來表示「過去的過去」。**(D) had completed**：過去完成式，正確表達「在報告之前完成了財務分析」。

其他選項：
- **(A) will complete**：未來式，表示未來的動作，與主要子句的過去背景不符。
- **(B) completed**：過去式，表示與主句「報告」同時發生的動作，但這裡需要表達的是更早發生的動作。
- **(C) have completed**：現在完成式，與主要子句過去時態不符。

單字 analysis (n.) 分析

18. **(C)** Conducting a survey to gather customer feedback, the marketing department aimed to identify key areas for improvement.

中譯 行銷部門進行顧客意見調查，旨在找出需要改進的關鍵領域。

說明 句子的主要子句是 "**the marketing department aimed to identify key areas for improvement**"。空格部分需要填入一個補充說明的分詞，描述進行調查這個動作與主要子句之間的關係。由於此句為分詞構句，**省略的主詞為 the marketing department**（行銷部門）**會主動做調查**，所以要選擇**表主動的現在分詞 (V-ing)**，**(C) Conducting**：現在分詞，用來說明「為了蒐集顧客意見而進行的調查」，修飾主要子句。

其他選項：
- **(A) To conduct**：不定詞表目的，不符合此處的語境。
- **(B) Conduct**：原形動詞，語法不符合。
- **(D) Conducted**：過去分詞，通常表示被動或已完成的狀態，與句子意思不符。

單字 survey (n.) 問卷　aim (v.) 旨在　improvement (n.) 改善

19. **(B)** After several months of negotiation, the final contract was signed by both parties, ensuring all terms were agreed upon.

中譯 經過數月的談判，最終合約由雙方簽署，確保所有條款達成一致。

說明 句子的主詞是 "**the final contract**"，動作是 "**signed**"。這是一個被動語態的句子，因為「合約」是被簽署的對象，而不是主動執行這個動作的人。
(B) was signed 過去簡單被動語態，表示「合約被簽署」。

其他選項：
- **(A) signed**：過去分詞，但缺少 be 動詞 **was**，不是被動語態。
- **(C) sign**：動詞原形，不符合語法。
- **(D) signing**：現在分詞，不符合句子的語法結構。

單字 negotiation (n.) 協商　ensure (v.) 確保　term (n.) 條款　agree (v.) 認同

20. **(D)** The project that was completed by our research team will be presented at the conference next month.

中譯 由我們研究團隊完成的專案將於下個月的會議上報告。

說明 句子中的空格部分需要一個關係代名詞，來指代 "the project"，描述這個專案的完成情況。主詞是事件，由於這個關係子句 "_____ was completed by our research team" 對語意很重要，不可省略，為限定用法，所以要用

075

關係代名詞 **that** 來取代前面的主詞 the project。

其他選項：
- **(A) when**：用來引導時間的從屬連接詞，表示時間，與句子結構不符。
- **(B) what**：用來引導名詞子句，通常表示「什麼」，不適用於此處。
- **(C) which**：用在非限定用法，也就是關係子句不放也不影響語意的情況。

單字 complete (v.) 完成

21. **(B)** Although she had little experience in the field, her enthusiasm and willingness to learn impressed the hiring manager during the interview.

中譯 儘管她在該領域經驗不足，但她的熱忱和學習意願在面試時打動了招聘經理。

說明 句子的意思是：儘管她在這個領域的經驗很少，但她的熱情和學習意願卻給面試官留下了深刻印象。**(B) Although**：表示意外的結果，「儘管」，用來表示在某種情況下，另一個結果仍然成立，這正是句子的意思。

其他選項：
- **(A) Because**：表示原因，通常用於解釋「為什麼」某事發生，與這句表示讓步的語氣不符。
- **(C) Even if**：表示即使在某些情況下，但不完全符合這裡的語境。通常用來表達假設。
- **(D) Unless**：表示「除非」，通常用於條件句，這與句意思不符。

單字 field (n.) 領域　enthusiasm (n.) 熱誠　willingness (n.) 意願
impress (v.) 留下好印象　interview (n.) 面試

22. **(C)** By the time the manager arrives, the team will have already completed the task.

中譯 當經理抵達時，團隊將已完成該任務。

說明 句子中的 "**By the time**" 表示「到某個時間點為止」，是未來的某個時間。"**the team will have already completed the task**" 描述的動作（完成任務）會在未來的某一時間點之前發生。因此，這需要使用**未來完成式（will have + 過去分詞）**，答案 **(C) will have**。

其他選項：
- **(A) had**：過去完成式，表示在過去某一時間之前完成的動作，與句子的時間背景不符。

- **(B) has**：現在完成式，表示過去發生的動作與現在有關，與句中未來的時間背景不符。
- **(D) will be**：將來進行式，表示某個動作在未來的某一時間點正在進行，不符合句子的語境。

單字 arrive (v.) 抵達

23. **(A)** <u>Finishing</u> the report, she felt a sense of accomplishment and was eager to present her findings to the board.

中譯 完成報告後，她感到一種成就感，並渴望向董事會發表她的研究結果。

說明 句子描述的是完成報告後的感受，"_____ **the report**" 需要一個現在分詞來表達完成某動作後的狀態或行為。由於<u>附屬子句的主詞也是 she</u>，所以要使用 **(A) Finishing**，表示<u>「主動」完成報告</u>。

其他選項：
- **(B) Finished**：過去分詞，通常用於被動語態或作形容詞。
- **(C) Has completed**：現在完成式，語法結構錯誤。
- **(D) Had completed**：過去完成式，描述在過去某一時刻之前完成的動作。

單字 accomplishment (n.) 成就　eager (adj.) 渴望的　finding (n.) 研究、調查結果　board (n.) 董事會

24. **(D)** The team needs to submit the plan by Friday <u>so that</u> they will have sufficient time to review it before the meeting.

中譯 團隊需要在星期五之前提交計劃，以便他們有足夠的時間在會議前進行審查。

說明 句子中 "**The team needs to submit the plan by Friday**" 表示「團隊需要在星期五之前提交計劃」，後面的部分 "_____ **they will have sufficient time to review it before the meeting**" 解釋了為什麼需要這樣做，即是為了讓他們有足夠的時間來審查計劃。**(D) so that** 表示目的或結果。

其他選項：
- **(A) even if**：表示「即使」，通常用於假設或讓步的情況，這不符合句子的目的。
- **(B) in case**：表示「以防」，通常用來表達某種預防措施，與句子含義不符。
- **(C) now that**：表示「既然」，通常用於某些情況已經發生的情境，這與句意不符。

單字 submit (v.) 繳交　sufficient (adj.) 足夠的

3-2 改善句子結構和清晰度的技巧

良好的文法基礎是多益考試成功的關鍵之一。透過熟悉關鍵語法規則、避免常見錯誤，以及改善句子結構和清晰度的技巧，能夠提升自己的寫作能力。在準備過程中，建議定期進行文法練習，以便持續改進。以下是一些提高句子結構和清晰度的技巧：

1. 簡化句子
使用簡單明瞭的句子結構，避免使用過於複雜的句子，這樣可以增強可讀性。

範例
- 複雜 Due to the fact that the weather was bad, we decided to cancel the picnic.
- 簡化 We decided to cancel the picnic because of bad weather.
（我們決定取消野餐，因為天氣不好。）

2. 使用主動語態
主動語態通常比被動語態更直接，能使句子更具活力。

範例
- 被動 The presentation **was given by** the team.
- 主動 The team **gave** the presentation.
（團隊報告了簡報。）

3. 避免冗長的修飾語
過多的修飾語會使句子顯得繁瑣，應保持簡潔。

範例
- 冗長 The very talented and skilled graphic designer created a stunning logo.

- 簡化 The talented graphic designer created a stunning logo.
（這位才華橫溢的平面設計師設計了一個令人驚艷的標誌。）

4. 使用清晰的轉承詞

適當使用轉承詞可以幫助讀者理解句子之間的關係，增強句子的流暢性。使用 "To begin with" 或 "Initially" 強調開頭，能讓句子層次更分明，並使句子的邏輯結構更清晰。使用不同的轉承詞，如 "After that," "followed by," 或 "subsequently"，可提升句子流暢性並避免重複。

範例

First, we will discuss the goals. **After that**, we will review the budget.

To begin with, we will discuss the goals, **followed by** a review of the budget.

Initially, we will focus on discussing the goals, and **subsequently**, we will examine the budget.
（首先，我們會討論目標。之後，我們會審查預算。）

5. 檢查拼寫和標點

錯誤的拼寫和標點會影響句子的清晰度和專業性，因此在寫作時應仔細檢查。

建議
- 使用拼寫檢查工具和語法檢查軟體來發現錯誤。
- 閱讀文章時，特別注意標點的使用，確保句子的結構正確。

第 4 章

口說和發音

4-1 用口說練出聽懂的能力
4-2 英澳腔的基礎加強版
4-3 辦公室常見句型練習

本章節會跟你分享練習口說的技巧和方法以聽懂母語人士說話，針對台灣學生普遍較為陌生的英國澳洲腔，教你應對的方法。最後提供辦公室裡常見的句型，並附上情境對話練習！

4-1 用口說練出聽懂的能力

以語塊學習法提升口說練習

語塊學習法的核心理念是將短語或片語作為完整的單元來學習，而非逐字記憶或背誦單詞。這種方法鼓勵學習者集中於語言的實際使用情境，模仿自然的語言流動。例如，與其逐字練習「The man whose beard caught on fire when he lit a cigarette.（點燃香煙時鬍子著火的男子。）」，學習者應將整句話拆解成 chunk（語塊），我把語塊比喻為樂高積木，必須一個一個堆疊，才能成為完成品，也就是這裡指的完整句子。

舉例來說這裡的語塊有：The man（男子）whose beard（他的鬍子）caught on fire（著火）when he（當他）lit a cigarette（點燃香煙）。

學習者需把自己不熟悉的語塊，拆開單獨練習，不斷地重複單詞，並反覆練習，專注於其語音節奏和語意連貫性。

這種方法的優勢在於，它更貼近母語者的語言學習方式。母語者在學習語言時，並不是逐字解讀，而是將整個語塊（例如短語或固定搭配）當作單位來理解和使用。通過語塊學習法，學習者不僅能更快速地適應自然語速，還能掌握常用的語言結構，提升流暢度。

此外，語塊學習還能幫助學習者更好地掌握語法和詞彙。在特定語境中學習短語，如 "I haven't thought about it."（我還沒想過這件事。）或 "We haven't thought of that."（我們還沒想到這個。），可以讓語言的運用更具實用性。語塊作為完整的記憶單位，有助於在實際對話中快速說出，減少語言停頓或不自然的拼湊現象。

大家練習一下這兩個例句裡的語塊有：I haven't（我還沒）thought about it.（想到）以及 We haven't（我們還沒）thought of that.

為了加強效果，建議學習者搭配重複練習和模仿技巧，例如跟讀 (shadowing)。透過模仿母語者的語速、語音和語調，學習者可以將語塊的學習內化為自身的語言能力。這種方法不僅提升學習效率，還能幫助學習者在實際對話中表現得更自然、更自信。

透過重複訓練提升發音與流暢度

重複練習是一種極為有效的語言學習技術，不僅能幫助學習者強化發音，還能顯著增強口語表達的信心進而『聽懂』。當學習者透過反覆練習像 "I didn't really enjoy the food as much as I thought I would."（我其實沒我想像中那麼享受這樣食物）這樣的句子時，能逐步內化英語的語調、節奏和語音細節，使語音輸出更加自然流暢。這種方法讓語音習慣深植於大腦中，幫助自己能夠自然、快速並正確地說出。

重複練習的另一個關鍵優勢在於，它能建立發音所需的肌肉記憶。發音涉及一系列微妙的口腔動作，而通過反覆練習這些動作，可以讓學習者的嘴唇、舌頭和聲帶更加熟練，輕鬆應對挑戰性詞彙或句子。例如，學習者在練習 "What would you like to eat?"（您想吃什麼？）這類連讀和音調複雜的句子時，重複的次數越多，發音的流利度和正確性就越高。

將重複練習融入日常學習習慣中，能有效地鞏固語言技能。建議學習者每天花幾分鐘專注於短語或句子練習，並逐步挑戰更長、更複雜的句子。搭配錄音工具，自我檢查發音進步，效果更佳。透過持之以恆的努力，學習者不僅能減少口語中的錯誤，也能在實際對話中提升流暢度與增添自信。

掌握包含無聲字母的發音 🎧 014 美

英語中無聲字母極為常見，想要正確掌握也很具挑戰性，對於學習者而言，很容易發音錯誤並影響流利度。像 comb（梳子）、climb（攀爬）和 thumb（拇指）中的 "b"，在字母 "m" 後通常是不發音的。同樣，像 knife（刀）、know（知道）和 knee（膝蓋）中的 "k" 也是無聲的，這些規則對母語者來說是自然習得的，但對非母語者可能需要特別注意。此外，像 hour（小時）、honest（誠實的）和 herb（香草）開頭的 "h" 也不發音，這種特例對於學習者來說往往是需要反覆記憶和練習的項目。

如果學習者不熟悉這些無聲字母的發音，他們可能會在聽力測試或實際溝通時誤解單詞的拼寫與發音。因此，掌握這些特性有助於減少困惑，並提升學習者的聽說能力。

為了有效克服，學習者應針對無聲字母做練習。例如，對於包含無聲字母的單詞，可以反覆朗讀，並用錄音設備檢查自己的發音是否正確。同時，將這些詞彙放入句子中練習，比如 "I know how to climb that mountain."（我知道如何攀登那座山），可以幫助學習者在真實語境中鞏固發音技巧。配合語音軟體或聽母語者的發音範例，也能進一步提高準確性。

總之，理解並掌握無聲字母的發音規律對提升英語流利度和清晰度至關重要。透過持續練習和科學方法，學習者不僅可以避免常見的發音錯誤，還能在實際溝通中更加自信、自然。

4-2 英澳腔的基礎加強版

台灣的教育機構所使用的英語，都是美式英語，因此在台灣一般提到「學英文」，絕大多數是指學「美式英文」，不僅學習美式英語的發音、文法、拼字，連跟語言密不可分的風俗、文化，也都是「美國式」的風格，因此許多英語學習者在第一次聽到英式英語時，多少都會感到有點不太一樣，甚至覺得英式英語比較難。一般來說，美式英語的標準發音，是以 General American Pronunciation (GAP) 為準。這是美國中西部地方人的發音，中西部各州約占美國國土的 75％。

一般稱為英式英語的發音，則是 Received Pronunciation (RP)「標準發音」，這是英國南部有教養的人所說的英語。在英國，由於教育水準、出身地區等個人背景的差異，因此可以根據口音的不同，大概推斷所屬的社會階級（大致分為上流階級、中產階級以及勞工階級）。RP 是 Oxbridge 腔（在牛津 Oxford 或是劍橋 Cambridge 等大學接受教育或知識份子所說的腔調）或 British Broadcasting Corporation (BBC)「英國廣播公司」腔等所謂菁英份子說話腔調的代表發音。由於 BBC 是官方的電視公司，甚至還有 BBC English 這個名詞產生。

英國腔特色　英 🎧 015

英國腔具有一些獨特的語音特徵，其中包括緊母音（tense vowels）和小嘴母音（o sound）等發音特點。首先，英國腔中的緊母音，如 [æ]，在單詞如 hand（手）、can't（不能）和 man（男人）中表現得尤為明顯。這些音的發音較為拉長和清晰，讓聽者能夠清楚區分發音中的每個元素。其次，英國腔的 o 音，如 [ɑ]，在單詞 stop（停止）、Oxford（牛津）和 job（工作）中常見，發音時口形會稍微圓形，且發音較為圓潤，由於和美式發音相比口型較小，所以稱為小嘴母音。

此外，英國腔通常不捲舌（non-rhotic），這意味著在某些音節中，字母 r 不會被發音。例如，在單詞 car（車）、bird（鳥）和 world（世界）中，r 的發音會被省略或顯得較弱，這是英國腔的典型特徵。

最後關於英式 T 發音與半母音的使用，英國腔的一個顯著特徵是 T 音的清晰發音，相較於美式發音中，T 音時常被弱化，在英式發音中，T 音通常很清楚。例如，單詞 *little*（小的）、*matter*（問題）和 *better*（更好）中，T 音都會清楚地發出，與美式英語中常見的 T 音弱化或失音情況不同。

另外，英國腔中還經常使用半母音（schwa vowel）[ə]，這種音通常出現在音節不強調的部分。例如，單詞 *answer*（答案）、*where*（哪裡）中的 /ə/ 音使得語音聽起來更加流暢和自然。這樣的發音方式有助於增強語言的節奏感，使英語聽起來更為平穩。

加強對英澳腔的聽懂能力和口說技巧

1. 了解英澳腔的特點　　英　澳　🎧 016

- **發音**：英澳腔有其獨特的母音和子音發音方式。了解一些常見的發音特點，例如：

  - "a" 的發音：在單詞如 "baby" 中，可能會聽起來有點像嘴巴比較往下壓的 "a + ei" 一起的發音。

  - "u" 的發音：在 "dude" 中，發音可能更接近 "jood"。即嘴巴更小、雙唇更撅起來像 O 字型的發音。

- **重音和語調**：美國腔的重音和語調與英國或澳洲腔調不同，通常較為平緩，語調上升的情況較少。

2. 聽力練習

- **播客和廣播**：收聽澳洲本地的播客或廣播節目，如 ABC Radio 或 Triple J，這些都是非常好的英澳腔聽力資源。

- **電影和電視劇**：觀看串流平台上英國 BBC 或澳洲製作的電影或電視劇（如 *After Life*（終極後人生）、*Black Mirror*《黑鏡》（第一、二季）、*Heart Break High*《心碎高中》等），注意角色的對話和用詞。

3. 口說練習

- **模仿練習**：選擇一些英澳腔的演講者或角色，模仿他們的發音和語調。可以使用 YouTube 上的影片來幫助你。
- **語言交換**：找一位講英澳腔的語伴，進行語言交換，互相練習口說和聽力。

4. 學習詞彙和俚語　　澳 🎧 017

- **澳洲俚語**：學習一些常用的澳洲俚語（如 "arvo" 代表下午，"bikkie" 代表餅乾等），這能幫助你理解日常對話中的非正式用語。
- **閱讀本地材料**：閱讀英國及澳洲的新聞、文章或書籍，了解當地文化和用語。

總結來說，澳洲腔的發音接近英國腔，但與英國腔不同，澳洲腔的發音較為輕柔，不會像英國腔那樣強烈。以發音 [æ] 和 [ɑ] 為例，這是美國腔與英國腔之間的區別。美國腔發 [æ] 的時候，英國腔則會將其發成 [ɑ]，但澳洲腔在這個發音上更接近美式發音，發音更偏向 [æ]。此外，英國腔較少捲舌，而澳洲腔則會有些微的捲舌現象，不過其捲舌的程度較美國腔為輕微。因此，澳洲腔在發音上綜合了英國腔與美國腔的特點，但又有其獨特的語音風格。

4-3 辦公室常見句型練習

在辦公室環境中，掌握一些常見的句型可以幫助你更有效地與同事和客戶溝通。以下是一些辦公室常見句型的練習，可以用來增強你的口語和聽力能力。

1 問候語　美 🎧 018

- How was your weekend?（你的周末過得怎麼樣？）
- Good morning! How are you today?（早安！你今天怎麼樣？）
- Hi, how have you been?（嗨，你最近過得怎麼樣？）
- I hope you had a good day yesterday.（我希望你昨天過得很好。）

2 會議開始　澳 🎧 019

- Let's get started.（我們開始吧。）
- Thank you all for coming.（謝謝大家光臨。）
- I'd like to welcome everyone to today's meeting.（我想歡迎大家來參加今天的會議。）
- Let's go over the agenda for today.（讓我們來看看今天的議程。）

3 會議進行中　英 🎧 020

- Does anyone have any updates?（有誰有最新消息嗎？）
- Let's focus on the main points.（讓我們專注於要點。）
- Can you elaborate on that?（你能詳細說明一下嗎？）
- I'd like to hear your thoughts on this.（我想聽聽你對此事的看法。）

4 結束會議　美 🎧 021

- Thank you for your contributions.（謝謝大家的貢獻。）

- We'll follow up on this next week.（我們下週再跟進這件事。）
- Let's summarize what we discussed.（讓我們總結一下我們所討論的內容。）
- Have a great day, everyone!（祝大家今天愉快！）

5 日常交流　英 🎧 022

- Could you please send me that report?（你能把那份報告發給我嗎？）
- I need your input on this project.（我需要你對這個項目的意見。）
- Can we schedule a meeting for next week?（我們可以安排一個下週的會議嗎？）
- Let me know if you need any assistance.（如果你需要任何幫助，請告訴我。）

6 提問與回答　澳 🎧 023

- What's the deadline for this task?（這項任務的截止日期是什麼時候？）
- I'm not sure about that. Let me check.（我不太確定。讓我查一下。）
- That's a great idea! Let's implement it.（那是個好主意！讓我們開始做。）
- I appreciate your feedback.（我很感謝你的意見。）

7 解決問題　美 🎧 024

- There seems to be a misunderstanding.（似乎有些誤解。）
- Let's brainstorm some solutions.（讓我們集思廣益，找出一些解決方案。）
- I think we should revisit this issue.（我認為我們應該重新檢視這個問題。）
- Can we address this concern?（我們可以解決這個問題嗎？）

8 安排會議　美 🎧 025

- Can we set a time to meet?（我們可以約個時間見面嗎？）
- What time works best for you?（你什麼時候最方便？）

辦公室常見句型練習

089

- I'll send out a calendar invite.（我會發送日曆邀請。）
- Let's make it a video call.（我們改成視頻通話吧。）

9 工作進度報告　英 🎧 026

- I wanted to give you a quick update.（我想簡單向你報告最新進度。）
- We're on track to meet the deadline.（我們正按計劃趕上截止日期。）
- I encountered some challenges with this task.（我在這項任務上遇到了一些挑戰。）
- I'll keep you posted on any developments.（有任何進展我會隨時告訴你。）

10 表達意見　澳 🎧 027

- In my opinion, we should consider a different approach.（在我看來，我們應該考慮不同的方法。）
- I believe this is a good opportunity for us.（我相信這對我們來說是個好機會。）
- I see your point, but I have some reservations.（我明白你的觀點，但我有一些顧慮。）
- That's a valid concern.（那是個合理的擔憂。）

11 建議與提議　美 🎧 028

- How about we try this strategy?（我們試試這個策略怎麼樣？）
- I suggest we look into that option.（我建議我們考慮一下那個選項。）
- Let's not overlook the potential benefits.（讓我們不要忽視潛在的好處。）
- It might be helpful to gather more information.（收集更多訊息可能會有幫助。）

12 處理衝突　英 🎧 029

- Let's address this issue calmly.（讓我們冷靜地解決這個問題。）
- I think we need to find common ground.（我認為我們需要找到共同點。）
- Can we discuss this further?（我們可以進一步討論這個嗎？）
- I appreciate your willingness to resolve this.（感謝你願意解決這個問題。）

13 工作分配　澳 🎧 030

- Who will take the lead on this project?（誰來負責這個項目？）
- I'll assign you to this task.（我會把這項任務分配給你。）
- Let's divide the work evenly.（讓我們平均分配工作。）
- Can you handle this part?（你能處理這部分嗎？）

14 意見與評估　美 🎧 031

- Could you provide feedback on my presentation?（你能對我的演講給點意見嗎？）
- I appreciate your constructive criticism.（我感謝你的建設性批評。）
- What do you think we could improve?（你覺得我們可以改進什麼？）
- Let's evaluate our performance regularly.（讓我們定期評估我們的表現。）

15 談論工作生活平衡　美 🎧 032

- It's important to maintain a work-life balance.（保持工作與生活的平衡是很重要的。）
- How do you manage stress at work?（你怎麼在工作中管理壓力？）
- Taking breaks can improve productivity.（休息可以提高生產力。）
- Let's prioritize our well-being.（讓我們優先考慮自己的健康。）

辦公室常見句型練習

091

16 尋求幫助　英 🎧 033

- Could you assist me with this task?（你能幫我完成這項任務嗎？）
- I could use some guidance on this project.（我需要一些這個項目的指導。）
- Is there someone who can help with this?（有沒有人能幫忙這件事？）
- I appreciate any support you can provide.（我感謝你能提供的任何支持。）

練習方法

- **角色扮演**：找一位語伴進行角色扮演，模擬辦公室對話，使用上述句型。
- **錄音回放**：錄下自己的口說練習，然後回放來檢查發音和流利度。
- **日常應用**：在實際工作中嘗試使用這些句型，增強記憶。

透過這些句型的練習，你可以在辦公室等工作環境更加自信地交流。

情境對話範例 ①：在會議中發言 　美英 🎧 034

角色：Alice（發言者）和 Bob（主持人）

Alice: Good morning, everyone. Before we dive into today's agenda, I'd like to share some findings from the recent market analysis.

Bob: Thank you for that introduction, Alice. Please proceed.

Alice: According to the data we collected, our competitor's sales have seen a significant increase of 15% over the last quarter. I believe it would be prudent for us to reconsider our pricing strategy to maintain our market position.

Bob: That's a valuable insight. Does anyone have any comments or suggestions regarding Alice's proposal?

John: I concur with Alice. Adjusting our pricing could definitely help us attract more customers. Perhaps we could also enhance our marketing efforts alongside that?

Bob: Excellent suggestion, John. Let's make a note to explore both pricing adjustments and marketing strategies in our next discussion.

艾莉絲：大家早安。在我們進入今天的議程之前，我想分享一些最近市場分析的結果。
鮑勃：謝謝你的介紹，艾莉絲。請繼續。
艾莉絲：根據我們收集的數據，我們的競爭對手在上一季度的銷售額增長了 15%。我認為我們應該重新考慮定價策略，以維持我們的市場地位。
鮑勃：這是一個有價值的見解。大家對艾莉絲的提議有任何意見或建議嗎？
約翰：我同意艾莉絲的看法。調整我們的定價肯定能幫助我們吸引更多的顧客。也許我們可以同時加強市場推廣工作？
鮑勃：約翰，這是一個很好的建議。我們在下次討論中記得探討定價調整和市場策略。

辦公室常見句型練習

情境對話範例 ②：與同事協作　澳 英 🎧 035

角色：Sarah（同事 A）和 David（同事 B）

Sarah: Hi, David. Do you have a few minutes to discuss the presentation we're working on for the client meeting next week?

David: Absolutely, Sarah. What specific aspects do you want to focus on?

Sarah: I'm currently drafting the design slides, but I'm feeling uncertain about the layout and how to best convey our key points. Would you mind reviewing them?

David: I'd be happy to help! I think incorporating more visuals could really enhance our presentation and engage the audience better.

Sarah: That's a great idea! Perhaps we can add some charts and infographics to make the data more digestible.

David: Definitely! Let's collaborate on this—if you can send me what you have so far, I'll start working on the visuals.

莎拉：嗨，戴維。你有幾分鐘時間討論一下我們下週客戶會議的報告文稿嗎？

大衛：當然可以，莎拉。有哪個部分是你特別想討論的嗎？

莎拉：我目前正在草擬設計幻燈片，但對於版型以及如何最好地傳達我們的重點有些不確定。你介意幫我檢查一下嗎？

大衛：我很樂意幫忙！我認為加入更多的視覺元素可以讓我們的報告更優秀，更能吸引觀眾。

莎拉：這是個好主意！也許我們可以添加一些圖表和信息圖表，讓數據更易於理解。

大衛：當然！讓我們一起合作吧——如果你能把目前正在做的檔案傳給我，我就可以開始處理視覺效果。

情境對話範例 ③：處理顧客問題　澳 美 🎧 036

角色：Emily（客服人員）和 Mr. Chen（顧客）

Emily: Good afternoon, Mr. Chen. Thank you for reaching out to us. My name is Emily. How may I assist you today?

Mr. Chen: Hi, Emily. I'm contacting you regarding an issue with my recent order. I received an incorrect item.

Emily: I'm sorry to hear that, Mr. Chen. I'd like to help resolve this for you. Could you please provide me with your order number?

Mr. Chen: Certainly, it's 12345.

Emily: Thank you for that information. I'm checking your order details now. It seems there was a mix-up at our warehouse. I sincerely apologize for the inconvenience.

Mr. Chen: I appreciate your prompt response. How soon can I expect the correct item to arrive?

Emily: We'll expedite the shipping of the correct item today, and you should receive it within 3-5 business days. Is there anything else you'd like assistance with?

Mr. Chen: No, that covers everything. Thank you for your assistance!

艾蜜莉：陳先生，午安。謝謝您聯繫我們。我是愛蜜莉，我今天能為您做什麼？
陳先生：嗨，艾蜜莉。我聯繫您是因為最近的訂單有問題。我收到的商品不正確。
艾蜜莉：抱歉，陳先生。我想幫您解決這個問題。您能告訴我您的訂單號碼嗎？
陳先生：當然可以，訂單號碼是 12345。
艾蜜莉：謝謝您提供的資訊。我正在檢查您的訂單詳情。看來我們的倉庫弄錯了。我對此造成的不便深表歉意。
陳先生：感謝您迅速的回應。正確的商品多久能送到？
艾蜜莉：我們今天會加快出貨正確的商品，您應該會在 3-5 個工作日內收到。還有其他需要幫助的地方嗎？
陳先生：沒有，所有問題都解決了。謝謝您的優秀服務！

第 5 章

聽力部分解題攻略

5-1 Part 1　照片描述
　　　　　　新制多益模擬試題
5-2 Part 2　應答問題
　　　　　　新制多益模擬試題
5-3 Part 3　簡短對話
　　　　　　新制多益模擬試題
5-4 Part 4　簡短獨白
　　　　　　新制多益模擬試題

> 本章節先介紹聽力部分考試題型，再提供獨家搶分關鍵，最後搭配解題技巧教學，清楚示範解題技巧，各題型後皆提供模擬試題，幫助考生正確答題。

5-1 Part 1 照片描述

■ **題型介紹**

多益第一部分「照片描述題」，首先你會看到一個圖片，裡面可能會有場景、人物、這個人物正在做的動作。接著題目就會問你，這個人正在做什麼，或是這是在哪裡。

（圖片標示：場景、人物、動作、物品）

■ **搶分關鍵**

解題技巧 聽力和觀察力同樣重要

考生務必要看清楚圖片裡面的場景、擺設、人物、動作等，接著再聽選項裡面哪一項敘述最符合照片的描述。這個部分是多益聽力最簡單的部分，考生務必在本部分盡量拿高分，以便拉高整體分數。

1. **觀察訓練**：練習觀察圖片，快速掌握關鍵信息。
2. **聽力模擬**：實作模擬測驗提升聽力和反應速度。
3. **描述練習**：日常用英文描述場景，增強應試能力。
4. **計時訓練**：計時答題，模擬考試壓力，提升速度和準確率。

解題技巧教學

你會看到一張圖片,請聽四個選項,選出最符合圖片敘述的答案,**題目不會出現在試題本上。**

照片描述範例 ①

(聽力稿範例,僅供參考。)

Look at the picture marked number 1 in your test book. 美 🎧 037

(A) He's moving some dirt.
(B) He's standing near a tube.
(C) He's cutting the grass.
(D) He's pushing a wheelbarrow.

(A) 他正在搬運泥土。
(B) 他正站在管子旁邊。
(C) 他正在除草。
(D) 他正在推著手推車。

範例解析

照片描述題最常出現的時態就是現在進行式,因為圖片往往會出現一個人正在做某件事,**答案必須正確敘述他正在做的動作。**現在進行式的公式是「am/are/is + V-ing」,以上四個選項全部都是現在進行式,(A) 無法看見手推車裡是否有泥土,所以無法斷定男子是否在搬運泥土。(B) 旁邊直立的部分看起來是樹幹,並非管子。(C) 男子沒有在除草,**所以正確答案是 (D)。**

高頻多益單字 dirt (n.) 泥土　tube (n.) 管子　wheelbarrow (n.) 手推車

片語 cut the grass (phr.) 除草

照片描述範例 ②

（聽力稿範例，僅供參考。）

Look at the picture marked number 2 in your test book. 澳 🎧 038

(A) They are sitting in a car.
(B) The man is reading a book.
(C) The couple are standing in front of a bar.
(D) The children are playing in the park.

(A) 他們坐在車內。
(B) 這個男人在讀一本書。
(C) 這對情侶站在酒吧前面。
(D) 孩子們在公園玩。

範例解析

在照片描述題裡，也經常用相似發音的單字作為選項。例如這裡就是用 car 和 bar 還有 park 和 book 這些相似發音的單字來讓你混淆。這道題依舊是看圖說故事，**因此答案是 (C)**。其他三個選項都不是正確敘述。

描述地方、位置的介系詞也是經常出現在聽力部分的考題，常見的 in front of (phr.) 就是「在⋯的前面」。in 指的是「在⋯空間的裡面」，例如在這裡的 in a car (phr.) 在車內；in the park (phr.) 在公園裡。on 通常指的是在某個空間的上面，在公車上 on a bus、在火車上 on a train、在飛機上 on the plane，我們就要用 on。

使用 in 的交通工具

通常用 in 表示位於小型、封閉的交通工具內。常見例子包括：

- in a car（在車內）
- in a taxi（在計程車裡）

- in a truck/van（在卡車/廂型車裡）
- in a helicopter（在直升機裡）
- in a boat（在小船裡）
- *in a hot air balloon（在熱氣球內），因為熱氣球的籃子較小，通常用 in。

使用 on 的交通工具

當交通工具較大且可以走動，或有開放空間時，使用 on。例如：
- on a bus（在公車上）
- on a train（在火車上）
- on a plane（在飛機上）
- on a ship（在船上）──對於大型船隻。
- on the metro（在捷運上）
- on a bike（在腳踏車上）
- *on a motorcycle 或 on a scooter（在機車上），這是因為像機車、腳踏車這樣的交通工具是在開放空間，騎乘者坐在車座上，所以用 on。

▶ **訣竅**
- in：適用於小型、封閉的交通工具。
- on：適用於大型、可以走動或有開放空間的交通工具。

高頻多益單字 stand (v.) 站立　bar (n.) 酒吧

片語 in front of (phr.) 在…的前面

照片描述範例 ③

（聽力稿範例，僅供參考。）

Look at the picture marked number 3 in your test book.　英🎧 039

(A) She's folding her arms.
(B) She's holding a folder.
(C) She's crossing the street.
(D) She's waiting at the light.

(A) 她雙手抱胸。
(B) 她正拿著檔案夾。
(C) 她正穿越街道。
(D) 她正等紅綠燈。

📝 範例解析

在照片描述題裡，人物的動作和場景為出題的關鍵。像選項 (A) folding her arms 和選項 (B) holding a folder，就很容易在聽力測驗的時候混淆。此外，雖然這裡有街景，然而無法看出這位女子是否有 cross the street 穿越街道，所以答案亦不能選 (C)。最後的 (D) 選項，雖然有看到公車站牌的燈，但是考生不要過度推論，以為女子正在 waiting at the light 等紅綠燈。**考生須根據照片上人物實際的動作，選出最正確的敘述。因此這道題選擇的答案就是 (B)。**

高頻多益單字　fold (v.) 折疊　　hold (v.) 握著　　cross (v.) 穿越

片語　folding arms (phr.) 交疊手臂　　cross the street (phr.) 穿越街道

照片描述範例 ④

（聽力稿範例，僅供參考。）

Look at the picture marked number 4 in your test book. 美 🎧 040

(A) The man is playing a song for his family while they enjoy their beverages.
(B) The couple is setting up their camping equipment and preparing breakfast.
(C) The man is taking photographs of the scenery while the woman organizes their supplies.
(D) The family is using a portable grill to cook a meal over an open flame.

(A) 男子正在為家人演奏音樂，而家人在享用他們的飲品。
(B) 這對情侶正在搭建露營設備和準備早餐。
(C) 男子正在拍攝風景照片，而女子在整理他們的物品。
(D) 這家人正在用便攜式烤架在明火上烹煮食物。

範例解析

根據描述，男子彈吉他，女子和孩子正拿著咖啡杯，顯示男子正在為家人演奏音樂，而家人則在享用飲品。因此，最準確的選擇是 **(A) 選項**。

高頻多益單字 beverage (n.) 飲品　supplies (n.) 供應品、物品

照片描述範例 ⑤

（聽力稿範例，僅供參考。）

Look at the picture marked number 5 in your test book. 英 🎧 041

(A) The man is demonstrating how to drive and the woman is observing.
(B) The woman is making a call and the man is reviewing her driving record on a tablet.
(C) The woman is taking a driving test and the man, who is the examiner, is holding a score sheet.
(D) The woman is fixing a malfunction in the car and the man is assisting her.

(A) 男子正在示範如何駕駛，而女子在觀察。
(B) 女子正在打電話，而男子正在用平板檢查她的駕駛記錄。
(C) 女子正在考駕照，而男子（考官）手上拿著計分板。
(D) 女子正在修理汽車的故障，而男子在協助她。

範例解析

根據描述，女子正在考駕照，**男子作為考官，手上拿著計分板**。因此，正確的選擇是 **(C) 選項**。

高頻多益單字 examiner (n.) 考官

片語 driving test (phr.) 駕駛考試　score sheet (phr.) 計分板、成績單

照片描述範例 ⑥

（聽力稿範例，僅供參考。）

Look at the picture marked number 6 in your test book. 澳 🎧 042

(A) He is likely managing multiple tasks simultaneously without difficulty.
(B) He is mainly focused on organizing files and is not using electronic devices.
(C) He is primarily engaged in a meeting and is not using any technology.
(D) He appears to be reading printed materials while taking notes on a notepad.

(A) 他可能能夠毫不費力地同時處理多個任務。
(B) 他主要專注於整理文件，並未使用電子設備。
(C) 他主要參加會議，沒有使用任何科技產品。
(D) 他似乎在閱讀印刷材料的同時在筆記本上做筆記。

📌 範例解析

根據描述，這位男子**在辦公室內同時使用筆電和手機，顯示他能夠輕鬆地處理多個任務**，因此答案**選 (A)**。

高頻多益單字 printed (adj.) 印刷的　material (n.) 材料
　　　　　notepad (n.) 筆記本、筆記型電腦

片語 take notes (phr.) 做筆記

Part 1 照片描述

Practice Test

新制多益模擬試題 🎧 043
Part 1 照片描述

1. ☐

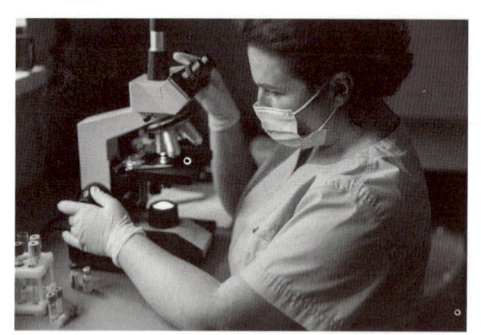

2. ☐

3. ☐

4. ☐

5. ☐

6. ☐

7. ☐

8. ☐

新制多益模擬試題

107

試題演練答案與翻譯

答案

1. (B)　2. (B)　3. (A)　4. (C)　5. (C)　6. (A)　7. (D)　8. (A)

1.

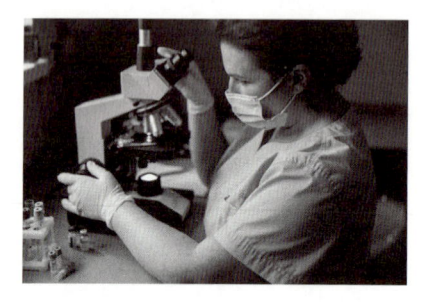

聽力內容
(A) The technician is assembling a piece of furniture.
(B) The technician is adjusting a microscope in a laboratory.
(C) The technician is cleaning a whiteboard.
(D) The technician is repairing a computer.

中譯
(A) 這位技術人員正在組裝家具。
(B) 這位技術人員正在實驗室裡調整顯微鏡。
(C) 這位技術人員正在清理白板。
(D) 這位技術人員正在修理電腦。

單字　technician (n.) 技術人員　adjust (v.) 調整　microscope (n.) 顯微鏡　laboratory (n.) 實驗室（簡稱為 lab）

2.

聽力內容　(A) The train is departing from the platform.
(B) The man is carrying a suitcase at the station.
(C) The passengers are boarding a bus.
(D) The man is purchasing a ticket from a vending machine.

中譯　(A) 火車正在離開月台。
(B) 這名男子正在火車站提著行李。
(C) 乘客們正在搭乘巴士。
(D) 這名男子正在從售票機購買車票。

單字　depart (v.) 離開　platform (n.) 月台　suitcase (n.) 行李箱
station (n.) 車站　passenger (n.) 乘客

3.

聽力內容　**(A) The people are gardening in a backyard.**
(B) The people are building a fence around a garden.
(C) The people are hiking through a forest trail.
(D) The people are arranging flowers in a vase.

中譯　**(A) 這些人在後院裡種植花木。**
(B) 這些人在花園周圍建造柵欄。
(C) 這些人在森林步道上健行。
(D) 這些人在花瓶裡插花。

單字　garden (v.) 種植花木　backyard (n.) 後院　fence (n.) 籬笆
trail (n.) 小徑　arrange (v.) 排列、布置

試題演練答案與翻譯

109

4.

聽力內容
(A) The students are writing an essay during a test.
(B) The students are watching a performance on stage.
(C) The students are conducting an experiment in a lab.
(D) The students are assembling desks in the classroom.

中譯
(A) 學生們正在考試時寫文章。
(B) 學生們正在舞台上觀看表演。
(C) 學生們正在實驗室做實驗。
(D) 學生們正在教室裡組裝桌子。

單字
essay (n.) 短文　performance (n.) 表演　experiment (n.) 實驗
assemble (v.) 組裝

5.

聽力內容
(A) The man is preparing food in a kitchen.
(B) The man is talking on his phone near a park.
(C) The man is typing on a laptop at a café.
(D) The man is reading a newspaper by the window.

中譯
(A) 這位男子正在廚房裡準備食物。
(B) 這位男子正在公園附近用手機講電話。
(C) 這位男子正在咖啡廳裡用筆記型電腦打字。
(D) 這位男子正在窗邊閱讀報紙。

單字　type (v.) 打字　laptop (n.) 筆記型電腦　café (n.) 咖啡廳

6.

聽力內容
(A) The photographer is taking pictures of the scenery.
(B) The photographer is cleaning his camera lens.
(C) The photographer is organizing photos on a computer.
(D) The photographer is setting up lights in a studio.

中譯
(A) 攝影師正在拍攝風景。
(B) 攝影師正在清潔相機鏡頭。
(C) 攝影師正在電腦上整理照片。
(D) 攝影師正在工作室裡安裝燈光設備。

單字　photographer (n.) 攝影師　scenery (n.) 風景　lens (n.) 鏡頭

7.

聽力內容
(A) The worker is unloading a truck on the street.
(B) The worker is assembling shelves in a store.
(C) The worker is painting a wall near a construction site.
(D) The worker is checking items in a warehouse.

中譯
(A) 工人正在街上卸載卡車。
(B) 工人正在商店裡組裝架子。
(C) 工人正在建築工地附近粉刷牆壁。
(D) 工人正在倉庫裡檢查商品。

單字
load/unload (v.) 裝載／卸載　　item (n.) 商品
warehouse (n.) 倉庫

片語
construction site (phr.) 建築工地

8.

聽力內容
(A) The passengers are waiting for their flight at the airport.
(B) The passengers are boarding an airplane.
(C) The passengers are lining up at a security checkpoint.
(D) The passengers are checking their luggage at the counter.

中譯

(A) 乘客正在機場候機室等候航班。
(B) 乘客正在登機。
(C) 乘客正在安檢口排隊。
(D) 乘客正在櫃檯托運行李。

單字
片語

flight (n.) 航班　　board (v.) 登機　　luggage (n.) 行李
security checkpoint (phr.) 安檢口　　line up (phr.) 排隊

5-2 Part 2 應答問題

■ 題型介紹

多益第二部分為「單一問答題」，在作答本上你看不到題目，只能用聽的方式記憶，有時候是 A 問了一個問題或是講了一件事情，那麼 B 就會針對 A 說的去回答，有的時候 B 會再提問。

who	誰	· Who is . . . ?	· David
where	哪裡	· Where is the marker? · Where is she going? · Where is . . . from?	· In the meeting room. · Downtown. · Italy.
when	何時	· When did Sam arrive? · When is Amy's birthday?	· Last night. · Next Friday.
why	為什麼	· Why did . . . ? · Why don't you . . . ?	· I have no idea. · I don't want to.
what	什麼	· What do/did you think . . . ? · What kind of . . . ? · What time . . . ? · What does . . . do for a living? · What's wrong with . . . ? · What color is . . . ?	· It's a good idea. · It's a monthly meeting. · 9:10 AM. · He's a college professor. · It's broken. · Green.
how	如何	· How did/do you . . . ? · How much . . . ? · How many . . . ? · How . . . get to . . . ? · How about . . . ? · How often . . . ? · How long . . . ?	· I like it a lot. · Two hundred dollars. · Two would be good. · Go straight and you'll see it. · Sounds good. · Three times a week · It takes 2 hours.

▰ 搶分關鍵

解題技巧 專注聽出疑問詞，理解要詢問的內容

由於這個部分有台灣學生比較不熟悉的英國、澳洲腔，因此在疑問句的時候常常會聽不懂到底是 when 還是 where 導致失分。對於 where 問題，通常會涉及地點或位置的描述；對於 why 問題，則需提供原因或解釋。

另外一種間接問句的問法，考生也很容易掉入陷阱，因為真正的問題是間接問句後面的那個疑問詞，而不是前面的 yes 或 no 問句。精準掌握間接問句的結構，尤其是當問題被嵌入在其他句子中時，如何識別和理解真正的疑問詞。此外注意問題的上下文和前後關聯，有助於更準確地理解問題的重點，並選擇最合適的回答。

最後加強語音辨識能力，練習辨認不同的語音變化和腔調，特別是英國腔和澳洲腔中的疑問詞發音。可以透過收聽不同來源的英語音檔來提升這方面的能力。

▰ 解題技巧教學

這個部分的題型像是問答題，**答案本不會出現題目和選項，請你聽問題和選項選出最正確的回答。**

應答問題範例 ①

（聽力稿範例，僅供參考。） 英 美 🎧 044

When did the fax machine arrive?　　傳真機何時送達呢？
(A) Earlier this afternoon.　　(A) 稍早的今天下午已經送達。
(B) I'll send it tomorrow.　　(B) 我明天將會送過去。
(C) I didn't place an order.　　(C) 我沒有下單。

✎ 範例解析

when 在英國腔的發音尾音會稍微提高。除了開頭的疑問詞，**問句所使用的時態也務必注意。如果題目是過去式，那麼通常回答也必須選擇過去時態的答案。**

注意題目是過去時態，因此選項 (B) 完全不符合題目問句的回答，而且主詞也不對。問句的主詞是 fax machine，選項 (B) 的主詞是 I，不符合題目在問的主詞。同理可證，選項 (C) 的主詞一樣也是 I，依舊不是正確的回答。

僅有選項 (A) 表示說稍早的今天下午已經送達。雖然選項 (A) 中沒有出現 fax machine，但已經清楚交代時間。

高頻多益單字 fax machine (n.) 傳真機　place (v.) 訂購

片語 place an order (ph.) 下訂單

應答問題範例 ②

（聽力稿範例，僅供參考。）　澳 美 🎧 045

Could you please tell me how to get to the nearest train station?
(A) That's right. There is one.
(B) No. It's not on Main Street.
(C) I'm sorry, I'm not from here, so I'm not sure.

可以告訴我最近的火車站在哪裡嗎？
(A) 沒錯。那裡有一個。
(B) 不。它不在大街上。
(C) 不好意思，我不是當地人，不太確定。

範例解析

這類題型還有一種考題是以間接問句當成疑問詞的開頭，考生也非常容易掉入陷阱。要特別注意，**間接問句開頭的句型，真正的疑問詞在後面**。

題目是以 Could you please tell me... 開頭的間接問句，當聽到 Could you please 估計很多考生就掉入陷阱了，會去選擇 yes 或 no，然而**真正的疑問詞卻是後面的 how**，所以答案不能選 (B)。這個選項除了 No 不正確以外，main 和 train 是相似音，也經常被放在答案選項裡混淆考生。選項 (A) 也是用來混淆同學在聽到 Could you please 之後，會傾向回答是或否的混淆選項。That's right 意思相近於 yes。

因此**正解就是 (C)**。I'm not from here. 我不是來自這裡，意思就是我不是本地人，所以不知道。

高頻多益單字 main (a.) 主要的　near (adj.) 靠近的，最高級為 nearest

片語 not from here (phr.) 非本地人

應答問題範例 ③

（聽力稿範例，僅供參考。）　美 英 🎧 046

Where was the ticket found?
(A) I've got a ticket.
(B) She is a travel agent.
(C) In the Terminal One concourse.

票是在哪裡找到的呢？
(A) 我已經買到票了。
(B) 她是一位旅行社代辦。
(C) 在第一航廈的大廳。

範例解析

又是經典英國腔發音的 where 當疑問句開頭的題型，台灣學生很容易掉入無法辨析 where 和 when 發音的陷阱。不過如果真的沒有聽到疑問詞的開頭，**記得一個解題原則，就是相似的發音或已經出現過的單字不要選，往往答對的機率還有 80%。**

(A) 選項的 ticket，和題目有一樣的單字，所以如果你真的沒有聽到疑問詞 where，那麼答題的原則就是不要選擇有同樣單字（ticket）的選項。(B) 選項的 travel agent 是多益高頻單字，經常搭配機場、旅遊等相關的考題一起出現。正確答案是**選項 (C)**。

高頻多益單字 ticket (n.) 票　terminal (n.) 航廈　concourse (n.) 大廳

片語 travel agent (phr.) 旅行社代辦人員

📝 Practice Test

新制多益模擬試題　🎧 047

Part 2 應答問題

1. ☐　2. ☐　3. ☐　4. ☐　5. ☐　6. ☐　7. ☐　8. ☐　9. ☐　10. ☐
11. ☐　12. ☐　13. ☐　14. ☐　15. ☐　16. ☐　17. ☐　18. ☐　19. ☐　20. ☐

試題演練答案與翻譯

答案

1. (A)　2. (C)　3. (B)　4. (A)　5. (A)　6. (A)　7. (A)　8. (B)　9. (C)　10. (A)
11. (B)　12. (B)　13. (A)　14. (A)　15. (C)　16. (B)　17. (B)　18. (A)　19. (A)　20. (C)

1. **聽力內容**　Where will the annual conference be held?
   (A) At the downtown convention center.
   (B) The dates are still being finalized.
   (C) We need to prepare the agenda

   中譯　年度會議將在哪裡舉行？
   (A) 在市中心的會議中心。
   (B) 日期仍在最後確定中。
   (C) 我們需要準備議程。

   單字　annual (adj.) 年度的　convention center (n.) 會議中心

2. **聽力內容**　Who is responsible for handling customer complaints?
   (A) The customer service department.
   (B) The new software.
   (C) The training session is next week.

   中譯　誰負責處理顧客投訴？
   (A) 客戶服務部門。
   (B) 新軟體。
   (C) 培訓課程在下週。

   單字　handle (v.) 處理　complaint (n.) 投訴

3. 聽力內容　What's wrong with the printer?
　　　　　　(A) It was repaired last month.
　　　　　　(B) There's a printer in my office.
　　　　　　(C) I think it's out of toner.

　　中譯　　印表機怎麼了？
　　　　　　(A) 上個月剛修過。
　　　　　　(B) 我辦公室有一台印表機。
　　　　　　(C) 我想它的碳粉用完了。

　　單字　　printer (n.) 印表機　　repair (v.) 修理
　　片語　　out of... 用完…

4. 聽力內容　How did the team handle the unexpected issue?
　　　　　　(A) The issue was unexpected.
　　　　　　(B) They worked late to resolve it.
　　　　　　(C) The team is preparing a report.

　　中譯　　團隊如何處理這個意外的問題？
　　　　　　(A) 這個問題是意外的。
　　　　　　(B) 他們加班解決了這個問題。
　　　　　　(C) 團隊正在準備報告。

　　單字　　unexpected (adj.) 意外的　　issue (n.) 問題　　resolve (v.) 解決

5. 聽力內容　Why was the meeting rescheduled?
　　　　　　(A) The meeting room was unavailable.
　　　　　　(B) The meeting will be held tomorrow.
　　　　　　(C) They need more participants.

　　中譯　　為什麼會重新安排會議？
　　　　　　(A) 會議室不可使用。
　　　　　　(B) 會議將於明天舉行。
　　　　　　(C) 他們需要更多的參與者。

　　單字　　reschedule (v.) 重新安排　　unavailable (adj.) 不可使用的

6. 聽力內容　What time will the conference start?
   (A) At 10 AM.
   (B) It will be held in the main hall.
   (C) We're still preparing the materials.

   中譯　會議何時開始？
   (A) 上午 10 點。
   (B) 會議將在主廳舉行。
   (C) 我們仍在準備資料。

   單字　prepare (v.) 準備

7. 聽力內容　How should we handle the delivery issues?
   (A) By contacting the shipping company.
   (B) They are still being shipped.
   (C) The delivery was scheduled.

   中譯　我們應該如何處理送貨問題？
   (A) 透過聯繫運輸公司。
   (B) 它們仍在運送中。
   (C) 送貨已經排定了。

   單字　delivery (n.) 送貨　　ship (v.) 運送　　schedule (v.) 為⋯安排時間

8. 聽力內容　How often should the equipment be serviced?
   (A) Every six months.
   (B) The equipment is out of stock.
   (C) A service report will be issued.

   中譯　設備應該多久維修一次？
   (A) 每六個月一次。
   (B) 設備已經缺貨。
   (C) 將會發出維修報告。

   單字　service (v.) 維修　　equipment (n.) 設備　　report (n.) 報告

9. **聽力內容** What is the company's new marketing strategy?
   (A) Enhanced customer service.
   (B) Expanded digital advertising.
   (C) Increased product inventory.

   中譯 公司新的市場行銷策略是什麼？
   (A) 提升客戶服務。
   (B) 擴展數位廣告。
   (C) 增加產品庫存。

   單字 strategy (n.) 策略　inventory (n.) 庫存

10. **聽力內容** Why was the event postponed?
    (A) I can't attend the event.
    (B) We posted the schedule.
    (C) Due to bad weather.

    中譯 為什麼活動被延期了？
    (A) 我無法參加這個活動。
    (B) 我們已經發布了時間表。
    (C) 因為天氣不好。

    單字 event (n.) 活動　weather (n.) 天氣

11. **聽力內容** What is the main goal of the new marketing campaign?
    (A) To upgrade office equipment.
    (B) To increase brand awareness.
    (C) To improve employee satisfaction.

    中譯 新行銷活動的主要目標是什麼？
    (A) 改善員工滿意度。
    (B) 提高品牌知名度。
    (C) 升級辦公設備。

    單字 goal (n.) 目標　campaign (n.) 活動　awareness (n.) 知名度

121

12. **聽力內容** What should employees do if they need to leave early on a workday?
(A) Attend a meeting.
(B) Submit a leave request form.
(C) Update their contact information.

中譯 如果員工需要在工作日提前離開，他們應該做什麼？
(A) 參加會議。
(B) 提交請假申請表。
(C) 更新聯絡資訊。

單字 leave (v./n.) 離開；請假　request (v.) 申請　form (n.) 表單
update (v.) 更新　contact information (n.) 聯絡資訊

13. **聽力內容** When will the report be finalized?
(A) By the end of the week.
(B) The team is brainstorming ideas.
(C) The office will be closed for maintenance.

中譯 報告何時會完成？
(A) 在本週結束前。
(B) 團隊正在腦力激盪想法。
(C) 辦公室將因維修而關閉。

單字 finalize (v.) 完成　brainstorm (v.) 腦力激盪

14. **聽力內容** Who should be contacted for technical support?
(A) The IT department.
(B) The administrative office.
(C) The customer service team.

中譯 應該聯繫誰來獲得技術支持？
(A) 資訊技術部門。
(B) 行政辦公室。
(C) 客戶服務團隊。

單字 contact (v.) 聯繫　technical support (n.) 技術支援
department (n.) 部門

15. **聽力內容**　Where will the annual company picnic be held?
    (A) At a local museum.
    (B) In the office meeting room.
    (C) At the city park.

    中譯　年度公司野餐會將在哪裡舉行？
    (A) 在當地博物館。
    (B) 在辦公室會議室。
    (C) 在市立公園。

    單字　picnic (n.) 野餐

16. **聽力內容**　How can employees request additional training?
    (A) The training schedule is online.
    (B) By submitting a formal request form.
    (C) The training program starts next month.

    中譯　員工如何申請額外的培訓？
    (A) 培訓時間表在線上。
    (B) 通過提交正式的申請表格。
    (C) 新的培訓計劃下個月啟動。

    單字　training (n.) 培訓　online (adj.) 線上的

17. **聽力內容**　What is the main objective of the business plan?
    (A) The campaign starts next week.
    (B) To improve our sales figures.
    (C) We need to finalize the budget.

    中譯　這份商業計劃的主要目的是什麼？
    (A) 活動下週開始。
    (B) 提高我們的銷售數字。
    (C) 我們需要確定預算。

    單字　objective (n.) 目標　figure (n.) 數字

18. 聽力內容　Where can employees find the new company policies?
(A) In the employee handbook.
(B) Attend a product launch event.
(C) The handbook will be printed soon.

中譯　員工可以在哪裡找到新的公司政策？
(A) 在員工手冊中。
(B) 參加產品發佈會。
(C) 手冊將很快印刷。

單字　handbook (n.) 手冊

19. 聽力內容　When will the next team meeting take place?
(A) On Thursday afternoon.
(B) We need to assign tasks.
(C) The agenda is still being prepared.

中譯　下一次團隊會議將在什麼時候舉行？
(A) 星期四下午。
(B) 我們需要分配任務。
(C) 議程仍在準備中。

單字　take place (v.) 舉行　　agenda (n.) 議程

20. 聽力內容　Why did the company decide to extend the project deadline?
(A) The team is preparing a presentation.
(B) The project is nearly complete.
(C) Due to unexpected delays.

中譯　公司為什麼決定延長專案截止日期？
(A) 團隊正在準備簡報。
(B) 專案幾乎完成了。
(C) 因為意外的延誤。

單字　extend (v.) 延長　　deadline (n.) 截止日期　　complete (adj.) 完整的
delay (n.) 延誤

試題演練答案與翻譯

5-3 Part 3 簡短對話

▰ 題型介紹

多益第三部分「兩人或三人的短對話」，這裡的題型你會直接看到作答的選項，因此在對話還沒有開始的時候，你可以先快速瀏覽過所有選項。

▰ 搶分關鍵

解題技巧 在聆聽時需特別注意**說話者男女間的關係**、**意圖**、**想法**和**立場**，因為這是必考的重點。

常見對話句型

- **詢問時間**：When is the meeting scheduled for?
- **詢問地點**：Where will the event take place?
- **詢問人物**：Who will be attending the conference?
- **詢問意圖**：What is the purpose of the report?

常見職業

- **客服代表**：customer service representative
- **會議主辦人**：meeting organizer
- **商業代表**：business representative
- **主管**：manager

常見問題類型

- **會議安排**：問題可能會涉及會議的時間、地點或參加者。
- **工作安排**：可能涉及工作的進度或責任分配。
- **日常事務**：如訂購商品、處理客戶查詢等。

回答技巧

- **邊聽邊作答**：切勿等到對話完全結束後再看選項。須**在對話中聽取關鍵信息的同時，快速選擇答案**。
- **辨別聲音**：分清楚對話中是男聲還是女聲，通常有助於理解對話的上下文。

▌解題技巧教學

這個部分的聽力考題，**你會聽到對話並看到三個問題和底下的四個選項，對話結束之後會朗讀第一個題目**，接著間隔 8 秒鐘再進行下一題，以此類推。

照片描述範例 ①

Questions 1 through 3 refer to the following conversation.

美 英 🎧 048

問題 1-3 請參考以下對話。

W: Hello. This is Rachael Green. I'm calling to see if the repairs on my car have been completed. I know you said it wouldn't be ready until this Friday, but I need to take an unexpected trip out of town tomorrow and was hoping I could drive it.

女：你好，我是 Rachael Green。我打電話來詢問我的車是否已經修好。我知道你們說了要到這個星期五才會完成，但我明天突然需要離開市區，我希望能開車。

M: Hi, Ms. Green. You're in luck. Even though we told you it would be Friday before we got the part ordered and installed, it arrived early, and I was able to finish the repair.

男：嗨，Green 女子。你運氣不錯。雖然我們告訴你需要到星期五才能訂購和安裝好零件，但我們提前取得零件，所以我能夠完成維修。

W: Oh, that's great! Fantastic news. Thank you. However, I'll need a ride to the shop in order to pick up my car.

女：哦，太好了！太棒了！謝謝你。不過，我需要搭車去你們店裡取車。

M: Unfortunately, it's almost 5 o'clock and we're closing for the day, but I'll arrange one for you first thing in the morning.

男：不幸的是，現在快到下午五點了，我們今天要關門了，但我們明天一早就會安排人去接你。

1. Why is the woman calling?
   (A) To check the repair status
   (B) To rent a car for a trip
   (C) To request a ride to work
   (D) To buy car parts

女子為什麼打電話？
(A) 確認修理狀況
(B) 租車去旅遊
(C) 叫車接送上班
(D) 購買汽車零件

2. What does the man say about the repair?
   (A) It is not covered.
   (B) It must be paid in full.
   (C) It wasn't necessary.
   (D) It has been completed early.

男子針對車子維修的部分說了什麼？
(A) 這沒有包含。
(B) 必須全額付款。
(C) 這不是必須的。
(D) 已經提早維修完成。

3. When can the woman pick up her car?
   (A) Today
   (B) Tomorrow
   (C) Friday
   (D) After 5 o'clock

女子何時可以取車？
(A) 今天
(B) 明天
(C) 星期五
(D) 五點過後

範例解析

汽車維修廠是多益頻繁出現的一個場景，不外乎就是客人打電話來詢問修車的進度以及維修的狀況，還有客人有什麼樣的事由和何時希望取車，並且要如何取車。

我總是交代考生，**每一題間隔的 8 秒鐘，你都要盯緊下一題的題目和選項。**播放對話的時候，甚至在還沒開始作答之前，就必須**先聽清楚關於這段對話有哪些 main ideas (主旨)**，當對話正在播放的時候，你也必須同步作答，千萬不能等到題目都已經唸完了，你才開始看選項選答案，因為多數時候你的記憶無法維持太久，尤其是在考場上，緊張的情緒更是無法讓你全部聽完，全都記得，然後才下筆圈選正確答案。因此邊聽邊作答的技巧，是要一直養成習慣的。

第一題答案選 (A)。女子並沒有 (B) 租一台車子去旅行，也沒有 (C) 預約接駁車去工作，或是 (D) 去買汽車零件。

第二題答案選 (D)。這裡用的是**現在完成式的被動語態 have/has + been + pp.，車子是物品，無法主動**，要有人來修理，故用被動語態。現在完成式也是在聽力對話當中最常考的時態。其他選項都不是正確答案，對話當中並沒有提及任何款項的事情，因此不要過度推論。

第三題要選出正確的時間，**答案是 (B)**。如果你沒有先看題目，對於答案選項有個譜，你很可能就因為忘記這個簡單的訊息而選錯。

高頻多益單字　check (v.) 確認　repair (v.) 維修　status (n.) 狀況、狀態
rent (v.) 租借　trip (n.) 旅途、旅行　ride (n.) 接駁、接送
part (n.) 零件　complete (v.) 完成　cover (v.) 涵蓋、包括
necessary (a.) 必須的

片語　pay in full (phr.) 全額付清

照片描述範例 ②

Questions 4 through 6 refer to the following conversation.
問題 4-6 請參考以下對話。

美 澳 英 🎧 049

M1: Have you two taken a look at the progress they've made upstairs with the new office renovations? It looks really good!

W: I know! It's exciting!! And the offices up there have amazing views of the city. I wonder which department will move up there when it's finished.

M2: I heard it's going to be research and development.

M1: Ah, that's a bummer, but it must be because they have the most people.

W: Probably. Although I'd love to have my office up there.

M2: It seems like the company must be doing well if they're adding that space!

W: Tell me about it! That can't be cheap.

男子1：你們兩個人有上樓去看一下重新裝修的辦公室了嗎？看起來真的很棒！

女子：我知道！太令人興奮了！而且樓上的辦公室還有驚豔的城市景觀，我很好奇是哪個部門會搬過去。

男子2：聽說是研發部門。

男子1：喔，太可惜了，但很可能是因為他們部門人數最多。

女子：可能吧。真希望我也能搬上去。

男子2：公司應該是賺了不少，才能有那個空間！

女子：就是啊！那一定不便宜。

4. What is the conversation mainly about?
　(A) Moving to a new location
　(B) Adding new office space
　(C) Hiring new employees
　(D) Changes in company policy

4. 這則對話主要在說什麼？
　(A) 搬去新的地點
　(B) 增加新辦公空間
　(C) 僱用新員工
　(D) 公司政策改變

5. What does the man imply about the company?
   (A) It is in a good financial situation.
   (B) It was recently founded.
   (C) It is downsizing.
   (D) It has offices in other cities.

6. Why does the woman say, "Tell me about it"?
   (A) She wants an explanation.
   (B) She needs to hear it again.
   (C) She strongly agrees.
   (D) She doesn't believe him.

5. 男子對於公司的推論是？
   (A) 財務狀況很好。
   (B) 最近增加資金。
   (C) 正在縮編。
   (D) 在其他城市有辦公室。

6. 女子說"Tell me about it"是什麼意思？
   (A) 她需要解釋。
   (B) 她想要再聽一次。
   (C) 她非常認同。
   (D) 她不相信他。

範例解析

新制多益在第三部分的聽力題型，會由兩個人的對話，擴充到三個人的對話，並且加上多國口音。

第 4 題考主旨大意，**答案要選 (B)**。三個人的對話都在討論辦公室的裝修、景緻，還有哪個部門會搬去，所以 (B) 選項最適合。(A) 選項比較混淆，因為對話裡女子有提到她好奇哪個部門會搬過去。(C) 完全沒有提到該內容，(D) 也沒有在對話中提到。

第 5 題考的是推論，**答案選 (A)**。由這句話 It seems like the company must be doing well if they're adding that space! 判斷出他認為公司的財務狀況相當良好。(B) 在對話中完全沒有提到。(C) 也與對話內容所提到的相反。(D) 也不對，內容提到的是辦公室有城市景觀，而非有辦公室在其他城市。

第 6 題 Tell me about it，這句話**中文翻譯可以說「可不是嗎！」**表示認同對方。**答案選 (C)**。

高頻多益單字 space (n.) 空間　location (n.) 地點　hire (v.) 僱用　company (n.) 公司　financial (adj.) 財務的、金融的　situation (n.) 情況　found (v.) 成立　downsize (v.) 縮減、縮編　explanation (n.) 解釋、說明

片語 do well (phr.) 成功、做得很好

📝 **Practice Test**

新制多益模擬試題 🎧 050

Part 3 簡短對話

1. Why is the woman calling?
   (A) To inquire about a delivery status
   (B) To request a refund
   (C) To make a new order
   (D) To complain about a service

2. When will the delivery arrive?
   (A) By the end of the week
   (B) Today
   (C) Tomorrow morning
   (D) Next week

3. What is the woman's reaction to the news?
   (A) She is disappointed.
   (B) She is indifferent.
   (C) She is grateful.
   (D) She is angry.

4. What is the conversation mainly about?
   (A) Scheduling issues
   (B) A new project
   (C) Team performance
   (D) Budget concerns

5. What does the woman say about the project?
   (A) It is behind schedule.
   (B) It is right on schedule.
   (C) It is ahead of schedule.
   (D) It has been canceled.

6. What kind of challenges is the woman facing?
   (A) Major obstacles
   (B) Budget cuts
   (C) Minor adjustments
   (D) Team conflicts

7. What does the woman want to do?
   (A) Cancel her reservation
   (B) Change the reservation date
   (C) Reserve additional seats
   (D) Confirm her reservation

8. When does the woman want to attend the conference?
   (A) This week
   (B) Next week
   (C) The week after next
   (D) In a month

9. What is the man going to do next?
   (A) Confirm the cancellation
   (B) Contact the conference organizers
   (C) Make a new reservation
   (D) Check availability

10. What is the man looking for?
    (A) A high-performance laptop
    (B) A new smartphone
    (C) A home appliance
    (D) A software program

11. What feature does the man want in the laptop?
    (A) Long battery life
    (B) Large storage
    (C) Lightweight design
    (D) Touchscreen capabilities

12. What does the woman recommend?
    (A) A laptop with a long battery life
    (B) A budget-friendly laptop
    (C) A laptop with a high-resolution display
    (D) A model with a 1TB hard drive

試題演練答案與翻譯

答案

1. (A)　2. (C)　3. (C)　4. (B)　5. (C)　6. (C)
7. (B)　8. (C)　9. (D)　10. (A)　11. (B)　12. (D)

聽力內容　Questions 1 through 3 refer to the following conversation.

W: Hi, I'm calling to check the status of the delivery I ordered. It was supposed to arrive by the end of the week, but I'm hoping to get it sooner if possible.

M: Hello! Let me check on that for you. Yes, it looks like your delivery will actually arrive tomorrow morning.

W: That's wonderful news! I really appreciate the update.

M: You're welcome. Is there anything else I can help you with today?

中譯　問題 1 到 3 請參考以下對話。

女子：你好，我打電話來確認我訂購的貨物配送狀態。應該會在本週末前送達，但我希望能儘早收到，如果有可能的話。

男子：你好！讓我幫您查詢一下。是的，看起來您的貨物實際上會在明天早上送達。

女子：這真是太棒了！非常感謝你告訴我最新的狀態。

男子：不客氣。今天還有其他需要我協助的地方嗎？

1. Why is the woman calling?　女子為什麼打電話？
   (A) To inquire about a delivery status　**(A) 查詢送貨狀況**
   (B) To request a refund　(B) 要求退款
   (C) To make a new order　(C) 下新訂單
   (D) To complain about a service　(D) 投訴服務

2. When will the delivery arrive?　貨物會在什麼時候到達？
   (A) By the end of the week　(A) 本週末
   (B) Today　(B) 今天
   (C) Tomorrow morning　**(C) 明天早上**
   (D) Next week　(D) 下週

136

3. What is the woman's reaction to the news? 女子對這個消息的反應如何？
   (A) She is disappointed.　　　　　　(A) 她很失望
   (B) She is indifferent.　　　　　　　(B) 她漠不關心
   (C) She is grateful.　　　　　　　**(C) 她很感激**
   (D) She is angry.　　　　　　　　　(D) 她很生氣

單字 inquire (v.) 查詢　appreciate (v.) 感激

聽力內容 **Questions 4 through 6 refer to the following conversation.**
M: I heard you're working on a new project. How's it going?
W: Yes, it's going well so far. We're actually ahead of schedule, which is great.
M: That's fantastic! Are there any challenges you're facing?
W: Nothing major, just some minor adjustments to the timeline.

中譯 **問題 4 到 6 請參考以下對話。**
男子：我聽說你正在做一個新專案。進展如何？
女子：是的，目前進展順利。我們實際上比預定進度超前，這很棒。
男子：那真是太好了！有遇到什麼挑戰嗎？
女子：沒有什麼大問題，只是對時間表做了一些小調整。

4. What is the conversation mainly about? 這則對話主要在討論什麼？
   (A) Scheduling issues　　　　　　　(A) 排程問題
   (B) A new project　　　　　　　　**(B) 新專案**
   (C) Team performance　　　　　　(C) 團隊表現
   (D) Budget concerns　　　　　　　(D) 預算問題

5. What does the woman say about the project? 女子說關於項目時間表的什麼？
   (A) It is behind schedule.　　　　　(A) 比計畫慢
   (B) It is right on schedule.　　　　(B) 正在按計畫進行
   (C) It is ahead of schedule.　　　**(C) 比計畫快**
   (D) It has been canceled.　　　　　(D) 已經取消

6. What kind of challenges is the woman facing?

   (A) Major obstacles

   (B) Budget cuts

   (C) Minor adjustments

   (D) Team conflicts

女子面臨什麼挑戰？

(A) 主要障礙

(B) 預算削減

(C) 小調整

(D) 團隊衝突

單字 challenge (n.) 挑戰　major (adj.) 重大的　minor (adj.) 輕微的
adjustment (n.) 調整

聽力內容 Questions 7 through 9 refer to the following conversation.

W: Hi, I need to change my reservation for the conference next month. Can you help me with that?

M: Certainly. What changes would you like to make?

W: I'd like to move it to a later date, preferably the week after next.

M: Let me check the availability for you.

中譯 問題 7 到 9 根據以下對話。

女子：你好，我需要更改下個月參加會議的預約。你能幫我處理嗎？

男子：當然可以。您想做哪些更改？

女子：我想將日期改到稍晚一點，最好是下下週。

男子：我幫您查一下有沒有空位。

7. What does the woman want to do?

   (A) Cancel her reservation

   (B) Change the reservation date

   (C) Reserve additional seats

   (D) Confirm her reservation

女子想要做什麼？

(A) 取消預訂

(B) 更改預訂日期

(C) 預訂額外座位

(D) 確認預訂

8. When does the woman want to attend the conference?

   (A) This week

   (B) Next week

   (C) The week after next

   (D) In a month

女子想在何時參加會議？

(A) 本週

(B) 下週

(C) 下下週

(D) 一個月後

138

9. What is the man going to do next?
   (A) Confirm the cancellation
   (B) Contact the conference organizers
   (C) Make a new reservation
   (D) Check availability

男子接下來要做什麼？
(A) 確認取消
(B) 聯繫會議主辦方
(C) 訂新的預訂
(D) 檢查可用性

單字 reservation (n.) 預訂　availability (n.) 空閒

聽力內容 **Questions 10 through 12 refer to the following conversation.**
M: I'm looking for a new laptop for work. Do you have any recommendations?
W: Certainly! We have several models that are popular among professionals. Are you looking for something specific?
M: Yes, I need a laptop with a high-performance processor and a lot of storage.
W: In that case, I'd recommend the model with the latest Intel processor and a 1TB hard drive.

中譯 **問題 10 到 12 根據以下對話。**
男子：我在找一台工作用的新的筆記型電腦。你有什麼推薦的嗎？
女子：當然！我們有幾款在專業人士中很受歡迎的型號。您有特別想要的規格嗎？
男子：是的，我需要一台有高效能處理器和大量儲存空間的筆記型電腦。
女子：如果是這樣的話，我建議您選擇搭載最新 Intel 處理器和 1TB 硬碟的型號。

10. What is the man looking for?
    (A) A high-performance laptop
    (B) A new smartphone
    (C) A home appliance
    (D) A software program

男子在尋找什麼？
(A) 高性能筆記本電腦
(B) 新智能手機
(C) 家用電器
(D) 軟體程式

11. What feature does the man want in the laptop?

(A) Long battery life

(B) Large storage

(C) Lightweight design

(D) Touchscreen capabilities

男子希望筆記本電腦具備哪些特點？

(A) 長效電池

(B) 大容量存儲

(C) 輕巧設計

(D) 觸控功能

12. What does the woman recommend?

(A) A laptop with a long battery life

(B) A budget-friendly laptop

(C) A laptop with a high-resolution display

(D) A model with a 1TB hard drive

女子推薦什麼？

(A) 電池壽命長的筆記本電腦

(B) 性價比高的筆記本電腦

(C) 高分辨率顯示屏的筆記本電腦

(D) 1TB 硬碟的款式

單字 laptop (n.) 筆記本電腦　processor (n.) 處理器　storage (n.) 存儲
recommend (v.) 推薦　high-performance (adj.) 高性能的

試題演練答案與翻譯

5-4 Part 4 簡短獨白

▍題型介紹

多益第四部分「長篇的單一獨白」，這裡往往是一個比較長篇的佈告、公告、電話留言，或者是超市廣告、機長報告、火車誤點，要不然就是一些會議宣達的事項。請注意獨白中出現的人事時地物與轉折詞。

多益聽力第四部分的「長篇單一獨白」通常會包括以下內容：
- **公告或佈告**：如公司公告、公共通知。
- **電話留言**：如服務通知、緊急通報。
- **廣告或宣傳**：如商店促銷、活動宣傳。
- **機長報告**：如航班狀況更新。
- **會議宣達事項**：如會議日程、注意事項。

▍搶分關鍵

1. **耐心與專注**：此部分考生常感疲憊，因此需要保持高度專注。
2. **邊聽邊作答**：聽到重要信息時，迅速筆記並選擇正確答案。

解題技巧

1. **先讀問題和選項**：在聽錄音前，**先快速閱讀題目和選項，了解問題所需的信息**，若有圖表也需以掃讀方式看過。
2. **專注聽取關鍵信息**：聽錄音時，對於重要細節須仔細聽，如**時間、地點、原因和主要內容**，須注意和圖表之間的關係。另外獨白的開頭句、主旨句、結尾句也是重點。**開頭句**：通常會**提供主要信息或目的**，例如 "Welcome to our annual sale event." **主旨句**：關鍵句子中**會清楚表達公告或通知的主要目的**，例如 "The library will be closed for renovations." **結尾句**：一般會**總結或給出後續指示**，例如 "We appreciate your patience during this time."
3. **跟隨題目順序作答**：答案通常按照錄音內容的順序，聽到題目時立即作答。
4. **注意轉折詞和關鍵詞**：**轉折詞**如 however、but、meanwhile 等，通常**提示信息的變化或重點**。

解題技巧教學

這個部分的聽力考題，你會看到三個問題和底下的四個選項，對話結束之後會朗讀第一個題目，接著間隔 8 秒鐘再進行下一題，以此類推。

照片描述範例 ①

Questions 1 through 3 refer to the following telephone message.
問題 1-3 請參考以下電話錄音。

美 🎧 051

M: Hello, Ms. Kim. This is Larry from Coffee Man Electronics calling with some information about your request. As per company policy, the warranty covers our products for up to a year, but, unfortunately, the warranty for your coffee machine has recently expired. We understand this is disappointing, but we are unable to replace it. However, as you're a valued customer, we're glad to offer you a coupon for forty percent off of your next purchase. It's been sent to your account and has no expiration date. Thank you again for shopping with us!

金女士您好，我是來自咖啡人電子產品公司的 Larry，我打電話來是要提供一些與您的要求相關的資訊。根據公司政策，我們的產品在一年內享有保固，但很遺憾，您的咖啡機最近已經過了保固期。我們明白這很令人失望，但我們無法更換咖啡機。然而，您是我們尊敬的客戶，我們很樂意為您提供下次購物的六折優惠券。該優惠券已經發送到您的帳號，並且沒有到期日。再次感謝您選擇我們的產品！

Part 4 簡短獨白

1. Why is the speaker calling?
   (A) To cancel an order
   (B) To offer a solution
   (C) To redeem a gift card
   (D) To renew a warranty

1. 說話者為何打電話來？
   (A) 取消訂單
   (B) 提供解決方法
   (C) 兌換禮物卡
   (D) 更新保固

143

2. For how long is the warranty valid?　　2. 保固期是多久？
　　(A) Indefinitely　　　　　　　　　　(A) 永久
　　(B) Six months　　　　　　　　　　 (B) 半年
　　(C) One year　　　　　　　　　　　 (C) 一年
　　(D) A bit over a year　　　　　　　　 (D) 稍微超過一年

3. What does the speaker offer to do?　　3. 說話者提供什麼？
　　(A) Issue a refund　　　　　　　　　(A) 退款
　　(B) Send a free sample　　　　　　　(B) 寄送免費樣品
　　(C) Cancel the order　　　　　　　　(C) 取消訂單
　　(D) Provide a discount　　　　　　　 (D) 提供折扣

> ✏️ **範例解析**
>
> 這是一則回覆客戶服務的電話語音留言。第 1 題考的是主旨大意。答案選 **(B)**。雖然內容中有提到保固和打折，但都不是留言內容的主要目的。
>
> 第 2 題答案是 **(C)**。留言當中有提到 the warranty covers our products for up to a year 產品涵蓋的保固期是一年為上限。
>
> 第 3 題答案是 **(D)**。說話者提供了一個 40% 折扣的優惠券作為對客戶的補償，並且這張優惠券已經發送到客戶的帳號中。

高頻多益單字　request (n.) 請求　　solution (n.) 解決方法　　cancel (v.) 取消
　　　　　　　　redeem (v.) 抵用　　gift card (n.) 禮物卡　　renew (v.) 更新
　　　　　　　　warranty (n.) 保固　　valid (adj.) 有效的

片語　up to (phr.) 接近於、至多

照片描述範例 ②

Questions 4 through 6 refer to the following announcement.
問題 4-6 請參考以下公告。

澳 🎧 052

F: Okay, folks! So, Wendy called in sick and likely won't be back for another couple of days. I know that it's frustrating since we've been short-staffed for a few weeks already, but, as always, we'll still do our best to serve our guests. We're looking at another full house tonight so Karen and Dylan will be in charge of the walk-ins at the front and the rest of you will be divided into four teams rotating among the tables. Please make sure to inform our guests of the new items on the menu, especially the veggie pie. That's all, everyone. Thank you!

好的，各位！Wendy 打電話來請病假，可能需要休息幾天。我知道最近人手不足，大家都相當心力交瘁。然而我們依舊會盡最大的努力來服務客人。今晚又是滿座的預約，因此 Karen 和 Dylan 在櫃檯接待沒有訂位的顧客。其他人就分成四組，輪流招呼每一桌客人。務必告訴我們的客人有新的菜色，特別是蔬菜派。以上，謝謝大家！

4. What is the location for this announcement?
   (A) A hospital
   (B) A restaurant
   (C) A hotel
   (D) A fitness center

5. Why is the speaker assigning work to the listeners?
   (A) An attendee is on leave.
   (B) Sales have gone down.
   (C) A staff member is unwell.
   (D) Many guests have left.

4. 這項公告的地點是哪裡？
   (A) 醫院
   (B) 餐廳
   (C) 飯店
   (D) 健身中心

5. 為什麼說話者分配工作給聽者？
   (A) 一位參加者休假。
   (B) 銷售下降。
   (C) 一位員工生病。
   (D) 很多客人離開。

6. What does the speaker ask the listeners to tell customers about?
(A) New business hours
(B) Discount coupons
(C) The staffing situation
(D) New dishes being offered

6. 說話者要求聽者告知客人什麼資訊？
(A) 新的營業時間
(B) 折價券
(C) 人員配置情況
(D) 提供新菜色

範例解析

這是一則在餐廳營業以前，向員工宣達事項的短獨白。由內容提到菜單、訂位及接待客人等等，可以判斷**第 4 題答案選的是 (B)**。

第 5 題問的是說話者為什麼要分配工作給聽者，從第一句 Wendy 請病假就可以得知，其中一位員工生病了，所以**答案選 (C)**。

第 6 題則是考細節，詢問說話者要求聽者告訴顧客什麼事情，在宣布結束前提到新的菜單，因此**答案選 (D)**。

高頻多益單字 location (n.) 地點　staff member (n.) 員工　unwell (adj.) 不舒服、生病　sales (n.) 銷售數字　guest (n.) 顧客、客人　item (n.) 品項　menu (n.) 菜單　dish (n.) 菜餚、菜色　business hours (n.) 營業時間　discount (n.) 折扣　coupon (n.) 優惠　frustrating (adj.) 沮喪的　front (n.) 前面、前台、櫃台

片語 go down (phr.) 下降、下滑　call in sick (phr.) 打電話請病假　short-staffed (adj.) 人手不足的　full house (phr.) 訂位額滿、滿座　in charge of (phr.) 負責　walk-in (phr.) 沒有訂位直接到場的客人　divide into (phr.) 切成、分成　make sure (phr.) 確認

Practice Test

新制多益模擬試題 🎧 053

Part 4 簡短獨白

1. What is the purpose of the call?
   (A) To remind about a late fee
   (B) To notify about a book pickup
   (C) To cancel a book reservation
   (D) To announce a library event

2. How long will the book be held?
   (A) Until the end of the day
   (B) Until the end of the week
   (C) For one month
   (D) Until next week

3. What happens if the book is not picked up?
   (A) It will be returned to the shelves
   (B) It will be sent to another library
   (C) A fine will be charged
   (D) It will be renewed automatically

4. What is the main reason for the message?
   (A) To inform about a service interruption
   (B) To announce a staff meeting
   (C) To update contact information
   (D) To promote a new service

5. When will the customer support line be unavailable?
   (A) From 4 PM to 6 PM
   (B) From 5 PM to 8 PM
   (C) From 8 AM to 10 AM
   (D) From 12 PM to 3 PM

6. How should urgent inquiries be handled?
   (A) By calling a different number
   (B) By visiting the office
   (C) By sending an email
   (D) By leaving a voicemail

7. What is the message about?
   (A) Performance evaluations
   (B) Changes in company policies
   (C) New training programs
   (D) Office relocation

8. When will the performance reviews take place?
   (A) This week
   (B) In two weeks
   (C) Next week
   (D) Next month

9. What should employees do to prepare?
   (A) Review their job descriptions
   (B) Check their calendar for the appointment time
   (C) Submit a report
   (D) Contact the HR department

10. What is the purpose of the call?
    (A) To confirm a meeting
    (B) To remind about a community event
    (C) To request volunteer help
    (D) To update contact information

11. What time will the health fair be held?
    (A) From 8 AM to 12 PM
    (B) From 9 AM to 1 PM
    (C) From 10 AM to 2 PM
    (D) From 10 pm to 2 AM

12. What activities will be available at the health fair?
    (A) Job interviews
    (B) Health tests
    (C) Cooking classes
    (D) Art exhibitions

試題演練答案、翻譯與解說

答案

1. (B)　2. (B)　3. (A)　4. (A)　5. (B)　6. (C)
7. (A)　8. (C)　9. (B)　10. (B)　11. (C)　12. (D)

聽力內容 Questions 1 through 3 refer to the following telephone message.

Hello, this is the City Library. We're calling to inform you that the book you requested is now available for pickup. The book will be held at the front desk under your name until the end of the week. If you don't pick it up by then, it will be returned to the shelves. Thank you for your patience!

中譯 問題 1-3 請參考以下電話錄音。

您好，這裡是市立圖書館。我們打電話通知您您要求的書籍現在可以取書了。書籍會在前台為您保留到本週末。如果您在那之前沒有取書，書籍將被歸還到書架上。感謝您的耐心等待！

1. What is the purpose of the call?　　此通話的目的為何？
   (A) To remind about a late fee　　(A) 提醒逾期費用
   (B) To notify about a book pickup　　**(B) 通知取書事宜**
   (C) To cancel a book reservation　　(C) 取消圖書預約
   (D) To announce a library event　　(D) 宣布圖書館活動

說明 這通電話的目的是通知顧客他們要求的書籍現在可以取書。說話者提到書籍已經準備好，並提供了取書的具體資訊。

2. How long will the book be held?　　書籍將保留多久？
   (A) Until the end of the day　　(A) 到當天結束為止
   (B) Until the end of the week　　**(B) 到本週結束為止**
   (C) For one month　　(C) 保留一個月
   (D) Until next week　　(D) 到下週為止

說明 書籍將被保留到本週末，顧客需要在這段時間內取書。

150

3. What happens if the book is not picked up? 如果書籍未被取走會怎麼處理？
   (A) It will be returned to the shelves (A) 它將被放回書架
   (B) It will be sent to another library (B) 它將被送往其他圖書館
   (C) A fine will be charged (C) 將收取罰款
   (D) It will be renewed automatically (D) 它將自動續借

   說明 如果顧客未能在指定時間內取走書籍，書籍將被歸還到書架上。

   單字 notify (v.) 通知　pickup (n.) 取貨　return (v.) 歸還　hold (v.) 保留
   shelf (n.) 書架

   片語 available for pickup (phr.) 可取貨　be held (phr.) 保留

聽力內容 **Questions 4 through 6 refer to the following announcement.**

Dear Team, due to a system upgrade, our customer support line will be unavailable from 5 PM to 8 PM today. Please direct any urgent inquiries to our email support. We apologize for the inconvenience and appreciate your understanding.

中譯 **問題 4-6 請參考以下宣布事項。**

親愛的團隊，由於系統升級，我們的客戶支持熱線將於今天下午 5 點至 8 點無法使用。請將任何緊急查詢發送至我們的電子郵件支持。我們為此帶來的不便深感歉意，感謝您的理解。

4. What is the main reason for the message? 此訊息的主要原因是什麼？
   (A) To inform about a service interruption (A) 通知服務中斷
   (B) To announce a staff meeting (B) 宣布員工會議
   (C) To update contact information (C) 更新聯絡資訊
   (D) To promote a new service (D) 推廣新服務

   說明 訊息的主要目的是告知顧客客戶支持熱線在特定時間內無法使用。這是因為服務中斷。

5. When will the customer support line be unavailable?　　客戶支援專線何時無法使用？
   (A) From 4 PM to 6 PM　　(A) 下午 4 點至 6 點
   (B) From 5 PM to 8 PM　　**(B) 下午 5 點至 8 點**
   (C) From 8 AM to 10 AM　　(C) 上午 8 點至 10 點
   (D) From 12 PM to 3 PM　　(D) 中午 12 點至下午 3 點

   說明　客戶支持熱線將在下午 5 點到 8 點無法使用。

6. How should urgent inquiries be handled?　　緊急詢問應如何處理？
   (A) By calling a different number　　(A) 撥打其他電話號碼
   (B) By visiting the office　　(B) 親自造訪辦公室
   (C) By sending an email　　**(C) 寄送電子郵件**
   (D) By leaving a voicemail　　(D) 留言語音信箱

   說明　在客戶支持熱線無法使用期間，顧客應通過電子郵件處理急需的查詢。

單字　interruption (n.) 中斷　inquiry (n.) 查詢　temporary (adj.) 暫時的
disrupt (v.) 擾亂

片語　direct to (phr.) 指引至

聽力內容　**Questions 7 through 9 refer to the following instructions.**
Hello, this is Jenna from the HR department. Please be reminded that the annual performance reviews will be conducted next Monday through Friday. Each employee will have a scheduled meeting with their manager to discuss their performance and future goals. Please check your calendar for your appointment time.

中譯　問題 7-9 請參考以下說明。
您好，我是 HR 部門的 Jenna。請記得年終績效評估將於下週進行。每位員工將與其經理安排會議，討論他們的表現和未來目標。請檢查您的日曆以查看您的預約時間。

7. What is the message about?
   (A) Performance evaluations
   (B) Changes in company policies
   (C) New training programs
   (D) Office relocation

   此訊息的內容是什麼？
   (A) 表現評估
   (B) 公司政策變更
   (C) 新培訓計劃
   (D) 辦公室搬遷

   說明　訊息主要關於即將進行的績效評估，並提供了相關的準備建議。

8. When will the performance reviews take place?
   (A) This week
   (B) In two weeks
   (C) Next week
   (D) Next month

   表現評估將於何時進行？
   (A) 本週
   (B) 兩週後
   (C) 下週
   (D) 下個月

   說明　績效評估將於下週進行。這提供了時間上的安排資訊。

9. What should employees do to prepare?
   (A) Review their job descriptions
   (B) Check their calendar for the appointment time
   (C) Submit a report
   (D) Contact the HR department

   員工應如何準備？
   (A) 檢視自己的職務描述
   (B) 查看行事曆上的預約時間
   (C) 提交報告
   (D) 聯繫人力資源部門

   說明　員工應檢查日曆以確認預約時間，這是準備績效評估的重要步驟。

   單字　review (n.) 審查　manager (n.) 經理、主管　discuss (v.) 討論
   appointed (adj.) 已定好的　evaluation (n.) 評估

   片語　HR (phr.) 人力資源（為 Human Resource 的簡稱）
   be reminded (phr.) 被提醒　check for (phr.) 查找

聽力內容　**Questions 10 through 12 refer to the following recorded message.**

Hi, this is the local community center calling to remind you about the health fair this Saturday from 10 in the morning till 2 in the afternoon. There will be free health screenings, informational booths, and activities for children. We hope to see you there!

中譯 問題 10-12 請參考以下錄音訊息。

您好，這裡是當地社區中心打來的，提醒您關於本週六上午 10 點至下午 2 點的健康博覽會。將提供免費健康檢查、資訊展位和兒童活動。希望見到您！

10. What is the purpose of the call?　　此通話的目的為何？
    (A) To confirm a meeting　　(A) 確認會議
    (B) To remind about a community event　　**(B) 提醒社區活動**
    (C) To request volunteer help　　(C) 請求志願者協助
    (D) To update contact information　　(D) 更新聯絡資訊

說明 這通電話的目的是提醒人們社區活動即將舉行，並提供了活動的時間和內容。

11. What time will the health fair be held?　　健康博覽會將於何時舉行？
    (A) From 8 AM to 12 PM　　(A) 上午 8 點至中午 12 點
    (B) From 9 AM to 1 PM　　(B) 上午 9 點至下午 1 點
    (C) From 10 AM to 2 PM　　**(C) 上午 10 點至下午 2 點**
    (D) From 10 pm to 2 AM　　(D) 晚上 10 點至凌晨 2 點

說明 健康博覽會的時間是上午 10 點到下午 2 點。這段時間提供了活動的具體時間。

12. What activities will be available at the health fair?　　健康博覽會將提供哪些活動？
    (A) Job interviews　　(A) 求職面試
    (B) Health tests　　(B) 健康檢查
    (C) Cooking classes　　(C) 烹飪課程
    (D) Art exhibitions　　**(D) 藝術展覽**

說明 健康博覽會上將提供免費健康檢查，這是主要的活動之一。

單字 fair (n.) 園遊會、市集　screening (n.) 檢查　booth (n.) 攤位　purpose (n.) 目的　confirm (v.) 確認

片語 community center (phr.) 社區中心

試題演練答案、翻譯與解說

第 6 章

閱讀部分解題攻略

6-1 Part 5 句子填空
6-2 Part 6 段落填空
6-3 Part 7 閱讀測驗

本章節會依照題型介紹，解說閱讀部分考試結構，再提供獨家搶分關鍵，最後搭配試題，清楚示範解題技巧，有效正確答題。

6-1 Part 5 句子填空

▸ 題型介紹

多益第五部分「句子填空題」，這部分就是單句填空的選擇題，找出空格中缺少的意思和詞性，有時候是考單字，有時候是考句子文法結構。有時可以從選項詞性判斷出正確答案，或從空格前後判定單字選項的意思。

▸ 搶分關鍵

解題技巧 作答速度快狠準

要在多益考試中得高分，閱讀的第五部分一定要在 15 - 20 分鐘內完成，以便將更多時間留給第六和第七部分的長篇閱讀，才能增加閱讀部分的總分。為此，作答時必須專心，既快速又準確地選出正確答案。每個選項不要猶豫過久；如果確實不會，就果斷猜測。然而，要真正致勝，必須有效掌握多益常考的高頻單字和基本的文法結構。

第五部分的題目設計通常針對詞性、字義和動詞變化來測驗考生。空格處常考的重點包括：

- **詞性判斷**：熟悉動詞、名詞、形容詞和副詞的正確位置和用途，選項中多數會提供不同詞性，要求考生選出語法正確的選項。
- **字義辨識**：須針對易混淆的詞義做選擇。具備高頻多益詞彙的理解能力，能幫助快速辨識正確選項。
- **動詞變化與時態**：時態一致性是多益的一個常考點，動詞的形式（如過去式、現在分詞等）需符合句意。熟悉基本的時態和主詞動詞一致性能提升解題速度。

解題技巧方面，建議在遇到熟悉句型的題目時快速作答，遇到不熟悉的題型時先跳過，完成後再回頭檢查。

最後，不論何種題型，養成練習快速掃讀句子結構的習慣、提高對文法和詞彙的敏感度，都是提升第五部分答題準確率的有效方式。

解題技巧教學

請從四個選項當中選出正確的答案。

句子填空範例 ①

Jo Wilson has received top performance reviews _____ she joined the marketing department three years ago.

(A) despite　(B) since　(C) while　(D) although

Jo Wilson 自從三年前加入行銷部門之後，績效考核優異。

範例解析

這個題目很明確，由於**動詞為 has received**，所以可以馬上得知是考**現在完成式** have/has + pp.，因此答案立刻選的**就是 (B) since 表示「自從哪一個時間點開始」**。

高頻多益單字　receive (n.) 收到　marketing (n.) 行銷

句子填空範例 ②

Customers _____ complete and return a feedback survey will receive a coupon for twenty percent off their next purchase.

(A) whose　(B) which　(C) whom　(D) who

顧客們完成並交回意見調查表，將得到下次消費的八折折價券。

範例解析

這題考關係代名詞，**前面的主詞是人 customers**，有 who、whom 或是 whose 幾種可能，**這裡需要代替先行詞『人』的主格關係代名詞**，因此答案立刻選 **(D) who**。關係代名詞絕對是經典必考題。

高頻多益單字　survey (n.) 調查表　coupon (n.) 折價券　purchase (n.) 購買

句子填空範例 ③

Having _____ in 1952, the convention center has undergone many expansions over the years.

(A) being built　(B) been built　(C) built　(D) build

會議中心自 1952 年完工，多年來已經擴建了很多次。

📝 範例解析

由於附屬子句主詞是主要子句的 **convention center**，會議中心無法自己蓋，因此 build 這個動詞要用被動語態。被動語態基本型式為「be + pp」，這裡再加上現在完成式就變成「have/has been + pp」，再從主要子句看到動詞是 has undergone 的現在完成式結構，那因此要選 **(B) been built** 才是現在完成式的被動語態。小心不要被 (A) 選項混淆，公式務必牢記才有快速答題的勝算。

高頻多益單字　undergo (v.) 經歷　　expansion (n.) 擴建、擴張

句子填空範例 ④

_____ having several years of experience in management, Mr. Parker did not get the promotion for which he applied.

(A) In spite of　(B) Unless　(C) Regardless　(D) Even so

Parker 先生即使已經有幾年的管理經驗，依舊沒有得到他申請的升遷機會。

📝 範例解析

這題考副詞子句裡，表示意外結果的介系詞片語。同學務必要記住這兩個可以互相替換的介系詞片語：**in spite of 和 despite**，它們後面都是接「名詞 N」或「動名詞 V-ing」。但和它們意思相同的 though、although 和 even though，後面就必須要接「句子」，也就是包含「主詞 S 和動詞 V」。所以這裡已經看到有 having 動名詞的結構，答案立刻選 **(A) In spite of 即使**。(B) Unless「除非」和 (C) Regardless「不管怎樣」的語意不符，(D) Even so「即使如此」，後面不可以接名詞 N 或動名詞 V-ing。

高頻多益單字　management (n.) 管理　　promotion (n.) 晉升　　apply (v.) 申請

句子填空範例 ⑤

Either the organization's sponsors will pay for the building addition _____ we will have to raise the money ourselves.

(A) or　(B) but　(C) and　(D) nor

不是組織的贊助商會支付擴建的部分，就是我們自己要募資。

範例解析

這題考連接詞裡的對等連接詞，"either… or…" 是常用的對等連接詞，意思為「不是 A 就是 B」，看到 either 馬上就可以選答案 (A) or。像這樣的秒殺解題千萬不要浪費時間去讀完題目，也絕對不能失分。記得我說過這個部份分秒必爭，愈快完成所有題目，正確率愈高，你就有更多時間作答第七部份的長篇、雙篇或是三篇閱讀，你獲得高分的勝算也越大。

高頻多益單字 sponsor (n.) 贊助者　addition (n.) 額外部分，這裡指建築物擴建

片語 raise money (phr.) 募資

句子填空範例 ⑥

The software will be updated _____ to keep the devices up to date.

(A) periodically　(B) formally　(C) respectively　(D) significantly

軟體將會定期更新，使設備維持在最新的狀態。

範例解析

這題考單字，根據句型可以判斷在動詞後面就是要選副詞，看起來選項皆為副詞，所以這裡要選出最符合語意的單字。由於 (B) formally「正式地」、(C) respectively「分別地」、(D) significantly「顯著地」，都不符合句意。因此答案選 **(A) periodically「定期地」**。

高頻多益單字 software (n.) 軟體　device (n.) 設備

片語 up to date (phr.) 包含最新資訊的

Practice Test

新制多益模擬試題

Part 5 句子填空

(　) 1. Due to budget constraints, we will need to _____ some expenses.
　　(A) reduce
　　(B) reduces
　　(C) reduced
　　(D) reducing

(　) 2. The marketing team is brainstorming ideas for the new campaign, _____ is expected to launch next month.
　　(A) who
　　(B) which
　　(C) where
　　(D) that

(　) 3. Since last quarter, the company _____ its profits by 20% due to strategic investments.
　　(A) increases
　　(B) increased
　　(C) has increased
　　(D) was increasing

(　) 4. Please ensure that the documents _____ before the meeting begins.
　　(A) prepare
　　(B) are prepared
　　(C) preparing
　　(D) have prepared

( ) 5. If the client _____ any changes to the contract, please let us know immediately.
(A) requests
(B) will request
(C) requested
(D) requesting

( ) 6. Despite _____ to improve the system, the team faced additional challenges during implementation.
(A) trying
(B) tries
(C) tried
(D) try

( ) 7. The report must be submitted no later than Friday, _____ the committee will review it the following Monday.
(A) while
(B) because
(C) when
(D) so

( ) 8. Had the team prepared more thoroughly, they _____ a better chance of securing the contract.
(A) have had
(B) would have had
(C) will have
(D) had

( ) 9. The CEO, along with her advisors, _____ to address the recent financial downturn.
(A) are planning
(B) plan
(C) is planning
(D) planning

( ) 10. Neither the supervisor nor the employees _____ satisfied with the new policy.
(A) are
(B) is
(C) was
(D) being

( ) 11. The consultant explained that the data was inaccurate because it _____ incorrectly during the analysis process.
(A) is processed
(B) processed
(C) had been processed
(D) has processed

( ) 12. The company's swift expansion into international markets required _____ planning and precise execution.
(A) strategic
(B) strategize
(C) strategically
(D) strategy

( ) 13. The committee is currently evaluating candidates, _____ performance evaluations will be completed next week.
(A) whose
(B) who
(C) whom
(D) which

( ) 14. The marketing team has been praised for their _____ approach to increasing brand awareness and attracting customers.
(A) creativity
(B) create
(C) creatively
(D) creative

( ) 15. The committee was applauded for its _____ handling of the complex negotiation process.
(A) judicious
(B) judiciary
(C) judiciously
(D) judgment

( ) 16. _____ the announcement of the new policy, management will provide additional details and answer questions from employees.
(A) Follow
(B) Followed
(C) Following
(D) To follow

( ) 17. The success of the new product launch can be attributed to the team's _____ execution of the marketing strategy.
(A) flaw
(B) flawless
(C) flawlessly
(D) flawlessness

( ) 18. The company is offering a discount to customers _____ purchases exceed $1,000 in total.
(A) who
(B) whose
(C) whom
(D) which

試題演練答案、翻譯與解說

答案

1. (A) 2. (B) 3. (C) 4. (B) 5. (A) 6. (A) 7. (B) 8. (B) 9. (C) 10. (A)
11. (C) 12. (A) 13. (A) 14. (D) 15. (A) 16. (C) 17. (B) 18. (B)

1. **(A)** Due to budget constraints, we will need to <u>reduce</u> some expenses.

   中譯　由於預算限制，我們將需要削減一些開支。
   說明　**need to** 前面的先行詞為主動時，**後面必須接動詞原形**。
   單字　constraint (n.) 限制　expense (n.) 開銷

2. **(B)** The marketing team is brainstorming ideas for the new campaign, <u>which</u> is expected to launch next month.

   中譯　行銷團隊正在為新活動集思廣益，該活動預計於下個月推出。
   說明　關係代名詞 "which" 用來補充說明先行詞 "the new campaign"。
   單字　expect (v.) 預計

3. **(C)** Since last quarter, the company <u>has increased</u> its profits by 20% due to strategic investments.

   中譯　自從上個季度以來，公司因為策略性投資而讓利潤多了 20%。
   說明　"**Since** last quarter" 表示的是從「上個季度」開始到現在的時間段，這屬於典型的**現在完成式用法**。
   單字　quarter (n.) 季度　profit (n.) 利潤
   片語　strategic investment (phr.) 策略性投資

4. **(B)** Please ensure that the documents <u>are prepared</u> before the meeting begins.

   中譯　請確保文件在會議開始之前準備好。
   說明　**因為文件不會自己主動準備，所以要用被動語態**。
   單字　document (n.) 文件

5. **(A)** If the client <u>requests</u> any changes to the contract, please let us know immediately.

   中譯　如果客戶要求對合約進行更改，請立即告知我們。
   說明　If 條件句搭配現在簡單式，表達未來可能發生的情況。
   單字　immediately (adv.) 立即地

6. **(A)** Despite trying to improve the system, the team faced additional challenges during implementation.

中譯 儘管團隊試圖改善系統，但在實施過程中仍面臨額外挑戰。
說明 **Despite 後接動名詞，表示儘管試圖做某事。**
單字 system (n.) 系統　additional (adj.) 額外的　implementation (n.) 實施

7. **(B)** The report must be submitted no later than Friday, because the committee will review it the following Monday.

中譯 報告必須在星期五之前提交，因為委員會將於下週一審查。
說明 **主要子句和附屬子句間有因果關係**，附屬子句表示原因，**需用 because 引導。**
單字 committee (n.) 委員會
片語 no later than... (phr.) 在…之前

8. **(B)** Had the team prepared more thoroughly, they would have had a better chance of securing the contract.

中譯 如果團隊當時準備得更充分，他們獲得合約的機率也會更大。
說明 與過去事實相反的假設句型使用「Had + 過去分詞」和「would have + 過去分詞」。
單字 secure (v.) 獲得

9. **(C)** The CEO, along with her advisors, is planning to address the recent financial downturn.

中譯 執行長與她的顧問正在計劃解決近期的財務下滑問題。
說明 **主詞為 "The CEO"（執行長）單數，動詞需用 "is planning"。along with her advisors 為附加資訊，不會影響動詞單複數。**
單字 advisor (n.) 顧問　address (v.) 對付、處理　downturn (n.) 衰退

10. **(A)** Neither the supervisor nor the employees are satisfied with the new policy.

中譯 主管和員工都對新政策感到不滿意。
說明 "Neither...nor" 後的**動詞和最靠近的主詞 "employees" 單複數形式一致**。
單字 supervisor (n.) 管理者

試題演練答案、翻譯與解說

167

11. **(C)** The consultant explained that the data was inaccurate because it had been processed incorrectly during the analysis process.

中譯　顧問解釋說數據是不準確的，因為在分析過程中處理不當。

說明　過去完成被動態表達在另一過去動作之前所發生的動作。

單字　consultant (n.) 顧問　inaccurate (adj.) 不準確的　process (n.) 階段、過程

12. **(A)** The company's swift expansion into international markets required strategic planning and precise execution.

中譯　公司迅速擴展到國際市場，這需要策略性規劃和精準執行。

說明　(A) **strategic 是形容詞，意為「策略性的」，正確修飾名詞 planning**，符合語法並表達「策略性規劃」。(B) strategize 是動詞，語法上不正確，因為需要的是形容詞修飾 planning。(C) strategically 是副詞，語法不正確，因為副詞不能修飾名詞 planning。(D) strategy 是名詞，語法上不正確，因為缺少與名詞 planning 的連接詞。

單字　swift (adj.) 迅速的　require (v.) 需要　precise (adj.) 精準的　execution (n.) 執行

13. **(A)** The committee is currently evaluating candidates, whose performance evaluations will be completed next week.

中譯　委員會正在評估候選人，其績效評估將於下週完成。

說明　**whose 為所有格代名詞，表示 candidates'**。

單字　candidate (n.) 候選人

14. **(D)** The marketing team has been praised for their creative approach to increasing brand awareness and attracting customers.

中譯　行銷團隊因用創意方法提升品牌能見度、吸引客戶而受到讚譽。

說明　(A) creativity 是名詞，意為「創造力」，但此處需要形容詞來修飾 approach。(B) create 是動詞，語法上不正確。(C) creatively 是副詞，語法上不正確，因為副詞無法直接修飾名詞 approach。**(D) creative 是形容詞，正確修飾名詞 approach**，表達「有創意的方法」。

單字　praise (v.) 讚揚

15. **(A)** The committee was applauded for its judicious handling of the complex negotiation process.

中譯　委員會因明智處理複雜談判過程，而受到讚揚。

說明　**(A) judicious 是形容詞，意為「明智的」，符合語法並修飾 handling**，表達「明智的處理方式」。(B) judiciary 是名詞，意為「司法機構」，與句意不符。

(C) judiciously 是副詞，語法不正確，因為副詞不能修飾名詞 handling。(D) judgment 是名詞，意為「判斷、判斷力」，但語法上需形容詞修飾 handling。

單字 applaud (v.) 讚許

16. **(C)** Following the announcement of the new policy, management will provide additional details and answer questions from employees.

中譯 在新政策公告後，管理層將提供更多細節並回答員工的問題。

說明 這題考分詞構句的使用，分詞可以用來表示時間、原因、條件或補充說明的關係。分詞的位置通常在主句前或主句後，用以修飾句子的主語。

主要子句為 "management will provide additional details and answer questions from employees."，主語是 management。前半句的分詞結構需修飾這個主語。分詞結構 "Following the announcement of the new policy" 的動詞用現在分詞 Following，表示「進行中的動作」或「補充說明」。(A) Follow 是原形動詞，不能直接做為分詞使用。(B) Followed 是過去分詞，通常用來表示被動或已完成的動作，語意不符，因為這裡要表達的是主動動作（管理層跟隨政策公告進一步行動）。**(C) Following 是現在分詞，表主動進行中的動作，正確。**(D) To follow 為不定詞，表目的或未來意圖，語意不符。

單字 announcement (n.) 公告、聲明

17. **(B)** The success of the new product launch can be attributed to the team's flawless execution of the marketing strategy.

中譯 新產品上市的成功歸功於團隊對行銷策略的完美執行。

說明 (A) flaw 是名詞，意為「缺陷」，語意與句子需求不符。**(B) flawless 是形容詞，意為「完美無瑕的」，正確修飾名詞 execution**，語法正確並表達「完美的執行」。(C) flawlessly 是副詞，語法不正確，因為副詞不能修飾名詞 execution。(D) flawlessness 是名詞，意為「完美」，但語法上需要形容詞來修飾 execution。

單字 attribute sth. to sb. (phr.) 將（某種特質）歸屬於（某人）

18. **(B)** The company is offering a discount to customers whose purchases exceed $1,000 in total.

中譯 公司為購買總額超過 1,000 美元的客戶提供折扣。

說明 whose 為所有格代名詞，指代 customers'。

單字 exceed (v.) 超過

6-2 段落填空

Part 6

▸ 題型介紹

多益第六部分「段落填空題」延長了第五部分的單一句子填空，變成了一篇短文，所以更需要注意上下文是否連貫。新制中增加的「插入句」題型，考生須根據上下文語意選出合適，且不影響文意的句子放在合適的空格裡。

▸ 搶分關鍵

解題技巧 注意上下文脈絡與關係

1. 預讀全文，快速理解上下文： 在閱讀完每個空格的前後句後，試圖在腦中形成段落的整體脈絡。先從主旨與文章的語氣出發，以大致推測選項的正確性，避免逐題單獨作答。

2. 帶入答案，確保文意通順： 在確定選項前，將答案帶入空格位置，檢查是否符合上下文的流暢性與邏輯性。以標準的句子結構來檢查是否符合英文語法的自然用法，並觀察句子間是否連貫。

3. 控制時間，盡量在 10 分鐘內完成： 保持閱讀速度的穩定性非常重要，避免在此部分花費過多時間，影響第七部分的作答。建議在答題時合理分配每題的時間，保持答題節奏的穩定，以利後續長篇閱讀的解題準備。

掌握段落填空題的考點與解題策略，並在實際考試中進行有效的時間管理，能夠顯著提升整體閱讀部分的答題效率與正確率。

▸ 常見考點

1. 連接詞與轉折詞： 段落填空題中，考題常涉及適當的連接詞或轉折詞，如 however、moreover、therefore 等，這些詞語用於連接句子，幫助文意更為連貫。解題時**須根據前後句的關係，判斷是轉折、因果、添加還是對比關係**，挑選出最適合的答案。

2. 時態一致性：根據文章的時態，選擇適當的動詞形式。若文章使用的是過去式，就應注意空格內動詞是否需要與之匹配的時態，避免時態不一致的情況。

3. 語氣與語境適合性：段落填空有時會考正式或非正式語氣的適切性，例如商務文書可能會使用較正式的語氣；而內部備忘錄可能會較口語化。根據文章的風格選擇合適的選項，可以提升段落的連貫性。

▎解題技巧教學

根據上下文從四個選項當中選出最正確的答案。

單句填空範例 ①

Questions 1 - 4 refer to the following notice.

Sun Group Dental Clinic is conducting a survey to help it improve the service provided to patients. The gathered __1__ will be used to establish a long-term plan to better serve the needs of local residents. __2__ . Alternatively, a paper version is also available from the reception counter.

All survey participants __3__ a complimentary toothbrush for their time. For further information, call 323 - 511 - 0960 __4__ regular business hours.

問題 1 - 4 請參考下面的公告。

太陽集團牙科診所正在做一項調查，以幫助改善提供給患者的服務。所收集的訊息將用於制定長期計劃，為了能更適當的滿足當地居民的需求。可以掃描 QR 碼在線上完成調查。此外，接待櫃檯也提供紙本版本。

所有參與調查的患者將獲得一支免費牙刷作為答謝。如需進一步資訊，請於正常營業時間撥打 323 - 511 - 0960 聯繫。

範例解析

1. (A) inform
   (B) informed
   (C) informative
   (D) information

這邊就算沒有看完整句子的題目，**你只要看到前面的形容詞 gathered（收集的），就應該要知道這個空格裡面應該選名詞**。這是非常基礎的文法概念，形容詞後面要加名詞，**答案為 (D) information**。

2. **(A) The survey can be completed online by scanning the QR code.**
   (B) Clinic hours will remain the same during construction.
   (C) Residents are asked to provide their contact info.
   (D) Based on the results, management is currently working on a plan.

   (A) 可以掃描 QR 碼在線上完成調查。
   (B) 在施工期間，診所的營業時間將保持不變。
   (C) 請居民提供聯絡資訊。
   (D) 根據結果，管理層目前正在制定計劃。

本題為新制多益的插入句子題，主要測試考生的上下文連貫能力。這個空格的後面一句提到 "a paper version is also available" 指的就是「有紙筆版本」，再接下來一句就提到 survey（問卷調查），**因此縱觀四個選項來看，選項 (A) 說明這個問卷也有線上版本，最符合承接上文連結下文**。選項 (B) 和 (C) 不符合文意。選項 (D) 完全沒有在文章中提到。

3. (A) received
   (B) will receive
   (C) are receiving
   (D) have received

這題考的就是很簡單的**主詞加上動詞未來式**，主詞為填寫問卷的人 (survey participants) 將獲得一支免費的牙刷，作為花時間填寫問卷的獎勵，因此**答案選 (B)「will + 原形動詞」will receive**。(A) received 為過去式動詞、

(C) are receiving 為現在進行式，或是 (D) have received 為現在完成式，都不符合句意及正確的時態使用。

4. (A) for
   (B) in
   (C) during
   (D) while

考表達時間的介系詞，**在 regular business hours（平日營業時間）這段時間來電，我們用的是 during，因此答案選 (D)**。(A) for 後面會加一段時間，(B) in 通常用在未來的時間，(D) while 則比較常用在指較長的時間的「當…」。

高頻多益單字 provide (v.) 提供　patient (n.) 病人　establish (v.) 建立
long-term (adj.) 長期的　serve (v.) 服務　resident (n.) 居民
alternatively (adv.) 或者　available (adj.) 可獲得的
complimentary (adj.) 免費的　further (adj.) 進一步的
regular (adj.) 正常的、規律的

片語 reception counter (phr.) 櫃台　business hours (phr.) 營業時間

新制多益模擬試題

Part 6 段落填空

Questions 1-4 refer to the following letter.

Subject: Upcoming Office Renovations

Dear Team,

I hope this message finds you well. I am writing to inform you about the upcoming office renovations scheduled to begin next month. These updates are aimed at creating a more comfortable and efficient workplace for everyone. __1__ improvements will focus on upgrading the furniture, installing modern equipment, and redesigning communal areas. We believe these changes will not only enhance productivity but also improve employee satisfaction.

During the renovation period, some teams may need to relocate to temporary workspaces. This __2__ relocation process will be coordinated by the project management team, who will provide detailed instructions on where you should set up and how to access essential resources.

To ensure a smooth transition, we encourage all employees to pack their personal belongings before the renovations commence. Please __3__ all items that need to be stored for the duration of the project. Additionally, ensure that fragile items are packed securely to prevent damage.

We understand that renovations can be disruptive, but we are confident that the end result will be worth the temporary inconvenience. __4__. If you have any questions or concerns, do not hesitate to reach out to the facilities department. Thank you for your understanding and cooperation.

Best regards,
Thomas Lee
Facilities Manager

1. (A) Planned
   (B) Completed
   (C) Estimated
   (D) Allocated

2. (A) short-term
   (B) complex
   (C) flexible
   (D) temporary

3. (A) label
   (B) move
   (C) collect
   (D) remove

4. (A) Your feedback will help us refine future renovation plans.
   (B) We aim to complete the project by the end of the quarter.
   (C) Thank you for your patience and support throughout this process.
   (D) This will allow us to create a workplace tailored to your needs.

Questions 5-8 refer to the following announcement.

Subject: Announcement of New Employee Benefits

Dear Team,

We are pleased to announce an update to our employee benefits program, which will take effect starting next month. These changes are designed to support your health, well-being, and professional growth.

__5__. For instance, all employees will now have access to a wider range of health insurance options, including plans that cover mental health services and wellness programs. In addition to healthcare benefits, we are introducing a new training reimbursement policy. This policy will allow employees to __6__ professional development courses related to their roles, with reimbursement of up to $1,000 per year.

To make the most of these benefits, we encourage all team members to familiarize themselves with the details. Please refer to the attached document for a __7__ overview of the new offerings, including eligibility criteria and enrollment procedures.

We are confident that these updates will have a positive impact on your overall experience at the company. __8__. If you have any questions or need assistance, please reach out to the HR team.

Best regards,

Sophia Chen
HR Manager

---

5. (A) Several new features are included in this update.
   (B) Employees should be aware of their responsibilities.
   (C) These benefits are available only for certain teams.
   (D) More details will be shared at the next meeting.

6. (A) enroll in
   (B) withdraw from
   (C) apply for
   (D) budget for

7. (A) broad
   (B) quick
   (C) limited
   (D) comprehensive

8. (A) We appreciate your feedback on these changes.
   (B) Thank you for your continued dedication to the company.
   (C) This initiative reflects our commitment to your success.
   (D) Participation in these programs is entirely optional.

Questions 9-12 refer to the following e-mail.

Subject: New Office Recycling Program

Dear Employees,

We are excited to announce the launch of our new recycling program. This initiative aims to promote sustainability and reduce waste. Starting next week, new recycling bins will be placed throughout the office.

__9__ for sorting will be explained. Each bin will be clearly labeled for specific materials, such as paper, plastic, and glass. We encourage everyone to participate actively in this program. Not only does recycling help the environment, but it also aligns with our company's commitment to social responsibility. It is __10__ that every employee follows the guidelines provided in the attached document.

Please remember that items like food waste and non-recyclable materials should be disposed of in the regular trash bins. __11__ can cause contamination of the recyclable materials, rendering them unusable.

Thank you for your cooperation in making this program a success. __12__. We look forward to your feedback on how we can improve this initiative in the future.

Best regards,

Anna Johnson
Facilities Manager

9. (A) Instructions
   (B) Placement
   (C) Distribution
   (D) Allocation

10. (A) appropriate
    (B) convenient
    (C) sufficient
    (D) essential

11. (A) Ignoring the rules
    (B) Proper sorting
    (C) Mixing trash
    (D) Recycling correctly

12. (A) We believe this will have a significant impact on our community.
    (B) Together, we can make a difference in reducing waste.
    (C) Let's work together to set an example for others.
    (D) Your participation is vital to the success of this program.

Questions 13-16 refers to the following letter.

> **Subject: Annual Team-Building Event**
>
> Dear Team,
>
> We are excited to announce that our annual team-building event will take place on Friday, June 16, at Greenfield Park. This event is a great opportunity for everyone to relax, connect, and strengthen our teamwork.
>
> The day will include activities such as a morning scavenger hunt, team sports in the afternoon, and a closing barbecue dinner. __13__. Participation in the event is voluntary, but we encourage all team members to join in. __14__ as soon as possible so we can plan meals and activities accordingly.

To ensure everyone has a good time, please come prepared. Wear comfortable clothing and 15 sunscreen and a reusable water bottle. The company will provide snacks, drinks, and all necessary equipment for the activities.

We look forward to seeing everyone there! 16 . If you have any questions, feel free to reach out to the event planning committee at events@ourcompany.com.

Best regards,

Emily Davis
Event Coordinator

13. (A) Activities will be canceled if it rains.
    (B) Please see the attached schedule for details.
    (C) We will provide transportation to the park.
    (D) Attendance is limited to 50 people.

14. (A) Pick up
    (B) Turn down
    (C) Check in
    (D) Sign up

15. (A) bring
    (B) hold
    (C) use
    (D) fetch

16. (A) Thank you for helping make this event a success.
    (B) This is a great chance to enjoy the outdoors together.
    (C) Don't forget to invite your family and friends.
    (D) Your suggestions for next year's event are welcome.

試題演練答案、翻譯與解說

答案

1. (A)   2. (D)   3. (A)   4. (C)   5. (A)   6. (A)   7. (D)   8. (C)
9. (A)   10. (D)   11. (C)   12. (D)   13. (B)   14. (D)   15. (A)   16. (B)

問題 1-4 請參考下面的信件

主題：即將進行的辦公室裝修

親愛的團隊：

希望你們一切安好。我寫這封信是為了通知大家，下個月即將開始的辦公室裝修計劃。這些更新旨在為每位員工打造一個更舒適、高效的工作環境。[1] **這些計劃好**的改變將著重於升級家具、安裝現代化設備以及重新設計公共區域。我們相信，這些變化不僅能提升生產力，還能提高員工的滿意度。

在裝修期間，一些團隊可能需要臨時遷移到其他工作區域。這些 [2] **臨時的**遷移過程將由專案管理團隊協調，他們會提供詳細的指導，包括新工作空間的位置以及如何獲取必要資源。

為了確保這段過渡時期順利，我們鼓勵所有員工在裝修開始前打包好個人用品。請 [3] **標記**所有需要在施工期間存放的物品。此外，請確保易碎物品包裝妥當，以防止損壞。

我們理解裝修可能會帶來一些不便，但我們相信最終的結果將值得這段暫時的不適。

[4] **感謝大家在這這段過程中的耐心和支持。**如果您有任何問題或疑慮，請隨時聯繫設施部門。感謝您的理解與合作！

設施經理
Thomas Lee 敬上

---

1. **(A)** Planned improvements will focus on upgrading the furniture, installing modern equipment, and redesigning communal areas.

   中譯 這些計劃好的改變將著重於升級家具、安裝現代化設備以及重新設計公共區域。

   說明 句子前面提到 "These updates are aimed at creating a more comfortable and efficient workplace"，後面則描述具體的改進措施。此處需要一個形容詞來修飾 improvements，表示這些改進是有計劃的。選項中 planned（計劃好的）最為合適，與上下文的語氣一致。

180

其他選項：
- completed (adj.) 已完成的：不符合文意，因為改進尚未開始。
- estimated (adj.) 估算的：多用於數字或數量，不適合形容改進措施。
- allocated (adj.) 分配的：不符合語境，與「改進」無直接關聯。

2. **(D)** This temporary relocation process will be coordinated by the project management team, who will provide detailed instructions on where you should set up and how to access essential resources.

中譯 這些臨時的遷移過程將由專案管理團隊協調，他們會提供詳細的指導，包括新工作空間的位置以及如何獲取必要資源。

說明 此空格位於 "relocation process" 之前，形容搬遷的性質。文中提到 "During the renovation period, some teams may need to relocate to temporary workspaces"，說明這種搬遷是暫時的，因此 temporary（暫時的）是正確答案。

其他選項：
- short-term (adj.) 短期的：雖然語意相近，但 temporary 在正式語境中更為常用。
- complex (adj.) 複雜的：與搬遷的性質不符。
- flexible (adj.) 靈活的：文中未提及靈活性。

3. **(A)** Please label all items that need to be stored for the duration of the project.

中譯 請標記所有需要在施工期間存放的物品。

說明 文中提到 "ensure that fragile items are packed securely"，說明需要標記物品以便存放或防止損壞，因此 label（標記）是最符合上下文的選項。

其他選項：
- move (v.) 搬動：雖然相關，但語意過於籠統，與句子要求不符。
- collect (v.) 收集：不符合文中要求標記的語意。
- remove (v.) 移除：並未提及移除物品，而是將其存放。

4. (A) Your feedback will help us refine future renovation plans.
   (B) We aim to complete the project by the end of the quarter.
   (C) Thank you for your patience and support throughout this process.
   (D) This will allow us to create a workplace tailored to your needs.

181

中譯　(A) 您的意見將幫助我們完善未來的翻修計劃。
　　　　(B) 我們的目標是在本季度結束前完成該項目。
　　　　(C) 感謝大家在這這段過程中的耐心和支持。
　　　　(D) 這將使我們能夠打造一個符合您需求的工作場所。

說明　文末總結段通常表達對員工帶來的不便所表達感謝，選項 (C) 傳遞出感謝與正向的語氣，為正解。選項 (A) 較適合放在針對未來規劃徵求建議時，非結尾語氣。選項 (B) 屬於描述時間表，與總結語氣不符。選項 (D) 雖然合理，但更適合作為文章中間對改進目標的補充說明。

單字　upcoming (adj.) 即將發生的　　renovation (n.) 整修　　inform (v.) 告知
　　　　upgrade (v.) 升級　　furniture (n.) 家具　　relocate (v.) 搬遷　　coordinate (v.) 協調
　　　　transition (n.) 轉變、過渡　　duration (n.) 期間　　disruptive (adj.) 混亂的

片語　focus on (phr.) 著重

問題 5-8 請參考下面的公告

主題：新員工福利公告

親愛的團隊：

我們很高興宣布，公司員工福利計劃將進行更新，並將於下個月開始生效。這些改變旨在支持大家的健康、福祉以及職業發展。

[5] **這次更新包含了幾個新特色**。例如，所有員工現在都可以選擇更多種類的健康保險計劃，其中包括涵蓋心理健康服務和健康計劃的選項。除了醫療福利之外，我們還引入了一項新的培訓費用補助政策。該政策允許員工 [6] **參加**與自身職務相關的專業進修課程，每年最高可獲得 1,000 美元的補助。

為了充分利用這些福利，我們鼓勵所有團隊成員熟悉具體細節。請參閱附件中的文件，其中包含新福利的 [7] **全面**概述，包括資格標準和註冊程序。

我們相信，這更新將對您在公司的整體體驗產生正面的影響。[8] **此舉體現了我們對於支持**您成功的承諾。如果您有任何問題或需要幫助，請隨時聯繫人力資源部門。感謝您的支持！

人力資源經理
Sophia Chen 敬上

182

5. **(A) Several new features are included in this update.**
   (B) Employees should be aware of their responsibilities.
   (C) These benefits are available only for certain teams.
   (D) More details will be shared at the next meeting.

   中譯 (A) 這次更新包含了幾個新特色。
   (B) 員工應了解自己的職責。
   (C) 這些福利僅適用於某些團隊。
   (D) 更多詳情將在下一次會議中分享。

   說明 空格後面描述了具體的新增保險選項，因此**最適合的選項是 (A)**，說明這次更新所包含的幾個新特色。

6. **(A)** This policy will allow employees to enroll in professional development courses related to their roles, with reimbursement of up to $1,000 per year.

   中譯 該政策允許員工參加與自身職務相關的專業進修課程，每年最高可獲得 1,000 美元的補助。

   說明 文意指員工可以參加與職務相關的課程，"enroll in"（參加）是最合適的搭配用語。
   其他選項意思如下：
   - withdraw from：(phr.) 退出、撤回
   - apply for：(phr.) 申請
   - budget for：(phr.) 制訂預算、安排資金

7. **(D)** Please refer to the attached document for a comprehensive overview of the new offerings, including eligibility criteria and enrollment procedures.

   中譯 請參閱附件中的文件，其中包含新福利的全面概述，包括資格標準和註冊程序。

   說明 此處需要形容文件內容涵蓋完整細節，**comprehensive（全面的）最符合語境。**
   其他選項意思如下：
   - broad：(adj.) 廣泛的
   - quick：(adj.) 快速的
   - limited：(adj.) 有限的

183

8. (A) We appreciate your feedback on these changes.
   (B) Thank you for your continued dedication to the company.
   (C) This initiative reflects our commitment to your success.
   (D) Participation in these programs is entirely optional.

中譯
(A) 我們感謝您對這些變更的意見反饋。
(B) 感謝您對公司的一貫奉獻。
(C) 此舉體現了我們對於支持您成功的承諾。
(D) 參與這些計畫完全是自願的。

說明 文中提到這些更新旨在提升員工體驗，因此此選項表達了公司對員工成功的承諾，符合文意和結尾語氣。

單字 insurance (n.) 保險　access (n.)（使用某物的）權利　option (n.) 選擇
reimbursement (n.) 報銷　professional (adj.) 職業的
development (n.) 成長、發展　encourage (v.) 鼓勵　overview (n.) 概觀
offerings (n.) 提供之物

片語 take effect (phr.) 生效

問題 9-12 請參考下面的電子郵件

主題：新的辦公室回收計劃

親愛的同事們：

我們很高興宣布推出新的回收計劃。此舉旨在促進可持續性並減少廢棄物。從下週開始，新回收桶將被放置在辦公室。

如何分類的 [9] **指導**稍晚會說明。每個回收桶都將清楚標示特定材料，例如紙張、塑料和玻璃。我們鼓勵每位員工積極參與這項計劃。回收不僅對環境有益，還體現了我們公司對社會責任的承諾。遵守指引是 [10] **相當重要的**，以確保每位員工遵守附件文件中提供的指導方針。

請記住，食物垃圾和不可回收的材料應該丟棄在普通垃圾桶中。[11] **混合垃圾**可能會導致可回收材料的污染，讓它們無法使用。

感謝您對成功推行此計劃的配合。[12] **您的參與是推行這項回收計劃的重要關鍵**。我們期待聽取您對如何改進這項倡議的意見。

設施經理
Anna Johnson 敬上

9. **(A)** Instructions for sorting will be explained.

中譯 如何分類的指導稍晚會說明。

說明 後面一句提到垃圾桶會清楚標示如何分類，因此選擇 Instructions（指導）最為合適，其他選項與文意不符。

其他選項：
- Placement：(n.) 放置、安排
- Distribution：(n.) 分配、分發
- Allocation：(n.) 分配、配置

10. **(D)** It is essential that every employee follows the guidelines provided in the attached document.

中譯 遵守準則是相當重要的，以確保每位員工遵守附件文件中提供的指導方針。

說明 此處強調遵守準則的重要性，因此 essential（至關重要的）最符合文意。

其他選項：
- appropriate：(adj.) 適當的
- convenient：(adj.) 方便的、便利的
- sufficient：(adj.) 充足的

11. **(C)** Mixing trash can cause contamination of the recyclable materials, rendering them unusable.

中譯 混合垃圾可能會導致可回收材料的污染，讓它們無法使用。

說明 文中提到混合垃圾會導致污染，"Mixing trash" 最符合這個意思，其他選項不符合上下文。

其他選項：
- Ignoring the rules：(phr.) 無視規則
- Proper sorting：(phr.) 正確分類
- Recycling correctly：(phr.) 正確回收

12. (A) We believe this will have a significant impact on our community.
    (B) Together, we can make a difference in reducing waste.
    (C) Let's work together to set an example for others.
    (D) Your participation is vital to the success of this program.

| 中譯 | (A) 我們相信這將對我們的社區產生重大影響。
(B) 一起努力,我們可以在減少浪費方面有所作為。
(C) 讓我們共同努力,為他人樹立榜樣。
(D) 您的參與是推行這項回收計劃的重要關鍵。 |
|---|---|
| 說明 | 作為結尾句,選項 (D) 強調了員工的參與對於成功推行回收計劃的重要性,符合文意。 |
| 單字 | recycle (v.) 回收再利用　initiative (n.) 新措施　sort (v.) 分類　plastic (n.) 塑膠
environment (n.) 自然環境　commitment (n.) 承諾　guideline (n.) 準則
dispose (v.) 丟掉　contamination (n.) 汙染　cooperation (n.) 合作 |
| 片語 | align with 想法和⋯⋯一致 |

問題 13-16 請參考下面的信件

主題:年度團隊建設活動

親愛的團隊:

我們很高興宣布,我們的年度團隊建設活動將於 6 月 16 日星期五在格林菲爾德公園舉行。這是一次極好的機會,讓大家放鬆身心、建立聯繫,並加強團隊合作。

一天的活動將包括早上的尋寶遊戲、下午的團隊運動,並以晚上的燒烤晚宴作為結束。

[13] **詳情請參閱附件中的時間表**。參與這次活動是自願的,但我們鼓勵所有團隊成員參加。請儘早 [14] **報名**,以便我們根據人數安排餐飲和活動。

為了確保每個人都能玩得開心,請準備好相應的物品。請 [15] **攜帶**舒適的服裝、防曬霜和可重複使用的水壺。公司將提供小吃、飲料和所有必要的活動設備。

我們期待著見到大家! [16] **這是一次很好的機會,一起享受戶外活動。** 如果有任何問題,隨時可以聯繫活動策劃委員會,郵箱地址是 events@ourcompany.com。

活動協調員

Emily Davis 敬上

---

13. (A) Activities will be canceled if it rains.
    (B) Please see the attached schedule for details.
    (C) We will provide transportation to the park.
    (D) Attendance is limited to 50 people.

| 中譯 | (A) 如果下雨,活動將取消。
(B) 詳情請參閱附件中的時間表。
(C) 我們將提供前往公園的交通服務。
(D) 出席人數限制為 50 人。 |
|---|---|

186

說明　上一句提到一天的活動安排，因此最佳選項是引導讀者查看附件以獲取具體細節。

14. **(D)** Sign up as soon as possible so we can plan meals and activities accordingly.

中譯　請儘早報名，以便我們根據人數安排餐飲和活動。

說明　**根據上下文，需要員工儘早報名，"sign up"（報名）是最符合語境的選擇。**
其他選項：
- Pick up：(phr.) 撿起、拿起
- Turn down：(phr.) 拒絕
- Check in：(phr.) 報到、登記

15. **(A)** Wear comfortable clothing and bring sunscreen and a reusable water bottle.

中譯　請攜帶舒適的服裝、防曬霜和可重複使用的水壺。

說明　此處列舉了需要攜帶的物品，**bring（攜帶）最適合。**
其他選項：
- hold：(v.) 拿
- use：(v.) 使用
- fetch：(v.) 拿來、取回

16. (A) Thank you for helping make this event a success.
    (B) This is a great chance to enjoy the outdoors together.
    (C) Don't forget to invite your family and friends.
    (D) Your suggestions for next year's event are welcome.

中譯　(A) 感謝您幫助使這個活動成功舉行。
　　　(B) 這是一次很好的機會，一起享受戶外活動。
　　　(C) 別忘了邀請您的家人和朋友。
　　　(D) 歡迎您對明年活動提出建議。

說明　**文末需要一個與活動氣氛相符的正向結語，表達期待與大家一起參加活動的心情，選 (B)。**

單字　connect (v.) 與…建立良好關係　strengthen (v.) 加強　participation (n.) 參加
　　　voluntary (adj.) 自願的、義務性的　accordingly (adv.) 依照
　　　sunscreen (n.) 防曬霜

片語　scavenger hunt (phr.) 尋物遊戲　look forward to (phr.) 期待

187

6-3 Part 7 閱讀測驗

▌題型介紹

多益第七部分「多篇閱讀」包含單篇和多篇閱讀題組，檢視考生在不同文本之間的綜合理解能力。

▌搶分關鍵

解題技巧 耐著性子就能找出答案

在多益閱讀測驗第七部分，掌握解題技巧至關重要。若能在 20 到 25 分鐘內完成第五和第六部分的題目，考生將有充裕的時間可以耐心分析每個問題並且檢查答案。

常見體裁和文本類型

本部分涵蓋多種體裁，包括通知、電子郵件、信件、廣告、行程表和會議紀錄等日常工作情境中常見的文本。這些題組中，有些是單篇閱讀，有些是多篇閱讀；單篇閱讀為閱讀一個文本，而多篇閱讀則是涉及多個相關文本的題目組合，例如比較兩封電子郵件的內容或關聯報告和通知等不同文本。

單篇和多篇閱讀的解題技巧

單篇閱讀題組的技巧是重點閱讀段落內容，特別是標題、開頭段和結尾段；題目常圍繞核心訊息或主要細節，因此可以先速讀，並根據題目尋找對應的關鍵資訊。**建議先看題目、標示關鍵字，再回到文本中搜尋相關句子。**

多篇閱讀則需要結合資訊，通常涉及跨文本的對照或訊息整合。這類題目考驗對多重資訊的理解與統整能力。建議逐步進行──先閱讀首個文本的標題和重點，回答與該文本有關的題目，然後進入下一文本；這樣可以避免在理解各篇文本時被干擾，也能有效整合多篇訊息。也要**特別注意代名詞指涉**：考題可能會考代名詞的指涉對象，如 it、they、this 代表的事物等。閱讀時需要明確知道代名詞所指的具體事物或主題，以確保理解正確。

時間分配與搶分技巧

搶分關鍵在於「先看題目再找答案」，運用所需時間將每個問題分階段完成。多篇閱讀部分尤其考驗耐心和穩定性，**請先確定解題方向，再以掃讀方式尋找文章關鍵字來加快速度**。如此一來，可以提高正確率並有餘力檢查答案，達到搶分的目的。

▼ 解題技巧教學

你會看到一至三篇閱讀文章與一些相關問題，請閱讀文章，並選出符合文章內容的答案。

Part 7 閱讀測驗

閱讀測驗範例 ①

Questions 1-2 refer to the following e-mail.

To: Sales Department
From: Nathan Collins, Sales Director
Date: March 20
Subject: New Product Launch - Brighten LED Desk Lamp

Dear Sales Team,

I am pleased to announce the launch of our latest product, the Brighten LED Desk Lamp. This lamp combines energy-efficient LED technology with a sleek, modern design, and features adjustable brightness levels. It's ideal for offices and home workspaces, providing high-quality lighting that reduces eye strain. The product will be available in stores and online starting April 5, and our marketing team has prepared a comprehensive campaign to promote it. Please familiarize yourself with its features to assist customers effectively.

Regards,

Nathan Collins

問題 1-2 請參考以下的電子郵件

銷售團隊你們好：

我很高興地宣布，我們的最新產品——Brighten LED 檯燈即將推出。[1] **這款檯燈結合了節能的 LED 技術和現代化的時尚設計，並具有可調亮度的功能。**[2] **它非常適合辦公室和家庭工作空間，提供高品質的照明，減少眼睛疲勞**。該產品將於 4 月 5 日正式在店內和線上上市，我們的市場團隊已經準備好了一個全面的宣傳活動來推廣它。請大家熟悉它的功能，以便有效地幫助顧客。

Nathan Collins 敬上

1. What feature does the Brighten LED Desk Lamp offer?
   (A) It allows the light to be adjusted to different levels.
   (B) It is designed exclusively for corporate environments.
   (C) It is constructed with environmentally sustainable materials.
   (D) It will only be available through online platforms.

2. What advantage does the Brighten LED Desk Lamp provide to users?
   (A) It is backed by a warranty against defects.
   (B) The color can be adjusted based on preference.
   (C) It includes a USB port for convenience.
   (D) It helps alleviate strain on the eyes.

範例解析

1. **(A)** It allows the light to be adjusted to different levels.

   中譯 它可以將燈光調整到不同的亮度級別。

   說明 本文中提到，這款燈具具有可調亮度的功能，因此**選項 (A) 為正確答案**。其他選項的描述都未提及。

2. **(D)** It helps alleviate strain on the eyes.

   中譯 它有助於減輕眼睛的疲勞。

   說明 文章提到這款燈具有助於**減少眼睛疲勞**（eye strain），這**與選項 (D) 最為相符**，其他選項提到的功能（保固、顏色調整、USB 接頭）並未在原文中提及。

高頻多益單字 combine (v.) 結合　energy-efficient (adj.) 節能的
sleek (adj.) 時尚的　adjustable (adj.) 可調整的
alleviate (v.) 減輕，緩解　familiarize (v.) 使熟悉

閱讀測驗範例 ②

Questions 3 - 7 refer to the following memo, schedule, and e-mail.

MEMO

To: All Employees　　　　From: Jackson Avery, Manager
Re: April Training　　　　Date: March 15

State lawmakers have recently issued new and stricter regulations on safety in food handling. The new guidelines, effective May 1 of this year, will apply to restaurants and other food service providers statewide. All Adela's employees are required to attend one of several training workshops, which will be conducted here at the restaurant throughout April, to ensure compliance with the new rules.

Also in May, Adela's will replace our old kitchen appliances with a full set of state-of-the-art Rosso brand cooking, refrigeration, and storage equipment. The units are operated using a programmable computerized system with functions such as inventory tracking and precision temperature control. Two training workshops on how to use the equipment will be held in April at the Rosso Pro Appliance showroom. Attendance at either session is mandatory only for members of the kitchen staff.

Once finalized, the April training schedule will be posted in the back office and the employee break room.

April Training Schedule			
Topic	**Location**	**Date**	**Time**
Safety Compliance	Adela's	April 8	8:00 A.M. to 11:00 A.M.
Equipment Functions	Rosso Pro Appliances	April 10	9:00 A.M. to 11:30 A.M.
Safety Compliance	Adela's	April 15	8:00 A.M. to 11:00 A.M.
Safety Compliance	Adela's	April 18	10:00 A.M. to 1:00 P.M.
Equipment Functions	Rosso Pro Appliances	April 24	9:00 A.M. to 11:30 A.M.
Safety Compliance	Adela's	April 25	10:00 A.M. to 1:00 P.M.

For questions or concerns, contact manager at javery@adelas.com

E-Mail

To: Jackson Avery <javery@adelas.com>
From: Candice Villalobos <cvillalobos@wheemail.com>
Re: April Training
Date: March 28

Dear Mr. Avery,

I am required to attend both training workshops, but I have a two-week vacation scheduled from April 14 to 28. Unfortunately, I am also unable to attend the session on April 10 as there is already an examination scheduled that morning for a course I am taking at the community college. I submitted a request to take the test on a different date, but it was denied. Would it be possible for me to undergo the equipment training individually on a different date?

Sincerely,

Stephanie Edwards

問題 3-7 請參考以下的備忘錄、時刻表和電子郵件

備忘錄

收件人：全體員工　　　發件人：經理 Jackson Avery

主旨：四月份培訓　　　日期：3月15日

[4]州立法機構最近頒布了有關食品處理安全的新規定，且規範更加嚴格。這些新的指導方針將於今年5月1日生效，適用於全州的餐館和其他食品服務提供者。[4]為確保遵守新規定，所有 Adela's 的員工必須參加4月份於本餐廳舉行的數場培訓工作坊之一。

此外，Adela's 將於5月份更換舊有廚房設備，並全面引進最先進的[3] **Rosso** 品牌烹飪、冷藏和儲存設備。這些設備透過可編程的計算機系統操作，並具備如庫存追蹤和精確溫度控制等功能。針對這些設備的兩場培訓將於四月份在 Rosso 專業設備展廳舉行。廚房員工必須參加其中一場培訓。

四月份的培訓時間表確定後，將張貼於後辦公室及員工休息室。

四月份培訓時間表			
主題	地點	日期	時間
遵行安全規範	Adela's	4月8日	上午8點~11點
設備功能介紹	Rosso 專業設備	4月10日	上午9點~11:30
遵行安全規範	Adela's	4月15日	上午8點~11點
遵行安全規範	Adela's	4月18日	上午10點~下午1點
設備功能介紹	Rosso 專業設備	4月24日	上午9點~11:30
遵行安全規範	Adela's	4月25日	上午10點~下午1點

如有疑問或需要協助，請聯繫經理，電子郵件：javery@adelas.com

收件人：Jackson Avery <javery@adelas.com>

寄件人：Candice Villalobos <cvillalobos@wheemail.com>

主旨：四月份培訓

日期：3月28日

親愛的 Avery 先生：

[5]**我需要參加兩場培訓工作坊，但我已安排於 4 月 14 日至 28 日進行為期兩週的假期**。不幸的是，我也無法參加 4 月 10 日的培訓，因為當天上午我在社區大學修讀的課程已安排了考試。我曾提交申請要求更改考試日期，但被拒絕。是否有可能讓我在不同的日期單獨接受設備培訓呢？

誠摯問候，

[5]**Stephanie Edwards 敬上**

3. According to the memo, what is true about the Rosso equipment?
   (A) It is technologically outdated.
   (B) It is computer controlled.
   (C) It is exceptionally delicate.
   (D) It is complicated to install.

4. What is indicated about the Safety Compliance workshops?
   (A) They all begin at the same time of day.
   (B) They all are taught by the same person.
   (C) They all take place at the restaurant.
   (D) They all are observed by state officials.

5. What is implied about Ms. Edwards?
   (A) She is a representative of a manufacturing firm.
   (B) She teaches at the community college.
   (C) She has been assigned to replace an instructor.
   (D) She is a member of the kitchen staff.

6. What is the purpose of the e-mail?
   (A) To request assistance with a scheduling conflict
   (B) To offer to provide an additional service
   (C) To seek reimbursement for an educational expense
   (D) To point out an error on a document

7. When will Ms. Edwards most likely be present at a training workshop?
   (A) April 8
   (B) April 10
   (C) April 15
   (D) April 24

範例解析

3. **(B)** It is computer controlled.

   中譯 它是電腦控制的。

   說明 先看題目再找答案，題目關鍵字 Rosso equipment 出現在備忘錄裡的第二段中間。放眼望去四個選項裡**只有選項(B)**和關鍵字 Rosso equipment 下方出現的 using a programmable computerized system **吻合，常常關鍵字的前一句或後一句往往也就是答案的所在**。這也是英文寫作邏輯的概念，會重複補充說明要解釋的關鍵詞。其餘選項都和題目不符。

4. **(C)** They all take place at the restaurant.

   中譯 它們都會在餐廳舉辦。

   說明 題目詢問 safety compliance workshops（與安全規範相關的工作坊）細節，須把四個選項看清楚後，再回去文章裡找。幾個關鍵字 safety、compliance 和 workshops 都出現在備忘錄的第一句以及第一段的中後方。四個選項當中**僅有 (C) 呼應了備忘錄第一段最後一句**的 "All Adela's employees... new rules."，這段內容不僅已直接說出這個工作坊會在餐廳舉行，也涵蓋了題目的關鍵字 workshops（工作坊）和 compliance（法規、規範）。至於其他選項都沒有出現在這則備忘錄所提及的內容裡。

5. **(D)** She is a member of the kitchen staff.

中譯 她是廚房工作人員的一員。

說明 看到題目關鍵字 Ms. Edwards 馬上掃讀發現 Ms. Edwards 出現在第三篇電子郵件最下面的署名。然後再略讀每一段的主旨句等部分，去看四個選項的敘述。電子郵件裡 Ms. Edwards 提到 "I am required to attend... scheduled from April 14 to 28." 她被要求參加工作坊，可是那段時間她排休，因此推論出來她是廚房的員工，這是第一則備忘錄所提供我們的資訊。因此正確答案是 (D)。

6. **(A)** To request assistance with a scheduling conflict

中譯 請求協助解決排程衝突

說明 本題詢問電子郵件的目的，通常內文的主旨大意 (purpose) 都會是在文章的第一句。承接上一題 Ms. Edwards 就已經提到訓練的時間她剛好排休了，她也繼續說明工作坊的上課時間與社區大學修課的考試時間衝突，因此她進一步解釋她想更換考試時間，但學校不准。因此她才寫信來詢問是否可以單獨接受培訓，選項 (A) 正確。

7. **(A)** April 8

中譯 4月8號

說明 詢問 Ms. Edwards 最可能出席培訓的日期。縱觀她在電子郵件裡的所提供的日期，再對照日程表的時間，可以馬上選出答案是 (A) April 8。因為在電子郵件裡她已經提到 April 14 to 28 她休假，April 10（四月十號）又有一個已經安排的考試。

高頻多益單字 issue (v.) 發布　effective (a.) 生效的　compliance (n.) 守規、合規　operate (v.) 運作　function (n.) 功能　attendance (n.) 出席　mandatory (a.) 必須的　post (v.) 張貼　session (n.) 某活動的一段時間　individually (adv.) 單獨地　representative (n.) 代表　manufacturing (n.) 製造業　conflict (n.) 衝突

片語 state-of-the-art (phr.) 最先進的　inventory tracking (phr.) 庫存追蹤　employee break room (phr.) 員工休息室

Practice Test

新制多益模擬試題

Part 7 閱讀測驗

Questions 1-2 refer to the following e-mail.

To: Ms. Harris

From: John Anderson

Date: October 10

Subject: Meeting Confirmation - October 15

Dear Ms. Harris,

I hope this message finds you well. I am writing to confirm the details of the upcoming meeting scheduled for next Wednesday, October 15, at 9 AM. The agenda will cover the progress of our current project, upcoming deadlines, and a discussion of potential improvements to the team's workflow. Please let me know if you require any additional materials prior to the meeting. I look forward to our discussion and hope to achieve our goals efficiently.

Best regards,
John Anderson

1. What is the primary objective of the e-mail?
   (A) To provide specific details regarding the project's timeline.
   (B) To request any additional materials needed before the meeting.
   (C) To offer suggestions on the team's performance.
   (D) To ensure that the meeting arrangements are properly confirmed.

2. What will be discussed at the meeting?
   (A) New project proposals
   (B) Upcoming team-building activities
   (C) Project progress and deadlines
   (D) Employee performance reviews

Questions 3-4 refer to the following e-mail.

To: All Employees

From: Human Resources Department

Date: November 10

Subject: Annual Company Retreat - December 15

Attention all employees,

Please be informed that the annual company retreat will take place on December 15th. The event will be held at the Fairmount Resort, starting at 8:30 AM. This year's retreat will focus on professional development and team collaboration. In addition to various workshops, there will be several networking opportunities with industry leaders. We look forward to seeing you there and encourage all of you to participate actively. Kindly RSVP by November 30th.

Best regards,
Human Resources Department

3. When will the company retreat be held?
   (A) November 30th
   (B) December 1st
   (C) December 15th
   (D) November 25th

4. What will be the primary emphasis of this year's company retreat?
   (A) Activities designed to strengthen team bonds
   (B) Discussions on the company's long-term goals
   (C) Opportunities for relaxation and informal networking
   (D) Enhancing job skills and fostering teamwork

Questions 5-9 refer to the following e-mail and review.

From: ShopEase Customer Support

To: Jennifer Wang

Subject: Order #5634921 Update

Dear Jennifer Wang,

Thank you for shopping with ShopEase! We are writing to inform you about the status of your recent order.

- Item: Wireless Noise-Cancelling Headphones
- Order Date: October 3, 2023
- Current Status: Shipped

Your package was shipped on October 5, 2023, via our standard delivery service. The estimated delivery date is October 10, 2023.

To track your order, click on the following link: Track My Order

If you have any questions or concerns, feel free to contact our customer support team. We are available 24/7 to assist you.

Thank you for choosing ShopEase!
Best regards,
ShopEase Customer Support

Product: Wireless Noise-Cancelling Headphones

Review by Michael L. ★★★★☆

I've been using these headphones for a week, and the sound quality is excellent. The noise-cancelling feature works well, especially in busy environments like coffee shops. However, I found the ear cushions slightly uncomfortable during extended use.

Review by Emma T. ★★★★★

This is my second pair of these headphones, and I absolutely love them! The battery life is impressive, lasting nearly 30 hours on a single charge. Highly recommended for frequent travelers.

Review by James K. ★★★☆☆

While the sound is clear and the design is sleek, I experienced some connectivity disruptions with my laptop. The headphones occasionally disconnect during calls, which can be frustrating.

5. What information is included in the e-mail from ShopEase?
   (A) A discount offer for the next purchase
   (B) The estimated delivery date of an order
   (C) Instructions for returning a product
   (D) A guide for using the product

6. When is Jennifer Wang expected to receive her order?
   (A) October 5, 2023
   (B) October 8, 2023
   (C) October 10, 2023
   (D) October 12, 2023

7. According to Michael L.'s review, what is a drawback of the headphones?
   (A) The noise-cancelling feature is ineffective.
   (B) The ear pads are aren't comfortable during long use.
   (C) The battery life is shorter than expected.
   (D) The headphones are too bulky for travel.

8. What does Emma T. like most about the headphones?
   (A) The long-lasting battery
   (B) The lightweight design
   (C) The sound quality
   (D) The affordable price

9. Based on James K.'s review, what issue did he experience with the headphones?
   (A) Poor sound quality during calls
   (B) Shorter battery life than advertised
   (C) Limited compatibility with mobile devices
   (D) Connectivity problems with his laptop

Questions 10-14 refer to the following menu, e-mail, and text messages.

Catering Menu

Welcome to Global Feast Catering Service! Whether it's a corporate gathering, a wedding, or any other special event, we provide exquisite catering services designed to satisfy a variety of tastes and dietary requirements. Below is our comprehensive catering menu for your consideration.

Appetizers

- Mini Beef Wellington – A bite-sized version of the classic dish, featuring tender beef wrapped in puff pastry.
- Shrimp Cocktail – Fresh shrimp served with a zesty cocktail sauce.
- Vegetarian Spring Rolls – Light and crispy, filled with seasonal vegetables and served with a tangy dipping sauce.

Main Courses

- Grilled Salmon with Herb Butter – Fresh salmon fillet grilled to perfection, served with a garlic herb butter sauce.
- Roast Chicken with Lemon and Rosemary – Succulent roast chicken, marinated with lemon and rosemary, and served with roasted vegetables.
- Vegan Stir-Fry with Tofu – A colorful stir-fry of seasonal vegetables and tofu, stir-fried in a savory sauce.

Sides

- Creamy Mashed Potatoes – Buttery mashed potatoes, whipped to a creamy consistency.
- Caesar Salad – Crisp romaine lettuce tossed with Caesar dressing, croutons, and parmesan cheese.
- Seasonal Roasted Vegetables – A mix of seasonal vegetables roasted to bring out their natural sweetness.

Desserts

- Chocolate Mousse – A rich mousse made with fine chocolate and whipped cream.
- Pastel de nata – A creamy Portuguese egg custard tart sprinkled with cinnamon.

All of our dishes are prepared with the highest quality ingredients and attention to detail. We also offer options for dietary restrictions, including gluten-free, vegan, and nut-free. For more information on our services and pricing, please contact us directly.

Inquiry Letter for Catering Services

To: catering@globalfeast.com

From: sarah.morris@techventures.com

Date: September 30, 2024

Subject: Inquiry about Catering Services for Company Launch

Dear Global Feast Catering Team,

I hope this e-mail finds you well. I am reaching out to inquire about your catering services for an upcoming event. Our company, Tech Ventures, will be holding its grand opening event on October 20th, and we are looking for a catering service that can provide a variety of food options for our guests.

We are expecting around 100 attendees, and we would like a menu that includes both vegetarian and non-vegetarian options. In particular, we are interested in your roast chicken and vegan stir-fry dishes, but we would also appreciate your recommendations for additional items that could complement the menu.

Could you please provide us with details on your pricing, the number of staff needed for the event, and any additional charges such as delivery or setup fees? Furthermore, we would like to know if you offer any packages for events of this size, and whether you can accommodate any special dietary requirements.

We would appreciate it if you could send us a proposal by October 5th, as we would like to finalize all the details well before the event. Thank you for your time, and we look forward to hearing from you.

Best regards,
Sarah Morris
Tech Ventures
456 Innovation Park, Suite 200
San Francisco, CA 94016
Phone: 415-555-1234

Budget Discussion via Text Messages

Tom (08:30 AM):

Hey, Rachel. About the catering for our upcoming event, do you think we should go with the full menu or choose a more budget-friendly option?

Rachel (08:32 AM):

I think we should go with a full menu. Our guest list is quite large, and we want to make a good impression. However, we should keep an eye on the budget.

Tom (08:35 AM):

That's true. The full menu will cost around $8,000. If we want to cut down a bit, we could reduce the number of main courses and stick to a few appetizers.

> **Rachel (08:37 AM):**
>
> I agree. We can also skip some of the expensive appetizers, like the smoked salmon rolls, and focus on the more affordable options. Maybe add a couple of vegetarian dishes as well.

Tom (08:40 AM):

> Sounds good. I'll contact the catering company to discuss these adjustments and get a revised quote.

> **Rachel (08:42 AM):**
>
> Great! Let me know if you need me to help with anything else.

10. According to the logic of the catering menu, if a third dessert option were to be added, which of the following would be most likely?
    (A) Chocolate cake
    (B) Vanilla milkshake
    (C) Fruit salad
    (D) Buttermilk pancakes

11. In Sarah Morris' e-mail, she asks for specific information about the catering service. Which of the following does she NOT request in the e-mail?
    (A) Pricing details
    (B) Recommended additional items
    (C) Delivery and setup fees
    (D) List of vegetarian dishes

12. What is the main reason that Rachel suggests modifying the catering order in the text message discussion?
    (A) Because there are too few guests for the full menu
    (B) To adhere to the company's budget constraints
    (C) To create a more diverse selection of appetizers
    (D) To impress a specific guest at the event

13. Which of the following best describes the dietary options offered by Global Feast Catering, as mentioned in both the menu and inquiry email?
    (A) Only vegan and gluten-free dishes
    (B) Custom-made dishes for each event
    (C) Options for common dietary restrictions
    (D) Exclusively vegetarian dishes

14. From the text message conversation, what can be inferred about Tom's role in the catering arrangement?
    (A) He is the primary decision-maker regarding menu selection.
    (B) He is responsible for contacting the catering company and managing costs.
    (C) He is the one in charge of handling the guest list and event logistics.
    (D) He is mainly concerned with guest satisfaction and preferences.

試題演練答案、翻譯與解說

答案

1. (D)　2. (C)　3. (C)　4. (D)　5. (B)　6. (C)　7. (B)
8. (A)　9. (D)　10. (C)　11. (D)　12. (B)　13. (C)　14. (B)

問題 1-2 請參考以下的電子郵件

收件人： 哈里斯女士
寄件人： 約翰·安德森
日期： 10 月 10 日
主旨： 會議確認 - 10 月 15 日
親愛的賀錦麗女士：
希望您一切安好。[1] **我寫這封信是為了確認即將於 10 月 15 日星期三上午 9 點舉行的會議細節。**[2] 議程將涵蓋目前項目的進展、未來的截止日期以及對團隊工作流程的潛在改進討論。如果會議前您需要任何其他材料，請告訴我。我期待我們的討論，並希望能高效達成目標。
John Anderson 敬上

1. **(D)** To ensure that the meeting arrangements are properly confirmed.

   中譯　確保會議安排已確認。

   說明　這封電子郵件的目的是確認即將舉行的會議細節和安排，確保雙方在會議的時間、議程和要求上沒有誤解，因此選 (D)。

2. **(C)** Project progress and deadlines

   中譯　專案進度和截止日期

   說明　電子郵件中提到的會議議程包括項目進展、截止日期以及團隊工作流程的改進，因此選 (C)。

   單字　progress (n.) 進展　discussion (n.) 討論　workflow (n.) 工作流程
   efficiently (adv.) 高效地

問題 3-4 請參考以下的電子郵件

收件人：全體員工
寄件人：人力資源部門
日期：11 月 10 日
主旨：年度公司員工旅遊
全體員工注意：
[3] 請注意，公司年度度假活動將於 12 月 15 日舉行。活動將在費爾蒙度假村舉行，開始時間為上午 8:30。[4] **今年的度假活動將專注於專業發展和團隊合作**。除了各種研討會外，還將有與行業領袖的多次聯誼機會。我們期待您的光臨，並鼓勵大家積極參加。請於 11 月 30 日前回覆是否參加。
人力資源部敬上

3. **(C)** December 15th

中譯　12 月 15 日

說明　文章中明確提到公司度假活動將於 12 月 15 日舉行，因此選 (C)。

4. **(D)** Enhancing job skills and fostering teamwork

中譯　提升工作技能並促進團隊合作

說明　今年的度假活動強調專業發展和團隊合作，這是文章中提到的主要重點，因此選 (D)。

retreat (n.) 度假活動　　workshop (n.) 研討　　networking (n.) 建立人脈

RSVP (v.) 回覆是否參加（為 "Répondez s'il vous plaît" 的簡稱）

問題 5-9 請參考以下的電子郵件和評論

寄件人：ShopEase Customer Support
寄件人：Jennifer Wang
主旨：訂單 #5634921 更新
親愛的 Jennifer Wang：
感謝您選擇在 ShopEase 購物！我們寫信通知您關於您最近訂單的狀態。

207

- 商品：無線降噪耳機
- 訂購日期：2023 年 10 月 3 日
- 當前狀態：已出貨

您的包裹於 2023 年 10 月 5 日出貨，並透過我們的標準配送服務運送。[5][6] **預計送達日期為** 2023 年 10 月 10 日。

若要追蹤您的訂單，請點擊以下連結：追蹤我的訂單

如有任何問題或疑慮，請隨時聯繫我們的客戶服務團隊，我們隨時為您提供幫助。

感謝您選擇 ShopEase！

ShopEase 客戶服務團隊敬上

產品：無線降噪耳機

[7]**Michael L. ★★★★☆**
我已經使用這款耳機一週了，音質非常好。降噪功能效果明顯，尤其是在像咖啡店這樣的繁忙環境中。[7] **然而，在長時間使用過後，我發現耳墊略感不適。**

[8]**Emma T. ★★★★★**
這是我第二次購買這款耳機，[8] **我非常喜歡它！電池壽命令人印象深刻，一次充電幾乎可以使用 30 小時。** 對於經常出差的人來說，強烈推薦。

[9]**James K. ★★★☆☆**
儘管音質清晰，設計也很時尚，[9] **但我在使用筆記型電腦時遇到了一些連接問題。耳機在通話過程中偶爾會斷線，這讓我感到有些沮喪。**

---

5. **(B)** The estimated delivery date of an order

   中譯　訂單預計的送達日期

   說明　根據第一篇電子郵件，ShopEase 提供了訂單的狀態更新，包括預計送達的日期（2023 年 10 月 10 日），其他選項（如折扣或產品指南）未在信件中提及。

6. **(C)** October 10, 2023

   中譯　2023 年 10 月 10 日

   說明　電子郵件中明確指出，Jennifer Wang 的訂單預計於 2023 年 10 月 10 日送達。其他日期不符合內容描述。

7. **(B)** The ear pads aren't comfortable during long use

中譯 耳墊在長時間使用時會讓人感到不適。

說明 Michael L. 在評論中提到，耳墊在長時間使用時會讓人感到不適。其他選項，如降噪效果不佳或電池壽命不足，並非他提到的缺點。

8. **(A)** The long-lasting battery

中譯 長效電池

說明 Emma T. 在評論中表示，電池壽命幾乎可以持續 30 小時，她認為這對於經常旅行的人來說非常棒。這是她特別喜歡的地方。

9. **(D)** Connectivity problems with his laptop

中譯 使用筆記型電腦時的連線問題

說明 James K. 提到耳機偶爾會在使用筆記型電腦時斷線，這是讓他感到困擾的問題。其他選項（如通話音質差或電池壽命不足）並未出現在他的評論中。

單字 estimated (adj.) 預計的、估計的　concern (n.) 疑慮、關心的事　assist (v.) 協助
noise-cancelling (adj.) 降噪的　connectivity (n.) 連接性　frequent (adj.) 頻繁的

問題 10-14 請參考以下的菜單、電子郵件和文字訊息。

餐飲服務菜單

歡迎來到全球宴席外燴服務！無論是公司聚會、婚禮還是任何其他特別活動，我們提供精緻的餐飲服務，旨在滿足各種口味和飲食需求。以下是我們綜合的餐飲菜單供您參考。

開胃菜

- **迷你牛肉威靈頓** – 經典菜式的迷你版，嫩牛肉包裹酥皮。
- **蝦雞尾酒** – 新鮮的蝦搭配辛辣的雞尾酒醬。
- **素春捲** – 輕盈酥脆，內含時令蔬菜，搭配酸辣蘸醬。

主菜

- **香草奶油烤三文魚** – 新鮮三文魚片，完美烤製，搭配蒜香奶油醬。
- **檸檬迷迭香烤雞** – 多汁的烤雞，檸檬和迷迭香醃製，並搭配烤蔬菜
- **素食炒時蔬豆腐** – 彩色時令蔬菜與豆腐同炒，醃製後呈現美味的醬汁。

配菜

- **奶油薯泥** – 入口即化的奶油薯泥，綿密光滑。
- **凱薩沙拉** – 新鮮的蘿蔓生菜搭配凱薩沙拉醬、麵包丁及帕瑪森芝士。
- **時令烤蔬菜** – 多種時令蔬菜烤至金黃，突顯自然甜味。

甜點

- **巧克力慕斯** – 用上等巧克力和鮮奶油製作的濃郁慕斯。
- **葡式蛋塔** – 一款奶油般濃郁的葡萄牙蛋塔，灑上肉桂粉。

我們的所有菜餚均使用最上等的食材並注重每一個細節。[13] **我們也提供符合不同飲食需求的選擇，包括無麩質、素食及不含堅果的選項。** 如需更多有關服務和價格的資訊，請直接聯繫我們。

詢價信件範例

收件人：	catering@globalfeast.com
寄件人：	sarah.morris@techventures.com
日期：	2024 年 9 月 30 日
主旨：	關於公司開幕活動餐飲服務的詢問

親愛的全球宴席餐飲團隊：

希望您收件愉快。我是 Tech Ventures 公司的 Sarah Morris，我們公司將於 10 月 20 日舉辦開幕活動，並希望能夠了解貴公司的餐飲服務。

此次活動預計將有約 100 位賓客，我們需要一份包含素食和非素食選項的菜單。我們特別對您提供的烤雞和素食炒豆腐感興趣，此外，我們也希望了解一些其他推薦菜品。

[11] 能否請您提供詳細的價格資訊、需要的工作人員數量，以及送餐或佈置的附加費用？同時，我們也想知道貴公司是否有針對這類型活動的套餐，並且能否適應特殊的飲食需求。

若能在 10 月 5 日之前提供提案，我們將非常感謝。期待您的回覆。

祝好，

[11]**Sarah Morris**
Tech Ventures
456 Innovation Park, Suite 200
San Francisco, CA 94016
電話：415-555-1234

透過訊息討論預算

Tom (08:30 AM):

嗨 Rachel，關於我們即將舉行的活動餐飲，你覺得我們應該選擇完整的菜單還是選擇較為經濟的選項？

[12]**Rachel (08:32 AM):**

我覺得我們應該選擇完整的菜單。我們的賓客名單還算不少，**我們希望能夠給他們留下好印象。不過我們也要關注預算問題。**

Tom (08:35 AM):

這倒是。完整的菜單費用大約是 $8,000。如果我們想節省些預算，可以減少主菜的數量，並集中於一些開胃菜。

[10]**Rachel (08:37 AM):**

我同意。[10] **我們也可以省去一些比較貴的開胃菜**，比如煙燻鮭魚卷，集中在更實惠的選項上。[10] **或許加幾道素食菜餚也不錯。**

[14]**Tom (08:40 AM):**

聽起來不錯。[14] **我會聯絡餐飲公司討論這些調整並要求更新報價。**

Rachel (08:42 AM):

好的！如果需要我幫忙其他的事，隨時告訴我。

10. **(C)** Fruit salad

中譯　水果沙拉
說明　根據訊息，由於女子想加幾道素食菜餚，只有 (C) 符合。

11. **(D)** List of vegetarian dishes

中譯　只列出素食菜品的清單
說明　在 Sarah 的郵件中，她要求了價格、推薦菜品以及送餐和佈置的附加費用，但並未要求只列出素食菜品的清單。

12. **(B)** To adhere to the company's budget constraints

   中譯　為了符合公司的預算
   說明　根據訊息對話，Rachel 建議減少菜單項目以符合預算，她強調了需要兼顧菜品多樣性，但也必須節省成本。

13. **(C)** Options for common dietary restrictions

   中譯　提供適合常見飲食限制的選項
   說明　根據菜單，外燴公司提供了適合常見飲食限制的選項，例如素食和無麩質選項，但並非僅限於這些選擇。

14. **(B)** He is responsible for contacting the catering company and managing costs.

   中譯　他負責與餐飲公司聯繫並管理費用。
   說明　根據對話，可以看出 Tom 負責與餐飲公司協商並調整菜單，以確保符合預算。
   單字　catering (n.) 食品供應服務　attendee (n.) 參加者
   　　　dietary restriction (n.)　飲食限制　proposal (n.) 提案

試題演練答案、翻譯與解說

新制多益模擬試題一回

🎧 054

Listening Test

In the Listening test, you will be asked to demonstrate how well you understand spoken English. The entire Listening test will last approximately 45 minutes. There are four parts, and directions are given for each part. You must mark your answers on the separate answer sheet. Do not write your answers in your test book.

Part 1

Directions: For each question in this part, you will hear four statements about a picture in your test book. When you hear the statements, you must select the one statement that best describes what you see in the picture. Then find the number of the question on your answer sheet and mark your answer. The statements will not be printed in your test book and will be spoken only one time.

1.

2.

3.

4.

5.

6.

Part 2

Directions: You will hear a question or statement and three responses spoken in English. They will not be printed in your test book and will be spoken only one time. Select the best response to the question or statement and mark the letter (A), (B), or (C) on your answer sheet.

7. ( ) 8. ( ) 9. ( ) 10. ( ) 11. ( ) 12. ( ) 13. ( ) 14. ( ) 15. ( )
16. ( ) 17. ( ) 18. ( ) 19. ( ) 20. ( ) 21. ( ) 22. ( ) 23. ( ) 24. ( )
25. ( ) 26. ( ) 27. ( ) 28. ( ) 29. ( ) 30. ( ) 31. ( )

Part 3

Directions: You will hear some conversations between two or more people. You will be asked to answer three questions about what the speakers say in each conversation. Select the best response to each question and mark the letter (A), (B), (C), or (D) on your answer sheet. The conversations will not be printed in your test book and will be spoken only one time.

32. What is the woman asking about?
    (A) The departure location
    (B) The ticket price
    (C) The platform number
    (D) The train schedule

33. What time does the last train leave?
    (A) At 10:30 p.m.
    (B) At 11:15 p.m.
    (C) At 11:45 p.m.
    (D) At midnight

34. Where will the train depart from?
    (A) Platform 1
    (B) Platform 2
    (C) Platform 3
    (D) Platform 4

---

35. What is the man looking for?
    (A) A bakery
    (B) An Italian restaurant
    (C) A coffee shop
    (D) A fast food place

36. Where is the restaurant located?
    (A) On Maple Street, two blocks away
    (B) Next to a bus stop
    (C) Across the street from a park
    (D) Near the train station

37. How does the woman describe the restaurant?
    (A) Expensive but worth it
    (B) A hidden gem
    (C) Usually crowded but affordable
    (D) Popular for its authentic dishes

38. What is the woman planning to buy?
    (A) A smartphone
    (B) A tablet
    (C) A laptop
    (D) A desktop computer

39. What does the man recommend?
    (A) The ABC brand
    (B) The XYZ Pro series
    (C) A refurbished model
    (D) The latest high-end model

40. Where does the woman plan to look for more information?
    (A) At a local store
    (B) By asking friends
    (C) In a catalog
    (D) Online

41. What are the speakers discussing?
    (A) A marketing campaign
    (B) A new office location
    (C) A staff meeting
    (D) A training session

42. When will the campaign begin?
    (A) This week
    (B) Early next month
    (C) By the end of the month
    (D) Next quarter

43. What is the man looking forward to?
    (A) Leading the project
    (B) Overseeing the campaign budget
    (C) Presenting his ideas
    (D) Joining the development team

44. What does the woman need help with?
    (A) Printing handouts
    (B) Preparing a projector
    (C) Preparing a presentation
    (D) Rearranging the meeting room

45. What does the man say he will do?
    (A) Get the cables
    (B) Check the sound system
    (C) Adjust the projector screen
    (D) Review the agenda

46. When does the presentation begin?
    (A) In a few minutes
    (B) In 10 minutes
    (C) In 15 minutes
    (D) At the top of the hour

---

47. What are the speakers discussing?
    (A) A company event
    (B) A training program
    (C) A team lunch
    (D) A new project

48. What is the woman concerned about?
    (A) The deadline
    (B) The project's budget
    (C) Team availability
    (D) The meeting time

49. What do the speakers decide to do?
    (A) Extend the deadline
    (B) Meet tomorrow
    (C) Cancel the project
    (D) Hire more staff

---

50. Where does this conversation most likely take place?
    (A) At a supermarket
    (B) At an office
    (C) At a restaurant
    (D) At a coffee shop

51. What does the man order?
    (A) A sandwich and tea
    (B) Coffee and a donut
    (C) A latte and a muffin
    (D) A cappuccino and a bagel

52. How much does the man have to pay?
    (A) $5.50
    (B) $6.25
    (C) $6.75
    (D) $7.00

---

53. Where does this conversation most likely take place?
    (A) At a bus stop
    (B) At an airport
    (C) At a train station
    (D) At a taxi stand

54. When does the next train to Central Station leave?
    (A) At 3:30
    (B) At 3:45
    (C) At 4:00
    (D) At 4:15

55. How long does it take to reach Central Station?
    (A) 20 minutes
    (B) 30 minutes
    (C) 40 minutes
    (D) 50 minutes

56. What is the purpose of the woman's visit?
    (A) To make a reservation
    (B) To check in
    (C) To request room service
    (D) To cancel her booking

57. What type of room did the woman book?
    (A) A deluxe suite
    (B) A twin room
    (C) A standard room with a queen bed
    (D) A room with a king bed

58. What additional request does the woman make?
    (A) A late check-out
    (B) An extra bed
    (C) Room cleaning service
    (D) A room upgrade

59. What are the speakers working on?
    (A) A project proposal
    (B) A financial report
    (C) A marketing strategy
    (D) A presentation for a client

60. What is the woman currently reviewing?
    (A) Annual revenue data
    (B) The budget for next year
    (C) Third-quarter figures
    (D) Department expenses

61. What additional task does the man ask the woman to do?
    (A) Prepare a presentation
    (B) Send the report to a client
    (C) Schedule a meeting
    (D) Verify the revenue projections

62. What is the woman looking for?
    (A) A book by James Grant
    (B) A gift card
    (C) A magazine
    (D) A non-fiction book

63. Where is the item the woman wants located?
    (A) On the first shelf
    (B) In the non-fiction section
    (C) Near the front counter
    (D) On the second shelf

64. What service does the business offer?
    (A) Free delivery
    (B) Gift wrapping
    (C) A discount on books
    (D) A membership program

Conference Room Schedule

Time	Room A	Room B
9:00-10:00	Marketing Meeting	IT Training
10:00-11:00	Project Planning	Client Presentation
11:00-12:00	Available	Team Building Workshop

65. Where will the client presentation be held?
    (A) Room A
    (B) The main hall
    (C) Room B
    (D) The cafeteria

66. What is happening in Room A at 10:00?
    (A) A marketing meeting
    (B) A project planning meeting
    (C) An IT training session
    (D) A team building workshop

67. What does the man suggest doing at 11:00?
    (A) Reserving Room B for a meeting
    (B) Attending the team building workshop
    (C) Moving the client presentation to Room A
    (D) Using Room A for a follow-up discussion

Monthly Sales by Region (Q3)

Region	July Sales	August Sales	September Sales
North America	$120,000	$135,000	$150,000
Europe	$95,000	$110,000	$130,000
Asia	$80,000	$85,000	$90,000

68. Which region had the highest sales in September?
    (A) Asia
    (B) Europe
    (C) North America
    (D) They all had similar sales

69. How much did Europe sell in August?
    (A) $95,000
    (B) $110,000
    (C) $130,000
    (D) $150,000

70. What do the speakers say about Asia's performance?
    (A) It showed the highest growth
    (B) It had steady growth
    (C) Its growth was slower than other regions
    (D) Its sales exceeded North America

Part 4

Directions: You will hear some talks given by a single speaker. You will be asked to answer three questions about what the speaker says in each talk. Select the best response to each question and mark the letter (A), (B), (C), or (D) on your answer sheet. The talks will not be printed in your test book and will be spoken only one time.

71. Who is most likely addressing the passengers?
    (A) A pilot
    (B) An instructor
    (C) A technician
    (D) A driver

72. What is the aircraft's current altitude?
    (A) 28,000 feet
    (B) 32,000 feet
    (C) 35,000 feet
    (D) 38,000 feet

73. How does the speaker describe the weather conditions?
    (A) Overcast
    (B) Favorable
    (C) Stormy
    (D) Rainy

---

74. What is the purpose of the event?
    (A) To hire employees
    (B) To build teamwork
    (C) To celebrate a holiday
    (D) To announce promotions

75. What is the first activity of the day?
    (A) A game
    (B) A lunch
    (C) A discussion
    (D) A workshop

76. What does the speaker recommend participants bring?
    (A) A notebook
    (B) A water bottle
    (C) A laptop
    (D) Comfortable clothes

77. What is being advertised?
    (A) A seasonal clearance
    (B) A limited promotion
    (C) A loyalty program
    (D) A new product release

78. What is the discount on appliances?
    (A) 10%
    (B) 15%
    (C) 25%
    (D) 40%

79. What time does the activity end?
    (A) At 7:30 p.m.
    (B) At 8:00 p.m.
    (C) At 8:30 p.m.
    (D) At 9:00 p.m.

80. Why will the library be closed?
    (A) For an inspection
    (B) For digital upgrades
    (C) For maintenance
    (D) For a holiday

81. When will the library reopen?
    (A) On Monday morning
    (B) On Tuesday morning
    (C) On Wednesday afternoon
    (D) On Thursday evening

82. What does the speaker suggest visitors do?
    (A) Use the library's digital resources
    (B) Call the library for assistance
    (C) Postpone their library visit
    (D) Visit other library branches

83. What type of business is being described?
    (A) A restaurant
    (B) A bank
    (C) A hotel
    (D) A retail store

84. When does the office close on weekends?
    (A) At 12 p.m.
    (B) At 1 p.m.
    (C) At 2 p.m.
    (D) At 3 p.m.

85. What can callers do if they stay on the line?
    (A) Talk to an employee
    (B) Make a payment
    (C) Leave a message
    (D) Listen to a recording

---

86. Who will board the flight first?
    (A) Passengers with special needs
    (B) Passengers in rows 10-20
    (C) Business class passengers
    (D) Frequent flyers

87. What should passengers prepare for boarding?
    (A) Luggage tags
    (B) Boarding passes and ID
    (C) Seat assignments
    (D) Flight itineraries

88. Where is the flight going?
    (A) New York
    (B) Los Angeles
    (C) Chicago
    (D) Dallas

---

89. What is the purpose of this announcement?
    (A) To provide operating hours and special events
    (B) To inform visitors about the zoo's feeding policies
    (C) To announce operating hours and an event
    (D) To inform visitors about feeding policies

90. At what time does the penguin feeding session begin?
    (A) 1:30 PM
    (B) 2:00 PM
    (C) 2:30 PM
    (D) 3:00 PM

91. Where can visitors find maps of the zoo?
    (A) At the ticket counter
    (B) Online or at the entrance
    (C) At the penguin exhibit
    (D) Near the snack bar

---

92. What is the announcement mainly about?
    (A) A new maintenance service
    (B) A water supply interruption
    (C) A change in apartment policy
    (D) A scheduled power outage

93. How long will the maintenance work take?
    (A) 4 hours
    (B) 6 hours
    (C) 8 hours
    (D) 10 hours

94. What are residents recommended to do?
    (A) Avoid using electricity
    (B) Contact the maintenance team
    (C) Move out temporarily
    (D) Store water in advance

95. What is the topic of the new exhibit?
    (A) Nature-inspired artworks
    (B) Historic architecture
    (C) Modern technology
    (D) Ancient artifacts

96. When is the last guided tour each day?
    (A) 11:00 AM
    (B) 12:00 PM
    (C) 2:00 PM
    (D) 3:00 PM

97. What is prohibited in the exhibit?
    (A) Eating and drinking
    (B) Talking loudly
    (C) Taking photographs
    (D) Using mobile phones

Schedule for Business Conference 2024:

Time	Session Title	Location
9:00 - 10:00	Keynote Speech	Hall A
10:15 - 11:15	Marketing Trends 2024	Room 101
11:30 - 12:30	Leadership Workshop	Room 102
1:30 - 2:30	Networking Strategies	Hall B

98. At what time does the Keynote Speech begin?
    (A) 8:00 AM
    (B) 9:00 AM
    (C) 10:15 AM
    (D) 11:00 AM

99. Where will the Leadership Workshop be held?
    (A) Hall A
    (B) Room 101
    (C) Room 102
    (D) Hall B

100. What session takes place in Hall B?
    (A) Networking Strategies
    (B) Marketing Trends 2024
    (C) Leadership Workshop
    (D) Keynote Speech

Reading Test

In the Reading test, you will read a variety of texts and answer several different types of reading comprehension questions. The entire Reading test will last 75 minutes. There are three parts, and directions are given for each part. You are encouraged to answer as many questions as possible within the time allowed.

Part 5

Directions: A word or phrase is missing in each of the sentences below. Four answer choices are given below each sentence. Select the best answer to complete the sentence. Then mark the letter (A), (B), (C), or (D) on your answer sheet.

101. The manager decided to _____ the meeting to next week due to scheduling conflicts.
    (A) approve
    (B) cancel
    (C) conduct
    (D) postpone

102. The new software update aims to _____ the overall performance of the system.
    (A) delay
    (B) improve
    (C) reduce
    (D) ignore

103. The annual company report was _____ to all employees via e-mail.
    (A) distributed
    (B) completed
    (C) collected
    (D) removed

104. Please make sure to read the _____ carefully before assembling the product.
    (A) opinions
    (B) recommendations
    (C) instructions
    (D) suggestions

105. The sales team has developed a strategy aimed at _____ potential clients away from their competitors.
    (A) abandoning
    (B) reducing
    (C) advancing
    (D) attracting

106. The company offers several _____ benefits, including health insurance and retirement plans.
    (A) employed
    (B) employer
    (C) employee
    (D) employable

107. The restaurant has gained a reputation for its _____ culinary offerings and impeccable service.
    (A) exquisite
    (B) excessive
    (C) indifferent
    (D) substantial

108. It is crucial to _____ important documents to ensure their security.
    (A) put away
    (B) take over
    (C) set up
    (D) turn in

109. The CEO emphasized the importance of _____ communication between departments.
    (A) reflective
    (B) elective
    (C) defective
    (D) effective

110. We are pleased to announce that the project was completed _____ schedule.
    (A) within
    (B) behind
    (C) ahead of
    (D) according to

111. The team leader asked if everyone _____ the agenda for the meeting.
    (A) received
    (B) has received
    (C) receiving
    (D) receive

112. By the time we arrived at the venue, the presentation _____.
    (A) had already started
    (B) starts
    (C) starting
    (D) was starting

113. Company policy requires all employees _____ their timesheets by Friday afternoon.
    (A) submits
    (B) submit
    (C) submitting
    (D) to submit

114. If we _____ the project by next month, we will receive a bonus.
    (A) are completing
    (B) completed
    (C) complete
    (D) have completed

115. The new regulations will _____ into effect starting next Monday.
    (A) go
    (B) went
    (C) going
    (D) gone

116. She is one of the employees who _____ consistently recognized for their hard work.
    (A) is
    (B) has been
    (C) was
    (D) are

117. Neither the manager nor the team members _____ satisfied with the outcome of the meeting.
    (A) was
    (B) were
    (C) is
    (D) being

118. The project is on schedule, _____ there are a few minor adjustments that need to be made.
    (A) despite
    (B) because
    (C) although
    (D) unless

119. The job posting indicates that candidates _____ a degree in computer science.
    (A) must have
    (B) must had
    (C) must has
    (D) must having

120. The project should be completed _____ the close of business today, so that we can meet the client's deadline.
    (A) on
    (B) at
    (C) in
    (D) by

121. The director, _____ the project proposal, decided to allocate additional resources to ensure its success.
    (A) reviewing
    (B) reviewed
    (C) having reviewed
    (D) review

122. To qualify for the position, applicants must _____ strong communication skills.
    (A) demonstrate
    (B) demonstrating
    (C) demonstrated
    (D) demonstrates

123. The new software update will _____ the user interface, making it more intuitive and easier to navigate.
    (A) refining
    (B) refinement
    (C) refined
    (D) refine

124. The company has consistently sought to _____ the efficiency of its production processes through innovative technology.
    (A) enhancing
    (B) enhanced
    (C) enhance
    (D) enhancement

125. The board of directors will meet next week to discuss the _____ of the proposal.
    (A) approval
    (B) approve
    (C) approving
    (D) approved

126. The CEO's decision to _____ the company's expansion strategy has resulted in significant growth in new markets.
    (A) recalibrated
    (B) recalibration
    (C) recalibrating
    (D) recalibrate

127. The team managed to complete the project on time _____ the unexpected delay.
    (A) although
    (B) because
    (C) in spite of
    (D) however

128. _____ the presentation, the team gathered feedback from the audience.
    (A) Have finished
    (B) Having finished
    (C) To finish
    (D) Finishing

129. The factory has increased production capacity to meet the growing _____ for its products.
    (A) demand
    (B) supply
    (C) request
    (D) offer

130. The manager's _____ in resolving the issue demonstrated his leadership skills.
   (A) competition
   (B) competent
   (C) competently
   (D) competence

Part 6

Directions: Read the texts that follow. A word, phrase, or sentence is missing in parts of each text. Four answer choices for each question are given below the text. Select the best answer to complete the text. Then mark the letter (A), (B), (C), or (D) on your answer sheet.

Questions 131 - 134 refer to the following letter.

> **Subject:** Office Renovation Notice
>
> Dear Team,
> We are pleased to inform you that our office will undergo renovations starting next Monday. The renovation project is expected to last for two weeks, during which some areas may be temporarily inaccessible. To minimize disruptions, we have __131__ alternative workspaces for employees. __132__ .
>
> Please note that construction noise may occasionally affect __133__ . We encourage everyone to use noise-cancelling headphones if needed.
>
> Additionally, the conference rooms on the third floor will be unavailable during this time. We appreciate your __134__ and understanding as we make these improvements to create a more comfortable and modern workplace.
>
> Should you have any questions or concerns, feel free to contact us at facility@company.com
>
> Sincerely,
> Facilities Management

131. (A) set up
   (B) set off
   (C) set out
   (D) set in

132. (A) We are excited to see the positive changes these renovations will bring.
   (B) All employees must vacate the building during the renovation period.
   (C) This project has been carefully planned to ensure minimal inconvenience to staff.
   (D) Construction permits have been approved by local authorities.

133. (A) productive
   (B) productivity
   (C) production
   (D) productively

134. (A) decision
   (B) information
   (C) consent
   (D) patience

Questions 135 - 138 refer to the following letter.

Subject: Customer Satisfaction Survey

Dear Valued Customer,

Thank you for your recent purchase with us. We strive to provide the best service possible, and ____135____ . Please take a few minutes to complete our online satisfaction survey.

Your responses will help us identify areas for improvement and ensure that our products meet your ____136____ . The survey should take no more than 5 minutes to complete, and all responses will remain ____137____ .

237

As a token of our appreciation, participants who complete the survey by May 15 will be entered into a draw to win a $50 gift card. To access the survey, please click on the link ___138___.

Thank you for your time and support.

Best regards,
Customer Service Team

135. (A) want to take this opportunity to tell you about our new line of products
    (B) we encourage you to be completely honest in providing feedback
    (C) your feedback will be used to improve our customer experience strategy
    (D) ask for your opinions about our latest advertising and marketing campaign

136. (A) exceptions
    (B) expectations
    (C) inspections
    (D) explanations

137. (A) protected
    (B) conditional
    (C) confidential
    (D) optional

138. (A) above
    (B) below
    (C) aside
    (D) near

Questions 139-141 refer to the following announcement.

Subject: Upcoming Workshop Registration

Dear Employees,

We are excited to announce a professional development workshop focused on enhancing teamwork and communication skills. The workshop will take place on June 10 at the downtown training center. Space is limited, so please register ___139___.

Participants will engage in interactive activities and group discussions. ___140___.
Lunch and refreshments will be provided.

To register, visit the HR portal and complete the registration form. A confirmation e-mail will be sent once your registration is ___141___.

If you have any questions, do not hesitate to reach out to HR. We look forward to seeing you at the workshop and hope you find it both informative and ___142___.

Sincerely,
Human Resources

139. (A) completely
 (B) immediately
 (C) occasionally
 (D) consistently

140. (A) These sessions will foster a collaborative environment for all participants.
 (B) Teamwork is one of the core values we strive to promote within the organization.
 (C) We believe this workshop will provide valuable insights for improving group dynamics.
 (D) Workshops like this are integral to building a strong and cohesive workforce.

141. (A) ignored
(B) declined
(C) postponed
(D) verified

142. (A) enjoyable
(B) convenient
(C) promising
(D) optional

Questions 143-146 refer to the following letter.

Subject: New Employee Orientation

Dear New Team Member,

Welcome to our company! We are thrilled to have you on board and look forward to working with you. To help you get started, we have scheduled a new employee orientation session for next Monday at 9:00 AM in the main conference room.

During the orientation, you will learn about company policies, benefits, and procedures. You will also meet key members of the team who will assist you in _____143_____ to your new role.

Please bring a government-issued ID and any documents that you have not yet _____144_____ to HR. _____145_____ If you are unable to attend the session, kindly inform us at least 24 hours in advance. We will do our best to arrange an alternative session.

Once again, welcome to the team! We are excited about the journey ahead and are confident you will find your time here both rewarding and _____146_____.

Sincerely,
HR Department

143. (A) agreeing
     (B) changing
     (C) converting
     (D) adapting

144. (A) permitted
     (B) submitted
     (C) returned
     (D) notified

145. (A) We appreciate your flexibility and understanding in scheduling this session.
     (B) Timely updates help maintain a smooth and organized orientation process.
     (C) Your prompt communication helps us better accommodate your onboarding needs.
     (D) This will allow us to plan effectively and ensure all necessary arrangements are made.

146. (A) effective
     (B) substantial
     (C) mutual
     (D) beneficial

Part 7

Directions: In this part you will read a selection of texts, such as magazine and newspaper articles, e-mails, and instant messages. Each text or set of texts is followed by several questions. Select the best answer for each question and mark the letter (A), (B), (C), or (D) on your answer sheet.

Questions 147 - 150 refer to the following e-mail.

Subject: Meeting Reschedule

Dear Team,

Due to unforeseen circumstances, our weekly meeting originally scheduled for Wednesday at 3:00 PM has been moved to Thursday at the same time. The agenda remains unchanged, and we will still meet in Conference Room A.

Please make the necessary adjustments to your schedule and notify me if you are unable to attend. Thank you for your understanding.

Best regards,

Emily Harper
Operations Manager

147. What is the purpose of this e-mail?
   (A) To confirm the location of a meeting
   (B) To share the meeting agenda
   (C) To introduce a new team member
   (D) To announce a change of schedule

148. When will the meeting take place?
   (A) Wednesday at 3:00 PM
   (B) Thursday at 3:00 PM
   (C) Wednesday at 4:00 PM
   (D) Thursday at 4:00 PM

149. What should recipients do if they cannot attend the meeting?
   (A) Reschedule the meeting
   (B) Inform Emily Harper
   (C) Change the agenda
   (D) Move to a different room

150. Where will the meeting be held?
    (A) The Operations Department
    (B) Conference Room B
    (C) Emily Harper's office
    (D) Conference Room A

Questions 151-155 refer to the following advertisement.

Introducing the New Aeroflex 2000 Vacuum Cleaner

The Aeroflex 2000 is now available at all major retail stores! Designed for maximum efficiency and ease of use, this innovative vacuum cleaner offers powerful suction, lightweight construction, and advanced air filtration technology.

Key Features:

- HEPA filtration system to capture 99.9% of dust and allergens
- Adjustable suction levels for various surfaces
- Detachable handheld unit for tight spaces

Purchase the Aeroflex 2000 by June 30 to receive a 20% discount. Visit www.aeroflex.com for more details.

151. What is the main purpose of this advertisement?
    (A) To promote a new product
    (B) To explain cleaning techniques
    (C) To announce store locations
    (D) To compare different vacuum models

152. What feature helps reduce allergens?
    (A) Adjustable suction levels
    (B) HEPA filtration system
    (C) Lightweight construction
    (D) Detachable handheld unit

153. Until when is the discount available?
    (A) June 1
    (B) June 15
    (C) June 30
    (D) July 1

154. How can customers learn more about the Aeroflex 2000?
    (A) By calling the customer service hotline
    (B) By visiting the website
    (C) By attending a demonstration
    (D) By reading the manual

155. What type of product is being advertised?
    (A) A cleaning product
    (B) A computer accessory
    (C) A fitness service
    (D) A home appliance

Questions 156-160 refer to the following notice.

> Subject: New Parking Regulations
>
> Dear Employees,
>
> Starting July 1, new parking regulations will be implemented to ensure a safer and more organized parking experience. All employees must register their vehicles with the HR department and display a valid parking permit on their windshield.
>
> Parking spaces are assigned based on department and seniority. Employees without a valid permit or parked in unauthorized areas will receive a warning notice. Repeated violations may result in fines or revocation of parking privileges.
>
> For questions or concerns, please contact HR at hr@company.com.

Thank you for your cooperation.

Sincerely,
Facilities Management

156. What is the purpose of the new parking regulations?
    (A) To increase parking fees
    (B) To ensure safety and organization
    (C) To reduce the number of vehicles
    (D) To provide more parking spaces

157. What must employees do to comply with the new regulations?
    (A) Pay a parking fee
    (B) Submit an application online
    (C) Register their vehicles with HR
    (D) Park in visitor spaces

158. What will happen to employees who violate the regulations repeatedly?
    (A) They will lose their parking privileges
    (B) They will be transferred to another department
    (C) They will receive a discount on parking permits
    (D) They will attend a training session

159. When will the new regulations take effect?
    (A) June 1
    (B) June 15
    (C) July 1
    (D) July 15

160. Where can employees send their questions?
    (A) To the Facilities Management office
    (B) To the security desk
    (C) To their immediate supervisor
    (D) To the HR department

Questions 161-165 refer to the following article.

Local Business Expands to New Markets

TechPro Solutions, a leading provider of software services, announced yesterday that it will expand its operations to three additional countries in Southeast Asia. This move is part of the company's long-term strategy to capture growing demand for digital transformation solutions.

The company plans to establish regional offices in Vietnam, Indonesia, and the Philippines by the end of the year. These offices will focus on providing customized software solutions for businesses in various industries, including retail, healthcare, and manufacturing.

According to CEO Michael Lee, "Our expansion reflects our commitment to delivering innovative solutions to our clients worldwide."

161. What is the main topic of this article?
    (A) A company's new product launch
    (B) A company's international expansion
    (C) A company's environmental initiatives
    (D) A company's leadership changes

162. Which countries will TechPro Solutions expand to?
    (A) Vietnam, Indonesia, and the Philippines
    (B) Thailand, Malaysia, and Indonesia
    (C) Singapore, Malaysia, and the Philippines
    (D) Vietnam, Thailand, and Singapore

163. What is the purpose of the new regional offices?
    (A) To conduct market research
    (B) To offer tailored software solutions
    (C) To recruit local talent
    (D) To reduce operational costs

164. When does the company plan to establish the new offices?
    (A) Mid-year
    (B) By the first quarter
    (C) Next year
    (D) By the end of the year

165. Who is quoted in the article?
    (A) A customer
    (B) A regional manager
    (C) The CEO of TechPro Solutions
    (D) A software engineer

Questions 166-170 refer to the following announcement.

Subject: New Health and Wellness Program

Dear Team,

We are excited to announce the launch of our new Health and Wellness Program, starting next month. This initiative is designed to promote a healthier work environment and support employees in achieving their fitness and wellness goals.

Key Benefits:
• Free weekly yoga and meditation sessions
• Discounts on local gym memberships
• Access to an online portal with fitness tips and healthy recipes

To participate, please sign up through the HR portal by March 20. Space is limited, so early registration is encouraged. For any questions, contact wellness@company.com.

We look forward to seeing you there!

Best regards,
Megan Carter
HR Director

166. What is the purpose of this announcement?
    (A) To recruit new employees
    (B) To promote a health program
    (C) To schedule a team meeting
    (D) To share company financial updates

167. Which benefit is mentioned in the announcement?
    (A) Free gym memberships
    (B) Weekly yoga sessions
    (C) Complimentary fitness equipment
    (D) Personal training services

168. What should employees do to participate in the program?
    (A) E-mail Megan Carter directly
    (B) Visit the HR office in person
    (C) Call the wellness hotline
    (D) Register on the HR portal

169. By when must employees sign up?
    (A) March 31
    (B) March 1
    (C) March 15
    (D) March 20

170. Which of the following is a feature of the new Health and Wellness Program?
    (A) It is a month-long exercise program.
    (B) It is available only for senior employees.
    (C) It includes discounts for gym memberships.
    (D) It requires employees to attend fitness classes.

Questions 171-175 refer to the following article.

City's Public Library Introduces 24/7 Book Return Service

The city's central public library announced the installation of an automated book return system that operates 24/7, providing greater convenience to its members. The new system, located at the library's main entrance, allows users to return books at any time, even outside regular library hours.

Library director Susan Perez stated, "This initiative reflects our commitment to enhancing accessibility for all members of the community." She added that the library plans to install similar systems at its branch locations in the coming months.

Members are reminded to return books on time to avoid late fees, which will still apply if items are overdue.

171. What is the main purpose of this article?
    (A) To promote a community event
    (B) To introduce a new library service
    (C) To announce extended library hours
    (D) To provide instructions for borrowing books

172. Where is the new system located?
    (A) In the central library's parking lot
    (B) At the library's main entrance
    (C) In the library near the information desk
    (D) At a branch library location"

173. What is the library's future plan?
    (A) To offer free memberships
    (B) To provide digital book rentals
    (C) To increase its book collection
    (D) To expand the system to other branches

174. What is mentioned about late fees?
    (A) They will no longer be charged.
    (B) They will be reduced for all members.
    (C) They still apply to overdue books.
    (D) They can be paid through the new system.

175. What is the main advantage of the 24/7 book return service?
    (A) It allows users to borrow books at any time.
    (B) It provides faster check-out services.
    (C) It makes returning books more convenient.
    (D) It offers free book delivery.

Questions 176-180 refer to the following announcement, advertisement, and e-mail.

To: All Employees

Subject: Annual Company Picnic

Date: June 5

Dear Team,

We are excited to announce that our annual company picnic will take place on Saturday, June 24, at Riverside Park, starting at 10:00 AM. This event is a great opportunity for employees and their families to enjoy a fun day together.

Activities will include games, a barbecue lunch, and live music. Please RSVP by June 15 by filling out the online form sent to your e-mail address.

We hope to see all of you there!

Best regards,
Human Resources Department

Make Your Event Unforgettable with PartyCaterers

Looking for delicious food for your next event? PartyCaterers offers a wide variety of catering options for corporate events, family gatherings, and parties.

Our packages include:
- Barbecue Buffet: Enjoy freshly grilled meats and sides.
- Vegetarian Options: Healthy and flavorful dishes for all.
- Custom Menus: Tailored to your needs and preferences.

Book your catering by June 10 and receive a 10% discount!

Call us today at 555-1234 or visit www.partycaterers.com for more details.

From: John Smith

To: Human Resources

Subject: Company Picnic Suggestions

Hi HR Team,

I'm thrilled about the upcoming company picnic at Riverside Park! I'd like to suggest a few additional activities, such as a team-building relay race or a small raffle for participants.

Also, will there be vegetarian options available for the barbecue lunch? I know several employees, including myself, who would appreciate it.

Looking forward to the event!
Best,
John

---

176. What is the main purpose of the announcement?
    (A) To request feedback on an event
    (B) To provide details about a picnic
    (C) To introduce a new park location
    (D) To advertise a catering service

177. According to PartyCaterers' advertisement, what is one benefit of booking early?
(A) Free delivery services
(B) A special gift with the order
(C) An extended menu selection
(D) A 10% discount on packages

178. What does John suggest adding to the company picnic?
(A) A vegetarian cooking class
(B) A relay race and a raffle
(C) A karaoke competition
(D) A dance performance

179. By what date should employees sign up for the company picnic?
(A) June 5
(B) June 10
(C) June 15
(D) June 24

180. What concern does John express in his e-mail?
(A) The location of the event
(B) The quality of the live music
(C) The timing of the picnic
(D) The availability of vegetarian options

Questions 181 - 185 refer to the following e-mail, advertisement, and analysis report.

From: Emily Brown, Marketing Manager

To: Product Development Team

Subject: Launch Plan for EcoSmart Bottle

Dear Team,

As we prepare for the launch of our new EcoSmart Bottle in July, I want to highlight key marketing strategies:

1. Social Media Campaign: Starting June 15, we'll use influencers to promote the product.
2. Retail Partnerships: Agreements with major retailers like GreenMart have been finalized.
3. Customer Feedback Initiative: Pre-launch product testing will involve 100 customers from our loyalty program.

Please ensure that the final product samples are ready by June 10 for testing. Let me know if there are any challenges.

Best regards,
Emily

Introducing the EcoSmart Bottle

Looking for a durable and eco-friendly solution to your hydration needs? The EcoSmart Bottle is made from 100% recycled materials and features an innovative design for convenient use.

Key Features:
- Leak-proof Cap: Ensures no spills in your bag.
- Temperature Retention: Keeps drinks hot or cold for up to 12 hours.
- Lightweight and Portable: Perfect for travel and outdoor activities.

Order now and enjoy an early bird discount of 15% before July 1!

Visit www.ecosmartbottle.com to place your order today.

> **Eco-Friendly Product Trends in 2023**
> Recent studies show that consumers are increasingly prioritizing sustainability when making purchases. Over 65% of surveyed shoppers prefer products made from recycled materials, with younger generations leading the trend.
> Key Insights:
> - Social media plays a crucial role in influencing purchasing decisions, especially for eco-friendly products.
> - Retail partnerships with eco-conscious stores have proven effective in boosting product visibility.
> - Customers value transparency about the environmental impact of products.
>
> The EcoSmart Bottle is well-positioned to capitalize on these trends, thanks to its recycled materials and strong online marketing strategy.

181. What is the purpose of Emily's e-mail?
    (A) To confirm the product launch date
    (B) To announce changes in product design
    (C) To request additional funding for promotions
    (D) To outline marketing strategies for a product

182. According to the brochure, what is one feature of the EcoSmart Bottle?
    (A) It is dishwasher-safe.
    (B) It has a built-in filter.
    (C) It holds temperature for 12 hours.
    (D) It comes in multiple sizes.

183. What deadline is mentioned in Emily's e-mail?
    (A) June 1
    (B) June 10
    (C) June 15
    (D) July 1

184. According to the market analysis, what is a key factor affecting eco-friendly product purchases?
    (A) Competitive pricing
    (B) Packaging design
    (C) Social media influence
    (D) Local manufacturing

185. What advantage does the EcoSmart Bottle have over competitors, based on the brochure and report?
    (A) Focus on recycled materials and sustainability
    (B) Lower production costs
    (C) Exclusive partnerships with luxury brands
    (D) Longer warranty period

Questions 186-190 refer to the following memo, website, and e-mail.

To: Sales Team

From: David Kim, Regional Manager

Subject: Preparations for the Global Trade Expo

Dear Team,

As you all know, the Global Trade Expo will take place from September 15 to September 18 in Frankfurt, Germany. This event is an excellent opportunity to showcase our new product line, network with international clients, and identify potential distributors.

Key Points:

1. Presentation Materials: Ensure that all promotional brochures and sample products are shipped to the venue by September 10.

2. Meeting Schedules: Please confirm appointments with key clients by August 25.

3. Cultural Sensitivity: Remember to familiarize yourselves with the customs and etiquette of the regions represented at the expo.

Feel free to reach out if you have any questions. Let's make this event a success!

Best regards,

David

Welcome to the Global Trade Expo 2023

The Global Trade Expo is the leading platform for international businesses to connect and collaborate. This year, we are excited to host over 500 exhibitors from 30 countries and welcome an estimated 20,000 attendees.

Event Highlights:

- Panel Discussions: Learn from industry leaders about the latest trends in global trade.
- Product Demonstrations: Experience cutting-edge innovations firsthand.
- Networking events: Build valuable business connections in a relaxed setting.

Don't miss the keynote speech by Dr. Elena Morales, CEO of InnovateCorp, on September 16 at 10:00 AM in Hall A.

Visit www.globaltradeexpo.com for more details and registration information.

From: John Taylor, Logistics Coordinator

To: David Kim

Subject: Shipping Arrangements for Expo

Hi David,

I wanted to update you on the shipping process for the Global Trade Expo. The promotional brochures and product samples have been packaged and will be shipped via express delivery on September 5. They are expected to arrive in Frankfurt by September 8, well before the September 10 deadline.

Additionally, I've spoken with the freight company to ensure proper handling of the materials during transit. Let me know if there's anything else you need.

Best regards,
John

186. What is the purpose of David Kim's memo?
    (A) To discuss important logistics issues
    (B) To provide a summary of the previous year's expo
    (C) To announce changes to the expo schedule
    (D) To outline the objectives of attending the expo

187. According to the expo website, what will happen on September 16 at 10:00 AM?
    (A) A networking event will take place.
    (B) A keynote speech will be delivered.
    (C) A product demonstration will begin.
    (D) A registration period will commence.

188. What is the deadline for confirming client appointments mentioned in David's memo?
    (A) August 25
    (B) September 5
    (C) September 8
    (D) September 10

189. According to John Taylor's e-mail, when are the promotional materials expected to arrive in Frankfurt?
    (A) September 5
    (B) September 8
    (C) September 10
    (D) September 15

190. What is one advantage of attending the Global Trade Expo mentioned on the website?
    (A) Access to exclusive business loans
    (B) Special discounts for exhibitors
    (C) Learning from industry leaders
    (D) Priority shipping for products

Questions 191-195 refer to the following news report, memo, and analysis.

GlobalTech and Innovatech Announce Merger Agreement

GlobalTech Inc. and Innovatech Solutions have officially announced their decision to merge, forming one of the largest technology firms in the industry. The merger, valued at $12 billion, is expected to be finalized by December 31 pending regulatory approval.

According to GlobalTech CEO Robert Lin, "This merger allows us to leverage Innovatech's expertise in software development while expanding our market reach globally." Innovatech's CEO, Maria Santos, added, "By joining forces, we can accelerate innovation and deliver better solutions to our clients."

The new company, to be named Global Innovate, will operate under a unified leadership team and is projected to achieve $1.5 billion in cost savings within three years.

To: Finance Department

From: CFO Office

Subject: Transition Plan for GlobalTech-Innovatech Merger

Dear Team,

As part of the upcoming merger, several financial and operational changes will take place:

1. Budget Integration: All departmental budgets must be aligned by November 15.

2. Staff Training: Training sessions on the new unified financial system will begin on October 1.
3. Quarterly Reports: The combined Q4 financial report will be prepared using the updated system and submitted by January 10.

Your cooperation during this transition is critical to ensure a smooth integration process. If you have questions, please contact the CFO Office.

Best regards,
Linda Chung
Chief Financial Officer

Industry Impact of the GlobalTech-Innovatech Merger

The merger of GlobalTech and Innovatech is expected to significantly alter the competitive landscape of the technology industry. Analysts predict that the new entity, Global Innovate, will become a market leader in both software and hardware solutions.

Key Impacts:
- Increased Competition: Smaller firms may struggle to compete with the combined resources of the two companies.
- Client Benefits: The merger could lead to lower prices and improved services due to increased efficiency.
- Innovation Potential: By pooling R&D efforts, Global Innovate is likely to introduce cutting-edge technologies faster than its competitors.

However, some experts caution that the integration process could pose challenges, such as merging corporate cultures and aligning operational systems.

191. What is one major benefit of the GlobalTech-Innovatech merger according to the news report?
    (A) Reduced operational costs
    (B) Improved employee benefits
    (C) Higher regulatory flexibility
    (D) Expanded legal resources

192. What deadline is mentioned in the memo for aligning departmental budgets?
    (A) October 1
    (B) November 15
    (C) December 31
    (D) January 10

193. According to the industry analysis, what is one potential challenge of the merger?
    (A) Declining customer satisfaction
    (B) Difficulty in merging corporate cultures
    (C) Increased competition from larger firms
    (D) Reduced investment in research

194. What is the projected cost saving of the new company within three years?
    (A) $12 billion
    (B) $2 billion
    (C) $15 billion
    (D) $1.5 billion

195. According to the industry analysis, how might clients benefit from the merger?
    (A) Extended warranties on products
    (B) Faster delivery of services
    (C) Improved services at lower prices
    (D) Exclusive access to new products

Questions 196-200 refer to the following announcement and review.

Welcome to the Grand Horizon Hotel

Dear Guests,

Thank you for choosing to stay with us at the Grand Horizon Hotel. To ensure you have a pleasant experience, please take note of the following services and amenities:

1. Complimentary Breakfast: Served daily from 6:30 AM to 10:00 AM in the Seaview Restaurant on the ground floor.
2. Fitness Center: Open 24/7 for all guests. Access cards are available at the front desk.
3. Shuttle Service: Free shuttle buses to the city center run every hour from 8:00 AM to 10:00 PM. Please reserve your seat at least 30 minutes in advance at the concierge desk.
4. Room Service: Available 24/7. Dial #101 from your room phone to place an order.

Should you have any questions or special requests, please contact our front desk team, available around the clock.

We hope you enjoy your stay!

Best regards,
Management Team

Review by Sarah P.

I recently stayed at the Grand Horizon Hotel for a business trip, and overall, it was a pleasant experience. The complimentary breakfast was a great start to my mornings, and I appreciated the variety of food options available.

The shuttle service was convenient for getting to the city center, though I wish the last bus departed later than 10:00 PM since my meetings sometimes ran late. The fitness center was well-equipped, but it would have been even better if yoga mats were provided.

The room was clean and comfortable, and the room service staff was prompt and courteous. I also liked that the front desk team was available 24/7 to address any questions.

Overall, I would recommend this hotel to other business travelers.

196. According to the announcement, what must guests do to use the shuttle service?
    (A) Show their key card to the driver
    (B) Confirm their reservation during check-in
    (C) Pay a small fee at the concierge desk
    (D) Book their seat in advance

197. What is one feature of the Grand Horizon Hotel that Sarah found inconvenient?
    (A) The fitness center's limited equipment
    (B) The shuttle service schedule
    (C) The lack of room cleaning services
    (D) The unavailability of breakfast options

198. When is the last shuttle bus to the city center scheduled to depart?
    (A) 8:00 PM
    (B) 9:30 PM
    (C) 10:00 PM
    (D) 11:00 PM

199. What is one service that both the announcement and review mention?
    (A) Parking availability
    (B) Laundry services
    (C) Room service
    (D) Late check-out options

200. How does Sarah suggest improving the fitness center?
    (A) Extending its hours
    (B) Adding more equipment
    (C) Offering personal trainers
    (D) Providing yoga mats

新制多益模擬試題一回解答、翻譯和解說

解答

Listening Test

Part 1

1. (A)　2. (C)　3. (A)　4. (B)　5. (A)　6. (D)

Part 2

7. (C)　8. (A)　9. (B)　10. (C)　11. (C)　12. (B)　13. (A)　14. (C)　15. (A)
16. (B)　17. (C)　18. (C)　19. (B)　20. (A)　21. (C)　22. (A)　23. (B)
24. (B)　25. (C)　26. (A)　27. (B)　28. (A)　29. (C)　30. (B)　31. (C)

Part 3

32. (D)　33. (C)　34. (C)　35. (B)　36. (A)　37. (D)　38. (C)　39. (B)　40. (D)
41. (A)　42. (B)　43. (D)　44. (B)　45. (A)　46. (B)　47. (D)　48. (A)　49. (B)
50. (D)　51. (C)　52. (C)　53. (C)　54. (B)　55. (B)　56. (B)　57. (C)　58. (A)
59. (B)　60. (C)　61. (D)　62. (A)　63. (D)　64. (B)　65. (C)　66. (B)　67. (D)
68. (C)　69. (B)　70. (C)

Part 4

71. (A)　72. (C)　73. (B)　74. (B)　75. (A)　76. (B)　77. (B)　78. (C)　79. (C)
80. (C)　81. (B)　82. (A)　83. (B)　84. (B)　85. (D)　86. (A)　87. (B)　88. (B)
89. (C)　90. (C)　91. (B)　92. (B)　93. (C)　94. (D)　95. (D)　96. (D)　97. (C)
98. (B)　99. (C)　100. (D)

Reading Test

Part 5

101. (D)　102. (B)　103. (A)　104. (C)　105. (D)　106. (C)　107. (A)　108. (A)
109. (D)　110. (C)　111. (B)　112. (A)　113. (D)　114. (C)　115. (A)　116. (D)
117. (B)　118. (C)　119. (A)　120. (D)　121. (C)　122. (A)　123. (D)　124. (C)
125. (A)　126. (D)　127. (C)　128. (B)　129. (A)　130. (D)

Part 6

131. (A) 132. (C) 133. (B) 134. (D) 135. (C) 136. (B) 137. (C) 138. (B) 139. (B)
140. (A) 141. (D) 142. (A) 143. (D) 144. (B) 145. (D) 146. (D)

Part 7

147. (D) 148. (B) 149. (B) 150. (D) 151. (A) 152. (B) 153. (C) 154. (B) 155. (D)
156. (B) 157. (C) 158. (A) 159. (C) 160. (D) 161. (B) 162. (A) 163. (B) 164. (D)
165. (C) 166. (B) 167. (B) 168. (D) 169. (D) 170. (C) 171. (B) 172. (B) 173. (D)
174. (C) 175. (C) 176. (B) 177. (D) 178. (B) 179. (C) 180. (D) 181. (D) 182. (C)
183. (B) 184. (C) 185. (A) 186. (D) 187. (B) 188. (A) 189. (B) 190. (C) 191. (A)
192. (B) 193. (B) 194. (D) 195. (C) 196. (D) 197. (B) 198. (C) 199. (C) 200. (D)

Part 1

1. **(A)** The man is sitting at a desk.
   中譯　這位男子正坐在桌子旁。
   說明　描述中提到 "The man is sitting at a desk."，圖片中的男子正坐在桌邊。其他選項的動作和圖片不符合。

2. **(C)** The woman is assisting a customer.
   中譯　這位女子正在幫助顧客。
   說明　描述中提到 "The woman is assisting a customer."，這符合圖片中的情境。

3. **(A)** The man is trying to fix his car.
   中譯　這位男子正試著修車。
   說明　描述中提到 "The man is trying to fix his car."，圖片中男子的引擎蓋打開，看起來正在修車，其他選項描述不符。

4. **(B)** The woman is working in her yard.
   中譯　這位女士正在院子裡工作。
   說明　描述中提到 "The woman is working in her yard."，圖片中女子正在院子掃落葉，符合敘述。

5. **(A)** The store shelves are fully stocked.
   - 中譯　商店的貨架已經被填滿。
   - 說明　描述中提到 "The store shelves are fully stocked"，圖片中貨架上擺滿了商品，描述和圖片相符。

6. **(D)** The woman is giving a presentation.
   - 中譯　那位女子正在做報告。
   - 說明　描述中提到 "The woman is giving a presentation"，圖片中女子正在做報告，描述和圖片相符。

Part 2

7. **(C)** What time does the meeting start?
   (A) I met him yesterday.
   (B) In the conference room.
   (C) At 2 p.m.
   - 中譯　會議幾點開始？
   (A) 我昨天見過他。
   (B) 在會議室裡。
   (C) 下午兩點。
   - 說明　問句詢問時間，只有選項 (C) 提供具體的時間。

8. **(A)** How do you usually commute to work?
   (A) By train, most of the time.
   (B) It's on the second floor.
   (C) No, I haven't met him.
   - 中譯　你通常如何通勤上班？
   (A) 大多數時候搭火車。
   (B) 在二樓。
   (C) 不，我沒見過他。
   - 說明　問句詢問交通方式，選項 (A) 回答火車，為合理回答。

9. **(B)** Why was the project delayed?
　　　(A) We are almost finished.
　　　(B) Because of technical issues.
　　　(C) The package will arrive soon.

中譯　為什麼專案被延遲了？
　　　(A) 我們快完成了。
　　　(B) 因為遇到技術問題。
　　　(C) 包裹很快會到。

說明　問句詢問原因，選項 (B) 提供發生問題的原因，為正解。

10. **(C)** Who is responsible for organizing the event?
　　　(A) It will be held on Friday.
　　　(B) At the main entrance.
　　　(C) I think it's Sarah from marketing.

中譯　誰負責籌劃活動？
　　　(A) 活動將在星期五舉行。
　　　(B) 在主入口。
　　　(C) 我想是行銷部的 Sarah。

說明　問句詢問人名，選項 (C) 提供具體人名。

11. **(C)** Have you submitted the report yet?
　　　(A) I'll leave around 6 p.m.
　　　(B) No, the room is already booked.
　　　(C) Yes, I e-mailed it this morning.

中譯　你已經提交報告了嗎？
　　　(A) 我大概六點左右離開。
　　　(B) 不，那間房已經預訂了。
　　　(C) 是的，我今天早上寄了電子郵件。

說明　問句為是非題，選項 (C) 明確回答並補充細節。

12. **(B)** Where can I find the customer service desk?
　　　(A) The order will arrive on Tuesday.
　　　(B) Near the entrance on the first floor.
　　　(C) Yes, they are very friendly.

中譯　我可以在哪裡找到客服櫃檯？
(A) 訂單將於星期二送達。
(B) 在一樓靠近入口的地方。
(C) 是的，他們非常友好。
說明　問句詢問地點，選項 (B) 提供位置的準確信息。

13. **(A)** What should I bring to the meeting?
    (A) Your laptop and the project file.
    (B) It's next to the break room.
    (C) The meeting starts at 10 a.m.

中譯　我應該帶什麼去開會？
(A) 你的筆電和專案文件。
(B) 在休息室旁邊。
(C) 會議於上午十點開始。
說明　問句詢問攜帶項目，選項 (A) 回答物品，直接回答問題。

14. **(C)** How long will the presentation take?
    (A) We'll use the large conference room.
    (B) It's about market trends.
    (C) Around 30 minutes.

中譯　簡報會持續多久？
(A) 我們將使用大會議室。
(B) 是關於市場趨勢的。
(C) 大約 30 分鐘。
說明　問句詢問時間長度，選項 (C) 告知一段時間。

15. **(A)** Have you seen the new product designs?
    (A) Yes, they were sent yesterday.
    (B) It's on the second shelf.
    (C) No, it hasn't arrived yet.

中譯　你看過新的產品設計嗎？
(A) 是的，昨天已經寄過來了。
(B) 在第二個架子上。
(C) 不，它還沒到。

說明　(C) 提到商品還沒到，但題目中商品設計是複數 (designs)，該選項 hasn't 為單數動詞，不正確。選項 (A) 的動詞也是複數，是合適的肯定回答。

16. **(B)** Where did you leave the keys?
    (A) Yes, they are working properly.
    (B) On the kitchen counter.
    (C) I'll return them tomorrow.

　中譯　你把鑰匙放在哪裡了？
    (A) 是的，它們運作正常。
    (B) 在廚房的檯面上。
    (C) 我明天會歸還它們。

　說明　問句詢問地點，選項 (B) 提供明確的地點。

17. **(C)** When is the project deadline?
    (A) In the manager's office.
    (B) By submitting the form.
    (C) Next Friday.

　中譯　專案的截止日期是什麼時候？
    (A) 在經理辦公室。
    (B) 提交表格即可。
    (C) 下星期五。

　說明　問句詢問時間，只有選項 (C) 提供了時間點。

18. **(C)** Can you send me the updated file?
    (A) The file is saved on the desktop.
    (B) No, you haven't sent it to me.
    (C) Yes, I'll e-mail it to you now.

　中譯　你能把更新的檔案寄給我嗎？
    (A) 檔案存放在桌面上。
    (B) 不能，你還沒寄給我。
    (C) 可以，我現在就寄郵件給你。

　說明　問句要求對方寄檔案，選項 (B) 用「你」回覆錯誤，應使用 I 回覆。選項 (C) 是直接肯定的回答。

19. **(B)** Why didn't you attend the meeting?
    (A) The agenda was about sales.
    (B) I was out of town.
    (C) It starts at 9 a.m.

中譯　你為什麼沒參加會議？
    (A) 議程是關於銷售的。
    (B) 我不在城裡。
    (C) 它在上午九點開始。

說明　問句詢問原因，選項 (C) 提到會議開始的時間，但沒有說明原因，只有選項 (B) 提供無法參加會議的理由，

20. **(A)** What is the address of the venue?
    (A) It's at 123 Main Street.
    (B) Yes, I'll send you an e-mail.
    (C) It will take about an hour.

中譯　活動場地的地址是什麼？
    (A) 在 123 主街。
    (B) 是的，我會寄電子郵件給你。
    (C) 大約需要一個小時。

說明　問句詢問地址，只有選項 (A) 提供了地址。

21. **(C)** Who will present the sales report?
    (A) It's a detailed analysis of sales data.
    (B) The presentation starts at 3 p.m.
    (C) Ms. Johnson from the finance department

中譯　誰會做銷售報告？
    (A) 是一份詳細的銷售數據分析。
    (B) 簡報於下午三點開始。
    (C) 財務部的 Johnson 女士。

說明　問句詢問人，選項 (C) 提供了明確的人名與部門。

22. **(A)** How often do you check your emails?
    (A) Every hour or so.
    (B) In my office.
    (C) Yes, I sent one yesterday.

中譯 你多久檢查一次電子郵件？
　　　(A) 大約每小時一次。
　　　(B) 在我的辦公室裡。
　　　(C) 是的，我昨天寄了一封。
說明 問句詢問頻率，選項 (A)「每小時一次」為頻率。

23．**(B)** Should I reschedule the meeting?
　　　(A) The meeting will be in Room 302.
　　　(B) Yes, please move it to next week.
　　　(C) I met him last week.
中譯 我應該重新安排會議嗎？
　　　(A) 會議將在302室。
　　　(B) 是的，請改到下周。
　　　(C) 我上週見過他。
說明 問句為建議性問題，選項 (B) 是針對該問題的肯定回答。

24．**(B)** Where can I park my car?
　　　(A) No, I didn't drive today.
　　　(B) In the garage behind the building.
　　　(C) The traffic was heavy this morning.
中譯 我可以在哪裡停車？
　　　(A) 不，我今天沒開車。
　　　(B) 在建築物後面的車庫裡。
　　　(C) 今天早上的交通很擁塞。
說明 問句詢問地點，只有選項 (B) 提供了「車庫」作為停車的地點。

25．**(C)** What did the manager say about the proposal?
　　　(A) Yes, I'll write the report today.
　　　(B) The proposal is on your desk.
　　　(C) She approved it immediately.
中譯 經理對提案說了什麼？
　　　(A) 是的，我今天會寫報告。
　　　(B) 提案在你的桌上。
　　　(C) 她立刻批准了。

說明 問句詢問經理針對提案說了什麼，可引申為對提案有什麼意見，選項 (C)「批准」就是經理對提案的意見。

26. **(A)** Is the museum open on weekends?
    (A) No, it's closed on Saturday and Sunday.
    (B) The office is on the third floor.
    (C) It's open until 5 p.m. on weekdays.
中譯 博物館週末開門嗎？
    (A) 不，周六和周日不開門。
    (B) 辦公室在三樓。
    (C) 平日開到下午五點。
說明 問句為是非題，詢問周末，選項 (C) 提供平日博物館關閉的時間，答非所問。選項 (A) 告知周六和周日關閉，為正解。

27. **(B)** Have you tried the new restaurant downtown?
    (A) It's located near the train station.
    (B) Yes, the food was excellent.
    (C) No, I haven't met him yet.
中譯 你試過市中心的新餐廳嗎？
    (A) 它位於火車站附近。
    (B) 是的，食物非常棒。
    (C) 不，我還沒見過他。
說明 問句為是非題，選項 (B) 是肯定回答，提供了對餐廳的評價。

28. **(A)** Can you help me with this report?
    (A) Sure, let me finish this e-mail first.
    (B) The report is due next Monday.
    (C) Yes, I saw it on my desk.
中譯 你能幫我處理這份報告嗎？
    (A) 好，讓我先完成這封電子郵件。
    (B) 報告的截止日期是下周一。
    (C) 是的，我在桌上看到它了。
說明 問句為請求，選項 (A) 正面回應並請對方先等一下，為正確答案。

271

29. **(C)** Why are the lights off in the meeting room?
- (A) The presentation starts at 2 p.m.
- (B) The switch is next to the door.
- (C) Because no one is using it right now.

中譯 為什麼會議室的燈關了？
- (A) 報告於下午兩點開始。
- (B) 開關在門旁邊。
- (C) 因為現在沒有人使用。

說明 問句詢問關燈的原因，選項 (C) 回答了原因，為正解。

30. **(B)** What should I do if the printer isn't working?
- (A) It's located near the copy machine.
- (B) Contact the IT department for support.
- (C) Yes, I've printed the document.

中譯 如果影印機壞了我該怎麼辦？
- (A) 它在影印機附近。
- (B) 聯繫資訊部門尋求支援。
- (C) 是的，我已經把文件印出了。

說明 問句詢問建議，選項 (B) 是明確的指示，最符合問句。

31. **(C)** When will the shipment arrive?
- (A) Yes, I'll confirm the order now.
- (B) The items are stored in the warehouse.
- (C) It's expected to arrive tomorrow afternoon.

中譯 貨物什麼時候到？
- (A) 是的，我現在確認訂單。
- (B) 貨物存放在倉庫裡。
- (C) 預計明天下午到達。

說明 問句詢問時間，選項 (C) 提供明確的時間答覆。

Part 3

Questions 32 through 34 refer to the following conversation.
Woman: Hi, could you tell me what time the last train leaves for the city?
Man: Sure, the last train departs at 11:45 p.m. from platform 3.
Woman: Thank you. I'll make sure to be there on time.

> **中譯** 問題 32-34 請參考以下對話。
> 女子：你好，請問能告訴我最後一班火車什麼時候開往市區嗎？
> 男子：嗯，最後一班火車在晚上 11:45 從 3 號月台開出。
> 女子：謝謝，我會準時到那裡的。

32. **(D)** What is the woman asking about?
    (A) The departure location
    (B) The ticket price
    (C) The platform number
    (D) The train schedule

> **中譯** 女子在詢問什麼？
> (A) 發車地點
> (B) 票價
> (C) 月台號碼
> (D) 火車時刻表
>
> **說明** 女子詢問火車的發車時間，對話內容沒有提到票價或其他資訊，因此選擇 (D) 最為正確。

33. **(C)** What time does the last train leave?
    (A) At 10:30 p.m.
    (B) At 11:15 p.m.
    (C) At 11:45 p.m.
    (D) At midnight

> **中譯** 最後一班火車什麼時候開？
> (A) 晚上 10:30
> (B) 晚上 11:15
> (C) 晚上 11:45
> (D) 午夜
>
> **說明** 對話中明確提到最後一班列車於 11:45 p.m. 出發，因此正確答案是 (C)。

34. **(C)** Where will the train depart from?
    (A) Platform 1
    (B) Platform 2
    (C) Platform 3
    (D) Platform 4

    中譯 火車會從哪個月台發車？
    (A) 1 號月台
    (B) 2 號月台
    (C) 3 號月台
    (D) 4 號月台

    說明 男子提到列車從第 3 月台出發，其他月台的選項均為干擾選項，因此正確答案是 (C)。

Questions 35 through 37 refer to the following conversation.

Man: Excuse me, I'm in the mood for some Italian food. Can you recommend a good place nearby?

Woman: Sure. There's a restaurant called "Luigi's" about two blocks from here, on Maple Street. It's very popular for its authentic dishes.

Man: That sounds perfect. Is it usually crowded?

Woman: During dinner hours, yes. But it's definitely worth the wait.

Man: Great, thanks for the suggestion.

中譯 問題 35-37 請參考以下對話。
男子：不好意思，我想吃義大利菜。你能推薦附近還不錯的餐廳嗎？
女子：可以。有一家叫 Luigi's 的餐廳，大約在這裡兩條街外的楓樹街上，因為菜餚口味道地而非常受歡迎。
男子：聽起來很棒。它通常會有很多人嗎？
女子：在晚餐時間是的。但絕對值得等候。
男子：太好了，謝謝你的建議。

35. **(B)** What is the man looking for?
    (A) A bakery
    (B) An Italian restaurant
    (C) A coffee shop
    (D) A fast food place

274

中譯　男子在找什麼？
(A) 一間麵包店
(B) 一家義大利餐廳
(C) 一間咖啡廳
(D) 一家速食餐廳
說明　男子詢問附近的義大利餐廳，因此正確答案是 (B)。

36. **(A)** Where is the restaurant located?
    (A) On Maple Street, two blocks away
    (B) Next to a bus stop
    (C) Across the street from a park
    (D) Near the train station
中譯　餐廳位於哪裡？
(A) 在楓樹街，距離這裡兩條街
(B) 在公車站旁邊
(C) 在公園的對面
(D) 靠近火車站
說明　女子提到餐廳位於楓樹街，距離這裡兩條街，因此正確答案是 (A)。

37. **(D)** How does the woman describe the restaurant?
    (A) Expensive but worth it
    (B) A hidden gem
    (C) Usually crowded but affordable
    (D) Popular for its authentic dishes
中譯　女子如何形容這家餐廳？
(A) 昂貴但值得
(B) 隱藏的寶石
(C) 通常人多但價格合理
(D) 以其道地菜餚聞名
說明　有提到人多，但並未提及價格合理，所以 (C) 不正確。其他選項均為干擾選項，未在對話中出現。女子提到這家餐廳「因為菜餚口味道地，而非常受歡迎」，因此答案是 (D)。

Questions 38 through 40 refer to the following conversation.

Woman: I'm planning to replace my old laptop. Can you suggest a good option?

Man: Sure, I'd recommend the XYZ Pro series. It's known for its durability and performance, and it's reasonably priced compared to similar models.

Woman: That sounds great. Do you think I can find it online?

Man: Definitely. Most major retailers carry it, and you might even find a discount.

> **中譯** 問題 38-40 請參考以下對話。
> 女子：我打算換掉我的舊筆電。你能推薦好的選擇嗎？
> 男子：可以，我推薦 XYZ Pro 系列。它以耐用性和性能著稱，與相似型號相比價格合理。
> 女子：聽起來不錯。你覺得我能在網路上找到它嗎？
> 男子：一定可以。大多數主要零售商都有賣，你甚至可能發現折扣商品。

38. **(C)** What is the woman planning to buy?
    (A) A smartphone
    (B) A tablet
    (C) A laptop
    (D) A desktop computer

> **中譯** 女子打算買什麼？
> (A) 智慧型手機
> (B) 平板電腦
> (C) 筆記型電腦
> (D) 桌上型電腦
>
> **說明** 女子提到她打算更換舊筆電，對話中未提及其他裝置，因此答案是 (C)。

39. **(B)** What does the man recommend?
    (A) The ABC brand
    (B) The XYZ Pro series
    (C) A refurbished model
    (D) The latest high-end model

中譯 男子推薦什麼？
(A) ABC 品牌
(B) XYZ Pro 系列
(C) 一台翻新的型號
(D) 最新的高端型號

說明 男子推薦了 XYZ Pro 系列，並提到其耐用性和性能，因此正確答案是 (B)。

40. **(D)** Where does the woman plan to look for more information?
(A) At a local store
(B) By asking friends
(C) In a catalog
(D) Online

中譯 女子計劃在哪裡尋找更多資訊？
(A) 在本地的商店
(B) 透過詢問朋友
(C) 在目錄中
(D) 在網路上

說明 女子詢問是否可以在網路上找到該型號，表明她計劃上網查詢更多資訊，因此答案是 (D)。

Questions 41 through 43 refer to the following conversation.

Man: Have you heard about the upcoming marketing campaign?
Woman: Yes, I read about it in the company newsletter. It's scheduled to kick off early next month.
Man: Exciting, right? I've already signed up to be part of the development team.
Woman: That's great. I'm sure it'll be a valuable experience for everyone involved.

中譯 **問題 41-43 請參考以下對話。**
男子：你有聽說即將開始的行銷活動嗎？
女子：有啊，我在公司的內部通訊中讀到，計劃會在下個月初開始。
男子：真令人興奮！對吧？我已經報名參加開發團隊了。
女子：太棒了，我相信這對所有參與的人來說都會是一次寶貴的經驗。

41．**(A)** What are the speakers discussing?
   (A) A marketing campaign
   (B) A new office location
   (C) A staff meeting
   (D) A training session

   中譯　對話者在討論什麼？
   (A) 一個行銷活動
   (B) 一個新辦公地點
   (C) 一場員工會議
   (D) 一場培訓會議

   說明　男子提到 "upcoming marketing campaign"，表示他們討論的是行銷活動，因此答案是 (A)。

42．**(B)** When will the campaign begin?
   (A) This week
   (B) Early next month
   (C) By the end of the month
   (D) Next quarter

   中譯　行銷活動何時開始？
   (A) 本週
   (B) 下個月初
   (C) 本月底前
   (D) 下一季度

   說明　女子提到活動計劃在 "early next month" 開始，因此答案是 (B)。

43．**(D)** What is the man looking forward to?
   (A) Leading the project
   (B) Overseeing the campaign budget
   (C) Presenting his ideas
   (D) Joining the development team

   中譯　男子期待什麼？
   (A) 領導這個專案
   (B) 監督活動預算
   (C) 報告他的想法
   (D) 加入開發團隊

說明 男子提到他已經報名加入開發團隊，因此答案是 (D)。

Questions 44 through 46 refer to the following conversation.

Woman: Excuse me, could you help me set up the projector for the presentation?
Man: Sure, I'll grab the cables and check if everything is connected properly.
Woman: Thanks. The presentation is scheduled to start in 10 minutes, so I don't have much time.
Man: No problem. I'll have it ready in just a few minutes.

中譯 問題 44 - 46 請參考以下對話。
女子：不好意思，你能幫我設置投影機在簡報時使用嗎？
男子：好，我可以拿連接線，並檢查是否全部連接妥當。
女子：謝謝。簡報預計在十分鐘後開始，所以我時間不多了。
男子：沒問題，我幾分鐘內就能準備好。

44．**(B)** What does the woman need help with?
　　(A) Printing handouts
　　(B) Preparing a projector
　　(C) Preparing a presentation
　　(D) Rearranging the meeting room
中譯 女子需要幫忙做什麼？
　　(A) 列印講義
　　(B) 準備投影機
　　(C) 準備簡報
　　(D) 重新佈置會議室
說明 女子提到需要男子幫忙準備投影機，因此答案是 (B)。

45．**(A)** What does the man say he will do?
　　(A) Get the cables
　　(B) Check the sound system
　　(C) Adjust the projector screen
　　(D) Review the agenda
中譯 男子說他會做什麼？

279

(A) 拿連接線
(B) 檢查音響系統
(C) 調整投影幕
(D) 檢查議程

說明 男子提到他會去拿連接線並檢查連接狀態，因此答案是 (A)。

46. **(B)** When does the presentation begin?
    (A) In a few minutes
    (B) In 10 minutes
    (C) In 15 minutes
    (D) At the top of the hour

中譯 簡報何時開始？
    (A) 幾分鐘內
    (B) 十分鐘內
    (C) 十五分鐘內
    (D) 整點時開始

說明 女子提到簡報計劃在十分鐘後開始，因此答案是 (B)。

Questions 47 through 49 refer to the following conversation.
Man: Hi, Lisa. Did you see the e-mail about the new marketing project?
Woman: Yes, I did. The deadline is pretty tight, isn't it?
Man: It is, but I think we can manage if we divide the tasks efficiently.
Woman: Agreed. Let's set up a meeting tomorrow to plan everything.

中譯 **問題 47-49 請參考以下對話**。
男子：嗨，Lisa。你有看到關於新行銷專案的電子郵件嗎？
女子：有的，我看到了。截止日期挺趕的，不是嗎？
男子：是的，但如果我們能有效分配任務，我覺得我們可以完成。
女子：同意。那我們明天開個會來共同計畫吧。

47. **(D)** What are the speakers discussing?
    (A) A company event
    (B) A training program
    (C) A team lunch
    (D) A new project

280

中譯 對話者在討論什麼？
(A) 一場公司活動
(B) 一個培訓計劃
(C) 一次團隊午餐
(D) 一個新專案

說明 對話中提到 "the new marketing project"（新行銷專案），所以答案是 (D)。

48. **(A)** What is the woman concerned about?
    (A) The deadline
    (B) The project's budget
    (C) Team availability
    (D) The meeting time

中譯 女子擔心的是什麼？
(A) 截止日期
(B) 專案預算
(C) 團隊的可用性
(D) 會議時間

說明 女子說 "The deadline is pretty tight, isn't it?"（截止日期很趕，對吧？）表示她對截止日期感到擔憂。

49. **(B)** What do the speakers decide to do?
    (A) Extend the deadline
    (B) Meet tomorrow
    (C) Cancel the project
    (D) Hire more staff

中譯 對話者決定做什麼？
(A) 延長截止日期
(B) 明天開會
(C) 取消專案
(D) 招募更多人員

說明 女子說 "Let's set up a meeting tomorrow to plan everything."（那我們明天開個會來共同計畫吧。）所以答案是 (B)。

281

Questions 50 through 52 refer to the following conversation.

Man: Good morning. Can I get a large latte, please?
Woman: Of course. Would you like anything else?
Man: Yes, I'll also take a blueberry muffin. How much is that altogether?
Woman: That will be $6.75.

> **中譯** 問題 50-52 請參考以下對話。
> 男子：早安。可以給我一杯大杯拿鐵嗎？
> 女子：當然，還需要其他東西嗎？
> 男子：需要。我再要一個藍莓瑪芬。請問總共多少錢？
> 女子：總共是 6.75 美元。

50. **(D)** Where does this conversation most likely take place?
    (A) At a supermarket
    (B) Ar an office
    (C) At a restaurant
    (D) At a coffee shop

> **中譯** 這段對話最有可能發生在哪裡？
> (A) 在超市
> (B) 在辦公室
> (C) 在餐廳
> (D) 在咖啡店

> **說明** 對話中提到 "Can I get a large latte, please?"（可以給我一杯大杯拿鐵嗎？）顯示對話是發生在咖啡店。

51. **(C)** What does the man order?
    (A) A sandwich and tea
    (B) Coffee and a donut
    (C) A latte and a muffin
    (D) A cappuccino and a bagel

> **中譯** 男子點了什麼？
> (A) 一個三明治和茶
> (B) 咖啡和一個甜甜圈
> (C) 一杯拿鐵和一個瑪芬
> (D) 一杯卡布奇諾和一個貝果

> **說明** 男子點了一杯拿鐵和藍莓鬆餅，答案是 (C)。

52. **(C)** How much does the man have to pay?
    (A) $5.50
    (B) $6.25
    (C) $6.75
    (D) $7.00

中譯　男子需要支付多少錢？
    (A) 5.50 美元
    (B) 6.25 美元
    (C) 6.75 美元
    (D) 7.00 美元

說明　女子說 "That will be $6.75."，所以答案是 (C)。

Questions 53 through 55 refer to the following conversation.

Woman: Excuse me, can you tell me when the next train to Central Station departs?
Man: Sure, the next train leaves at 3:45, and the one after that is at 4:15.
Woman: Great. How long does it take to get there?
Man: It takes about half an hour.

中譯　**問題 53-55 請參考以下對話。**
　　　女子：不好意思，你能告訴我下一班開往中央車站的火車何時出發嗎？
　　　男子：當然，下一班列車是 3:45，之後的那班是 4:15。
　　　女子：太好了。到達中央車站需要多久時間？
　　　男子：大約半個小時。

53. **(C)** Where does this conversation most likely take place?
    (A) At a bus stop
    (B) At an airport
    (C) At a train station
    (D) At a taxi stand

中譯　這段對話最有可能發生在哪裡？
    (A) 在公車站
    (B) 在機場
    (C) 在火車站
    (D) 在計程車站

說明　女子提到 "the next train to Central Station"（下一班開往中央車站的火車），顯示兩人是在火車站。

54. **(B)** When does the next train to Central Station leave?
    (A) At 3:30
    (B) At 3:45
    (C) At 4:00
    (D) At 4:15

中譯 下一班開往中央車站的列車何時出發？
    (A) 3:30
    (B) 3:45
    (C) 4:00
    (D) 4:15

說明 男子回答 "the next train leaves at 3:45"（下一班火車在 3:45 出發），所以答案是 (B)。

55. **(B)** How long does it take to reach Central Station?
    (A) 20 minutes
    (B) 30 minutes
    (C) 40 minutes
    (D) 50 minutes

中譯 到達中央車站需要多久時間？
    (A) 20 分鐘
    (B) 30 分鐘
    (C) 40 分鐘
    (D) 50 分鐘

說明 男子說 "It's about half an hour."（大約半個小時），所以答案是 (B)。

Questions 56 through 58 refer to the following conversation.

Woman: Hi, my name is Emily Carter, and I have a reservation for three nights.
Man: Welcome, Ms. Carter. Let me pull up your reservation. Okay, I see it here. You've booked a standard room with a queen bed.
Woman: That's correct. Could I also request a late check-out on the last day?
Man: Certainly. I'll add that to your booking. Is there anything else you need assistance with?
Woman: No, that'll be all for now. Thank you.
Man: You're welcome. I'll have someone show you to your room.

中譯 問題 56-58 請參考以下對話。

女子：你好，我的名字是 Emily Carter，我預訂了三晚的房間。
男子：歡迎，Carter 女士。讓我查一下您的預訂。好的，我找到了。您預訂的是一間雙人加大床的標準房。
女子：沒錯。我能請求最後一天延後退房嗎？
男子：當然，我會將這個要求加到您的預訂中。還有其他需要幫忙的地方嗎？
女子：沒有了，謝謝你。
男子：不客氣。我會派人帶您到您的房間。

56. **(B)** What is the purpose of the woman's visit?
    (A) To make a reservation
    (B) To check in
    (C) To request room service
    (D) To cancel her booking

中譯 女子來的目的是什麼？
    (A) 預訂房間
    (B) 辦理入住
    (C) 要求客房服務
    (D) 取消預訂

說明 根據對話前面女子確認入住的資訊，以及男子最後說 "I'll have someone show you to your room."（我會派人帶您到您的房間。）表示她是來登記入住的。

57. **(C)** What type of room did the woman book?
    (A) A deluxe suite
    (B) A twin room
    (C) A standard room with a queen bed
    (D) A room with a king bed

中譯 女子預訂的是什麼類型的房間？
    (A) 豪華套房
    (B) 雙人房
    (C) 一間有雙人加大床的標準房
    (D) 一間有特大雙人床的房間

說明　男子提到 "You've booked a standard room with a queen bed"（您預訂的是一間雙人加大床的標準房），所以答案是 (C)。

58. **(A)** What additional request does the woman make?
    (A) A late check-out
    (B) An extra bed
    (C) Room cleaning service
    (D) A room upgrade

中譯　女子提出了什麼額外的要求？
    (A) 延遲退房
    (B) 加床
    (C) 客房清潔服務
    (D) 升級房間

說明　女子說 "Could I also request a late check-out on the last day?"（我可以請求最後一天延遲退房嗎？）所以答案是 (A)。

Questions 59 through 61 refer to the following conversation.

Man: Have you finished reviewing the financial report yet? The deadline to submit it is tomorrow afternoon.

Woman: Not yet, but I should be done by lunchtime today. I just need to verify the figures for the third quarter.

Man: That's good. Can you also double-check the revenue projections for next year? There was some confusion about them during yesterday's meeting.

Woman: Sure, I'll make sure everything is accurate before I send it over.

中譯　**問題 59-61 請參考以下對話。**
男子：你完成了財務報告的審查了嗎？報告的提交截止日期是明天下午。
女子：還沒有，但我應該今天午餐前完成。我只需要核對第三季度的數字。
男子：很好。你能再檢查一下明年的收入預測嗎？昨天的會議上對這部分有些混淆。
女子：當然，我會確保在發送之前一切都準確無誤。

59. **(B)** What are the speakers working on?
    (A) A project proposal
    (B) A financial report
    (C) A marketing strategy
    (D) A presentation for a client

    中譯　對話者正在處理什麼工作？
    (A) 項目提案
    (B) 財務報告
    (C) 行銷策略
    (D) 客戶簡報

    說明　男子提到 "Have you finished reviewing the financial report yet?"（你完成財務報告的審查了嗎？），所以答案是 (B)。

60. **(C)** What is the woman currently reviewing?
    (A) Annual revenue data
    (B) The budget for next year
    (C) Third-quarter figures
    (D) Department expenses

    中譯　女子目前正在審查什麼？
    (A) 年度收入數據
    (B) 明年的預算
    (C) 第三季度的數字
    (D) 部門開支

    說明　女子說 "I just need to verify the figures for the third quarter"（我只需要核對第三季度的數字），所以答案是 (C)。

61. **(D)** What additional task does the man ask the woman to do?
    (A) Prepare a presentation
    (B) Send the report to a client
    (C) Schedule a meeting
    (D) Verify the revenue projections

    中譯　男子要求女子做什麼額外的工作？
    (A) 準備簡報
    (B) 把報告寄送給客戶
    (C) 安排會議
    (D) 核對收入預測

287

說明 男子說 "Can you also double-check the revenue projections for next year?"（你能再檢查一下明年的收入預測嗎？）所以答案是 (D)。

Questions 62 through 64 refer to the following conversation.

Woman: Excuse me, I'm looking for the latest novel by James Grant. Do you have it in stock?

Man: Let me check our system. Yes, we have a few copies left. You'll find them on the second shelf in the fiction section.

Woman: Great, thank you. Also, do you wrap gifts here?

Man: Yes, we do. You can bring the book to the front counter, and we'll wrap it for you.

中譯 問題 62 - 64 請參考以下對話。

女子：不好意思，我在找詹姆斯·格蘭特的最新小說。你們有庫存嗎？

男子：讓我查一下系統。是的，我們還剩幾本。你可以在小說區的第二個書架找到它們。

女子：太好了，謝謝。另外，你們有提供禮物包裝服務嗎？

男子：有的，你可以把書帶到櫃台，我們會幫你包裝。

62. **(A)** What is the woman looking for?
    (A) A book by James Grant
    (B) A gift card
    (C) A magazine
    (D) A non-fiction book

中譯 女子在找什麼？
    (A) 詹姆斯·格蘭特的書
    (B) 禮品卡
    (C) 一本雜誌
    (D) 一本非小說類的書

說明 女子說 "I'm looking for the latest novel by James Grant"（我在找詹姆斯·格蘭特的最新小說），所以答案是 (A)。

63. **(D)** Where is the item the woman wants located?
    (A) On the first shelf
    (B) In the non-fiction section
    (C) Near the front counter
    (D) On the second shelf

288

中譯 女子想要的書在哪裡？
(A) 在第一排書架
(B) 在非小說類書籍區
(C) 在前台附近
(D) 在第二個書架

說明 男子回答 "You'll find them on the second shelf in the fiction section"（你可以在小說區的第二個書架找到），所以答案是 (D)。

64. **(B)** What service does the business offer?
(A) Free delivery
(B) Gift wrapping
(C) A discount on books
(D) A membership program

中譯 公司提供了什麼服務？
(A) 免費送貨
(B) 禮物包裝
(C) 書籍折扣
(D) 會員計劃

說明 男子說 "You can bring the book to the front counter, and we'll wrap it for you."（你可以把書帶到櫃台，我們會幫您包裝。）所以答案是 (B)。

Questions 65 through 67 refer to the following conversation and conference room schedule.

Man: Hi, Sarah. Do you know which room we're using for the client presentation at 10:00?

Woman: Yes, it's in Room B. Room A is booked for the project planning meeting at that time.

Man: Got it. By the way, I noticed Room A is free at 11:00. Should we use it for the follow-up discussion?

Woman: That's a good idea. I'll reserve it now.

中譯 **問題 65-67 請參考以下對話和會議室日程表。**
男子：嗨，Sarah。你知道我們 10:00 的客戶簡報在哪個房間嗎？
女子：知道，會議在 B 室。A 室在那個時間已經預定給專案規劃會議了。
男子：了解。順便問一下，我注意到 A 室在 11:00 是空的。我們要不要用它來進行後續討論？
女子：這是個好主意。我現在就預訂。

Conference Room Schedule

Time	Room A	Room B
9:00-10:00	Marketing Meeting	IT Training
10:00-11:00	Project Planning	Client Presentation
11:00-12:00	Available	Team Building Workshop

會議室日程表

時間	A室	B室
9:00-10:00	行銷會議	IT培訓
10:00-11:00	專案規劃會議	客戶簡報
11:00-12:00	尚可使用	團隊建設工作坊

65. **(C)** Where will the client presentation be held?
    (A) Room A
    (B) The main hall
    (C) Room B
    (D) The cafeteria

中譯 客戶簡報會安排在哪裡？
    (A) A室
    (B) 主會場
    (C) B室
    (D) 自助餐廳

說明 日程表顯示"Client Presentation"在10:00-11:00的Room B，對話中女子確認這一資訊。

66. **(B)** What is happening in Room A at 10:00?
    (A) A marketing meeting
    (B) A project planning meeting
    (C) An IT training session
    (D) A team building workshop

中譯 10:00時，什麼活動正在A室進行？
(A) 行銷會議
(B) 專案規劃會議
(C) 資訊培訓課程
(D) 團隊建設工作坊

說明 圖表顯示 Room A 在 10:00-11:00 的活動是 "Project Planning"（專案規劃會議），對話也提到 Room A 當時被預訂。

67. **(D)** What does the man suggest doing at 11:00?
(A) Reserving Room B for a meeting
(B) Attending the team building workshop
(C) Moving the client presentation to Room A
(D) Using Room A for a follow-up discussion

中譯 男子在11:00時建議做什麼？
(A) 預訂B室開會
(B) 參加團隊建設工作坊
(C) 把客戶簡報移到A室
(D) 用A室進行後續討論

說明 男子提到 Room A 在 11:00 是空閒的，並建議用它來進行後續討論，女子同意了他的提議。

Questions 68 through 70 refer to the following conversation and table.

Woman: Have you looked at the Q3 sales report? North America performed really well in September.

Man: Yes, they had $150,000 in sales, the highest for any region that month. But Europe also showed consistent growth.

Woman: That's true. Their sales increased steadily each month, and they reached $130,000 in September.

Man: Asia's growth was slower, though.

Monthly Sales by Region (Q3)

Region	July Sales	August Sales	September Sales
North America	$120,000	$135,000	$150,000
Europe	$95,000	$110,000	$130,000
Asia	$80,000	$85,000	$90,000

各地區每月銷售（第三季度）

地區	七月銷售額	八月銷售額	九月銷售額
北美	120,000 美元	135,000 美元	150,000 美元
歐洲	95,000 美元	110,000 美元	130,000 美元
亞洲	80,000 美元	85,000 美元	90,000 美元

中譯 問題 68-70 請參考以下對話和表格。

女子：你看過第三季度的銷售報告嗎？北美在九月表現非常好。

男子：有的，他們在九月的銷售達到 150,000 美元，是所有地區中最高的。不過，歐洲也顯示出穩定的成長。

女子：沒錯，他們每個月的銷售都穩定增長，九月達到 130,000 美元。

男子：不過，亞洲的成長較慢。

68. **(C)** Which region had the highest sales in September?

    (A) Asia
    (B) Europe
    (C) North America
    (D) They all had similar sales

中譯 哪個地區在九月的銷售額最高？

    (A) 亞洲
    (B) 歐洲
    (C) 北美
    (D) 它們的銷售額類似

說明 圖表顯示北美在 9 月的銷售額為 $150,000，為當月所有地區中最高，對話中也提到這一點。

69. **(B)** How much did Europe sell in August?

    (A) $95,000
    (B) $110,000
    (C) $130,000
    (D) $150,000

中譯 歐洲在八月的銷售額是多少？
(A) 95,000 美元
(B) 110,000 美元
(C) 130,000 美元
(D) 150,000 美元

說明 表格顯示歐洲在 8 月的銷售額為 $110,000，對話未直接提及，但可從表格中得知答案。

70. **(C)** What do the speakers say about Asia's performance?
    (A) It showed the highest growth
    (B) It had steady growth
    (C) Its growth was slower than other regions
    (D) Its sales exceeded North America

中譯 對話者對亞洲的表現有何評價？
(A) 它增長最多
(B) 它的增長穩定
(C) 它的增長比其他地區慢
(D) 它的銷售超過北美

說明 對話中男子提到 "Asia's growth was slower"（亞洲的成長較慢），所以答案是 (C)。

Part 4

Questions 71 through 73 refer to the following announcement.

Good morning, everyone. This is your captain speaking. We are currently cruising at an altitude of 35,000 feet and expect to arrive at our destination punctually. The weather conditions are fair, and we anticipate a seamless flight. Please inform the cabin crew if you require any assistance.

中譯 **問題 71 - 73 請參考以下廣播。**

各位早安，我是各位的機長。我們目前正以 35,000 英尺的高度飛行，預計準時抵達目的地。天氣狀況良好，我們預期將有一段平穩的飛行。如果您需要任何協助，請通知機組人員。

71. **(A)** Who is most likely addressing the passengers?

  (A) A pilot
  (B) An instructor
  (C) A technician
  (D) A driver

中譯　誰最有可能正在對乘客說話？

  (A) 機長
  (B) 指導員
  (C) 技術員
  (D) 駕駛

說明　對話中提到 captain（機長）、destination（目的地）、flight（飛行），可判斷說話者為機長 (pilot)。

72. **(C)** What is the aircraft's current altitude?

  (A) 28,000 feet
  (B) 32,000 feet
  (C) 35,000 feet
  (D) 38,000 feet

中譯　飛機目前的高度是多少？

  (A) 28,000 英尺
  (B) 32,000 英尺
  (C) 35,000 英尺
  (D) 38,000 英尺

說明　根據 "cruising at an altitude of 35,000 feet"，可得知飛機目前的高度為 35,000 英尺。

73. **(B)** How does the speaker describe the weather conditions?

  (A) Overcast
  (B) Favorable
  (C) Stormy
  (D) Rainy

中譯 發言者如何描述天氣狀況？
(A) 多雲的
(B) 良好的
(C) 有亂流的
(D) 有降水的

說明 機長說 "The weather conditions are fair."（天氣狀況良好。）選項中只有 (B) Favorable 為「有利的、良好的」，其餘錯誤。

Questions 74 through 76 refer to the following talk.
Welcome to the annual company retreat. Today, we have a variety of team-bonding activities planned, starting with a treasure hunt at 10 a.m., followed by lunch at 12:30 p.m. Please make sure to wear comfortable clothes and bring a water bottle.

中譯 問題 74-76 請參考以下談話。
歡迎來到年度公司員工旅遊。今天，我們計劃進行多項團隊合作活動，首先是上午 10 點的尋寶遊戲，隨後是 12:30 的午餐時間。請確保穿著舒適的衣服並攜帶水壺。

74. **(B)** What is the purpose of the event?
(A) To hire employees
(B) To build teamwork
(C) To celebrate a holiday
(D) To announce promotions

中譯 這個活動的目的是什麼？
(A) 雇用員工
(B) 增進團隊合作
(C) 慶祝節日
(D) 公布晉升名單

說明 談話中提到活動是為了團隊合作 (team-building)，因此正確答案是 (B)。

75. **(A)** What is the first activity of the day?
(A) A game
(B) A lunch
(C) A discussion
(D) A workshop

295

中譯 今天的第一個活動是什麼？
(A) 遊戲
(B) 午餐
(C) 討論
(D) 工作坊

說明 第一個活動是尋寶遊戲 (scavenger hunt)，因此正確答案是 (A)。

76. **(B)** What does the speaker recommend participants bring?
(A) A notebook
(B) A water bottle
(C) A laptop
(D) formal clothing

中譯 發言者建議參與者攜帶什麼？
(A) 筆記本
(B) 水壺
(C) 筆記型電腦
(D) 正式衣物

說明 說話者建議員工攜帶水壺，因此正確答案是 (B)。

Questions 77 through 79 refer to the following advertisement.

Attention customers! Experience unbeatable deals during our exclusive flash sale. Selected appliances are discounted by 25%, and footwear purchases qualify for a free accessory with each pair bought. Visit the promotions counter to claim your voucher for additional savings. This limited-time offer ends promptly at 8：30 p.m. tonight.

中譯 **問題 77-79 請參考以下廣告。**

顧客請注意！快來參加我們獨家限時促銷活動。指定家電享 25% 折扣，購買鞋類商品即可免費獲得一個配件。請前往促銷櫃台領取額外優惠券。本活動將於今晚 8：30 準時結束。

77. **(B)** What is being advertised?
(A) A seasonal clearance
(B) A limited promotion
(C) A loyalty program
(D) A new product release

- **中譯** 廣告的活動是什麼？
  (A) 季節性清倉
  (B) 限量促銷
  (C) 忠誠計畫
  (D) 新產品發佈
- **說明** 廣告提到限時促銷活動，因此正確答案是 (B)。

78. **(C)** What is the discount on appliances?
    (A) 10％
    (B) 15％
    (C) 25％
    (D) 40％
- **中譯** 家電的折扣是多少？
  (A) 10％
  (B) 15％
  (C) 25％
  (D) 40％
- **說明** 電器產品折扣為 25％，因此正確答案是 (C)。

79. **(C)** What time does the activity end?
    (A) At 7:30 p.m.
    (B) At 8:00 p.m.
    (C) At 8:30 p.m.
    (D) At 9:00 p.m.
- **中譯** 活動何時結束？
  (A) 晚上 7:30
  (B) 晚上 8:00
  (C) 晚上 8:30
  (D) 晚上 9:00
- **說明** 促銷活動於晚上 8:30 結束，因此正確答案是 (C)。

Questions 80 through 82 refer to the following announcement.

This is a reminder that the downtown library will be closed on Monday for scheduled maintenance. Regular hours will resume on Tuesday at 9 a.m. We apologize for any inconvenience and encourage you to access our digital collection via the library website.

中譯 問題 80 - 82 請參考以下公告。

這是一則提醒，市中心圖書館將於星期一關閉進行例行性維修。圖書館將於星期二上午 9 點恢復正常開放。我們對此造成的不便深表歉意，並建議您透過圖書館網站觀看我們的數位館藏。

80. **(C)** Why will the library be closed?
    (A) For an inspection
    (B) For digital upgrades
    (C) For maintenance
    (D) For a holiday

中譯 為什麼圖書館將關閉？
    (A) 進行檢查
    (B) 進行數位升級
    (C) 進行維修
    (D) 放假

說明 公告提到關閉的原因是 "scheduled maintenance"（例行性維修），因此正確答案是 (C)。

81. **(B)** When will the library reopen?
    (A) On Monday morning
    (B) On Tuesday morning
    (C) On Wednesday afternoon
    (D) On Thursday evening

中譯 圖書館將於何時重新開放？
    (A) 星期一早上
    (B) 星期二早上
    (C) 星期三下午
    (D) 星期四晚上

說明 公告中提到圖書館將於週二上午 9 點恢復正常營業，因此正確答案是 (B)。

82. **(A)** What does the speaker suggest visitors do?
   (A) Use the library's digital resources
   (B) Call the library for assistance
   (C) Postpone their library visit
   (D) Visit other library branches

   中譯 說話者建議訪客做什麼？
   (A) 使用圖書館的數位資源
   (B) 打電話向圖書館尋求幫助
   (C) 延後圖書館參訪計畫
   (D) 去其他圖書館分館

   說明 公告建議訪客透過圖書館網站觀看數位館藏，因此正確答案是 (A)。

Questions 83 through 85 refer to the following telephone message.

Thank you for calling Sunrise Bank. Our office hours are Monday through Friday, 9 a.m. to 5 p.m., and Saturday, 9 a.m. to 1 p.m. Please stay on the line to speak with a representative or visit our website for more information.

中譯 問題 83 - 85 請參考以下電話留言。

感謝您撥打日出銀行。我們的營業時間是週一至週五，上午9點至下午5點，週六上午9點至下午1點。若您想與客服人員交談，請在線上持續等候，或您可上我們官網，了解更多資訊。

83. **(B)** What type of business is being described?
   (A) A restaurant
   (B) A bank
   (C) A hotel
   (D) A retail store

   中譯 這裡描述的是什麼類型的公司？
   (A) 餐廳
   (B) 銀行
   (C) 酒店
   (D) 零售店

   說明 電話留言內提到的是銀行的營業時間，因此正確答案是 (B)。

84. **(B)** When does the office close on weekends?
   (A) At 12 p.m.
   (B) At 1 p.m.
   (C) At 2 p.m.
   (D) At 3 p.m.

   中譯　這間辦公室在週末幾點關閉？
   (A) 中午12點
   (B) 下午1點
   (C) 下午2點
   (D) 下午3點

   說明　星期六營業至下午1點，因此正確答案是 (B)。

85. **(D)** What can callers do if they stay on the line?
   (A) Make a payment
   (B) Leave a message
   (C) Listen to a recording
   (D) talk to an employee

   中譯　如果來電者在線上持續等候，他們可以做什麼？
   (A) 進行付款
   (B) 留下訊息
   (C) 聽錄音
   (D) 與員工交談

   說明　說話者提到在線上持續等候可以與客服人員通話，客服人員也是該公司員工 (employee)，因此正確答案是 (D)。

Questions 86 through 88 refer to the following announcement.

Good afternoon, passengers. This is a pre-boarding announcement for Flight 723 from New York to Los Angeles with a stop in Chicago. We will begin boarding shortly, starting with passengers requiring special assistance and families with young children. After that, we will begin general boarding, starting with passengers in rows 10 through 20. Please have your boarding passes and identification ready.

中譯　問題 86-88 請參考以下廣播。

各位乘客午安。這是航班 723 從紐約前往洛杉磯，中途停靠芝加哥的登機前廣播。我們將很快開始登機，首先是需要特殊協助的乘客和帶有小孩的家庭。之後，我們將開始一般登機，首先是第 10 排到第 20 排的乘客。請準備好您的登機證和身分證明。

86. **(A)** Who will board the flight first?
    (A) Passengers with special needs
    (B) Passengers in rows 10-20
    (C) Business class passengers
    (D) Frequent flyers

中譯　誰將最先登機？
    (A) 需要特殊協助的乘客
    (B) 第 10 排到第 20 排的乘客
    (C) 商務艙乘客
    (D) 常旅客

說明　根據廣播，地勤會先讓需要特別協助的乘客和有小孩的家庭優先登機。

87. **(B)** What should passengers prepare for boarding?
    (A) Luggage tags
    (B) Boarding passes and ID
    (C) Seat assignments
    (D) Flight itineraries

中譯　乘客在登機時應準備什麼？
    (A) 行李標籤
    (B) 登機證和身分證明
    (C) 座位分配
    (D) 航班行程

說明　廣播中明確指出乘客需要準備登機證和身分證件才能登機。

88. **(B)** Where is the flight going?
    (A) New York
    (B) Los Angeles
    (C) Chicago
    (D) Dallas

中譯　這個航班的目的地是？
(A) 紐約
(B) 洛杉磯
(C) 芝加哥
(D) 達拉斯

說明　開頭提到這是從紐約前往洛杉磯，中途停靠芝加哥的航班，因此答案為 Los Angeles。

Questions 89 through 91 refer to the following announcement.

Thank you for visiting Green Valley Zoo. We are open daily from 9:00 AM to 5:00 PM, including weekends and holidays. Don't forget to check out our special penguin feeding session at 2:30 PM every day. Maps and schedules are available at the entrance or online. Enjoy your visit!

中譯　問題 89-91 請參考以下廣播。

感謝您參觀綠谷動物園。我們每天從上午9:00到下午5:00開放，包括週末和假日。別忘了參加我們每天2:30的特別企鵝餵食活動。地圖和時刻表可在入口處或線上獲取與觀看。祝您參觀愉快！

89. **(C)** What is the purpose of this announcement?
　　(A) To promote annual membership
　　(B) To notify about a schedule change
　　(C) To announce operating hours and an event
　　(D) To inform visitors about feeding policies

中譯　這段廣播的目的是什麼？
　　(A) 推廣年度會員
　　(B) 通知時刻表更動
　　(C) 宣布營業時間和活動
　　(D) 通知訪客有關餵食規定

說明　廣播提供了動物園的開放時間以及特別的企鵝餵食活動，目的是向訪客提供相關資訊。

90. **(C)** At what time does the penguin feeding session begin?
    (A) 1:30 PM
    (B) 2:00 PM
    (C) 2:30 PM
    (D) 3:00 PM

中譯　企鵝餵食活動在什麼時候開始？
    (A) 下午 1:30
    (B) 下午 2:00
    (C) 下午 2:30
    (D) 下午 3:00

說明　廣播中提到餵食活動的開始時間是每天下午 2:30。

91. **(B)** Where can visitors find maps of the zoo?
    (A) At the ticket counter
    (B) Online or at the entrance
    (C) At the penguin exhibit
    (D) Near the snack bar

中譯　遊客可以在哪裡找到動物園的地圖？
    (A) 在票務櫃檯
    (B) 在線上或入口處
    (C) 在企鵝展示區
    (D) 在小吃吧附近

說明　廣播中指出地圖可以在入口獲得或在線上觀看，因此答案為 (B)。

Questions 92 through 94 refer to the following announcement.

Attention, residents of Sunnydale Apartments: Maintenance work will be conducted tomorrow from 8:00 AM to 4:00 PM. The water supply will be temporarily shut off during this time. We apologize for any inconvenience and recommend that you store water in advance if needed. Thank you for your understanding.

中譯　**問題 92-94 請參考以下廣播。**

注意，陽光谷公寓的居民：明天上午 8:00 到下午 4:00 將進行維修工作。此期間將會暫時停止供水。我們對此帶來的不便表示歉意，並建議您如果需要請提前儲水。感謝您的諒解。

92．**(B)** What is the announcement mainly about?
　　　(A) A new maintenance service
　　　(B) A water supply interruption
　　　(C) A change in apartment policy
　　　(D) A scheduled power outage

中譯　這則廣播主要是關於什麼？
　　　(A) 一項新的維修服務
　　　(B) 供水中斷
　　　(C) 公寓政策變更
　　　(D) 計劃中的停電

說明　廣播的重點為 "The water supply will be temporarily shut off"，通知住戶維修期間會暫時停止供水。

93．**(C)** How long will the maintenance work take?
　　　(A) 4 hours
　　　(B) 6 hours
　　　(C) 8 hours
　　　(D) 10 hours

中譯　維修工作將持續多長時間？
　　　(A) 4 小時
　　　(B) 6 小時
　　　(C) 8 小時
　　　(D) 10 小時

說明　廣播中提到維修將從早上 8 點到下午 4 點，總共 8 小時。

94．**(D)** What are residents recommended to do?
　　　(A) Avoid using electricity
　　　(B) Contact the maintenance team
　　　(C) Move out temporarily
　　　(D) Store water in advance

中譯　建議居民做什麼？
　　　(A) 避免使用電力
　　　(B) 聯繫維修團隊
　　　(C) 暫時搬離
　　　(D) 提前儲水

說明 廣播建議住戶提前儲水以備不時之需,因此答案為 (D)。

Questions 95 through 97 refer to the following announcement.

Ladies and gentlemen, welcome to the City Art Museum. Our new exhibit, Impressions of Nature, features over 50 paintings and sculptures from renowned contemporary artists. Guided tours are available every hour from 11:00 AM to 3:00 PM. Please note that photography is not allowed in this exhibit. Enjoy your visit!

中譯 **問題 95 - 97 請參考以下廣播。**

女子們,先生們,歡迎來到城市藝術博物館。我們的全新展覽《大自然的印象》展示了來自知名當代藝術家的 50 多幅畫作和雕塑。導覽服務每天提供,每小時一次,時間為上午 11:00 至下午 3:00。請注意,該展覽內禁止拍照。祝您參觀愉快!

95. **(D)** What is the topic of the new exhibit?
 (A) Ancient artifacts
 (B) Historic architecture
 (C) Modern technology
 (D) Nature-inspired artworks

中譯 新展覽的主題是什麼?
 (A) 古代文物
 (B) 歷史建築
 (C) 現代科技
 (D) 以自然為靈感的藝術作品

說明 廣播提到展覽名稱為 Impressions of Nature,表示展覽內容是以自然為主題的藝術作品。

96. **(D)** When is the last guided tour each day?
 (A) 11:00 AM
 (B) 12:00 PM
 (C) 2:00 PM
 (D) 3:00 PM

中譯 每天最後一場導覽是何時?
 (A) 上午 11:00
 (B) 中午 12:00
 (C) 下午 2:00
 (D) 下午 3:00

說明　廣播指出導覽時間從 11:00 AM 到 3:00 PM，因此最後一場導覽是下午 3 點。

97. **(C)** What is prohibited in the exhibit?
　　(A) Eating and drinking
　　(B) Talking loudly
　　(C) Taking photographs
　　(D) Using mobile phones

中譯　展覽中禁止做什麼？
　　(A) 吃喝
　　(B) 大聲交談
　　(C) 拍照
　　(D) 使用手機

說明　廣播中特別提到展覽禁止拍照，因此答案為 (C)。

Questions 98 through 100 refer to the following announcement.

Thank you for attending the Business Conference 2025. We have an exciting schedule of events for you today. The day begins with a Keynote Speech in Hall A at 9:00 AM, where our distinguished speaker will discuss innovation in business. After a short break, Marketing Trends 2025 will take place in Room 101 at 10:15 AM, followed by a Leadership Workshop in Room 102 at 11:30 AM. And don't miss the Networking Strategies session in Hall B at 1:30 PM, which offers a great opportunity to connect with other professionals. Remember to arrive at least 10 minutes early for each session.

中譯　**問題 98-100 請參考以下廣播。**

感謝您參加 2025 年商業會議。我們今天有個令人興奮的活動安排。會議於上午 9 點在 A 廳開始，將有一場主題演講，主講人將討論商業創新。簡短的休息後，2025 年市場營銷趨勢會議將於上午 10:15 在 101 室舉行，隨後在 102 室有一場領導力工作坊，時間為上午 11:30。不要錯過下午 1:30 在 B 廳舉行的建立人脈策略會議，這是一個與其他專業人士聯繫的絕佳機會。請記得每場會議至少提前 10 分鐘到場。

Schedule for Business Conference 2025:

Time	Session Title	Location
9:00 - 10:00	Keynote Speech	Hall A
10:15 - 11:15	Marketing Trends 2024	Room 101
11:30 - 12:30	Leadership Workshop	Room 102
1:30 - 2:30	Networking Strategies	Hall B

2025年商業會議日程

時間	會議標題	地點
9:00 - 10:00	專題演講	A廳
10:15 - 11:15	2024市場營銷趨勢	101室
11:30 - 12:30	領導力工作坊	102室
1:30 - 2:30	建立人脈策略	B廳

98. **(B)** At what time does the Keynote Speech begin?
    (A) 8:00 AM
    (B) 9:00 AM
    (C) 10:15 AM
    (D) 11:00 AM

中譯　專題演講何時開始？
    (A) 上午8:00
    (B) 上午9:00
    (C) 上午10:15
    (D) 上午11:00

說明　根據圖表，Keynote Speech 的開始時間是 9:00 AM，答案為 (B)。

99. **(C)** Where will the Leadership Workshop be held?
    (A) Hall A
    (B) Room 101
    (C) Room 102
    (D) Hall B

中譯　領導力工作坊在哪裡舉行？
    (A) A廳
    (B) 101室
    (C) 102室
    (D) B廳

說明 圖表中顯示 Leadership Workshop 位於 Room 102，因此答案為 (C)。

100. **(D)** What session takes place in Hall B?
   (A) Keynote Speech
   (B) Marketing Trends 2025
   (C) Leadership Workshop
   (D) Networking Strategies

中譯 哪一場會議在 B 廳舉行？
   (A) 專題演講
   (B) 2025 市場營銷趨勢
   (C) 領導力工作坊
   (D) 建立人脈策略

說明 圖表指出 Networking Strategies 的地點是 Hall B，答案為 (D)。

Part 5

101. **(D)** The manager decided to postpone the meeting to next week due to scheduling conflicts.

中譯 經理因為日程衝突決定將會議延期到下週。

說明 postpone 表示「延期」，符合文意。

102. **(B)** The new software update aims to improve the overall performance of the system.

中譯 新的軟體更新旨在改善系統的整體性能。

說明 improve 表示「改善」，符合文意。

103. **(A)** The annual company report was distributed to all employees via e-mail.

中譯 年度公司報告已經透過電子郵件分發給所有員工。

說明 distributed 表示「分發」，符合文意。

104. **(C)** Please make sure to read the instructions carefully before assembling the product.

中譯 請在組裝產品之前仔細看指令。

說明 instructions 表示「指令」，其他選項不符合語境：opinions 表示「意見」，recommendations 和 suggestions 表示「建議」。

105. **(D)** The sales team has developed a strategy aimed at <u>attracting</u> potential clients away from their competitors.
- 中譯　銷售團隊實施了一項策略，旨在吸引競爭對手的潛在客戶。
- 說明　attract 表示「吸引」，其他選項不符合語境：abandon 表示「放棄」，reduce 表示「減少」，advance 表示「促進」。

106. **(C)** The company offers several <u>employee</u> benefits, including health insurance and retirement plans.
- 中譯　公司提供若干員工福利，包括健康保險和退休計劃。
- 說明　employee benefits 是固定搭配，指「員工福利」。

107. **(A)** The restaurant has gained a reputation for its <u>exquisite</u> culinary offerings and impeccable service.
- 中譯　這家餐廳因其精緻的菜餚和無可挑剔的服務而聲名遠揚。
- 說明　句意為 exquisite 表示「精緻的」，有「造型優美、細緻」的涵義，符合文意。其他選項不符合語境：excessive 表示「過度的」，indifferent 表示「冷漠的」，substantial 表示「大量的」。

108. **(A)** It is crucial to <u>put away</u> important documents to ensure their security.
- 中譯　將重要文件妥善放置以確保其安全是至關重要的。
- 說明　put away 是固定片語，表示「妥善收好」，符合句意。其他選項的意思分別是：take over 表示「接管」，set up 表示「建立」，turn in 表示「提交」。

109. **(D)** The CEO emphasized the importance of <u>effective</u> communication between departments.
- 中譯　CEO 強調部門間有效溝通的重要性。
- 說明　effective 表示「有效的」，符合文意。

110. **(C)** We are pleased to announce that the project was completed <u>ahead of</u> schedule.
- 中譯　我們很高興宣布項目提前完成。
- 說明　ahead of schedule 表示「提前」，符合文意。

111. **(B)** The team leader asked if everyone has received the agenda for the meeting.
- 中譯 組長詢問是否每個人都已經收到會議議程。
- 說明 asked 是過去式，問句需用現在完成式 "has received" 表示「是否已經收到」。

112. **(A)** By the time we arrived at the venue, the presentation had already started.
- 中譯 當我們到達時，演講已經開始了。
- 說明 看到 By the time，主要子句通常使用過去完成式。

113. **(D)** Company policy requires all employees to submit their timesheets by Friday afternoon.
- 中譯 公司政策規定所有員工必須在星期五下午前提交工時表。
- 說明 require 後要接不定詞 (to + V)，to submit 表示「要求提交」。

114. **(C)** If we complete the project by next month, we will receive a bonus.
- 中譯 如果我們在下個月之前完成這個專案，我們將會獲得獎金。
- 說明 if 引導條件子句，主要子句是未來式 will，條件子句需用現在簡單式 complete。

115. **(A)** The new regulations will go into effect starting next Monday.
- 中譯 新的規定將於下週一開始生效。
- 說明 will 後需接原形動詞，go into effect 是固定搭配，表示「生效」。

116. **(D)** She is one of the employees who are consistently recognized for their hard work.
- 中譯 她是其中一位因勤奮工作而持續獲得認可的員工。
- 說明 who 引導形容詞子句，指代 one of the employees，由於 employees 為複數，所以需用複數動詞 are。

117. **(B)** Neither the manager nor the team members were satisfied with the outcome of the meeting.
- 中譯 經理和團隊成員都對會議的結果不滿意。

310

說明　Neither ... nor 後的動詞與靠近的主詞一致，team members 為複數，須用 were。

118. **(C)** The project is on schedule, <u>although</u> there are a few minor adjustments that need to be made.
中譯　雖然需要進行一些小調整，但該專案仍在進度內。
說明　although 是連接副詞子句的正確選項，意思是「儘管如此」或「雖然如此」，表示兩個對比的情況，符合句意。

119. **(A)** The job posting indicates that candidates <u>must have</u> a degree in computer science.
中譯　職缺公告指出，應徵者必須擁有電腦科學相關學位。
說明　must 後接原形動詞，must have 表示「必須擁有」。

120. **(D)** The project should be completed <u>by</u> the close of business today, so that we can meet the client's deadline.
中譯　該專案應在今天下班前完成，以便我們能夠趕上客戶的截止日期。
說明　the close of business today 表示「表示在今天工作結束之前」，固定搭配。

121. **(C)** The director, <u>having reviewed</u> the project proposal, decided to allocate additional resources to ensure its success.
中譯　經過審查專案提案後，導演決定分配更多資源以確保專案的成功。
說明　這是分詞構句的正確使用，表示"在審核了項目提案之後"，用"having reviewed"來表達兩個動作的先後關係。

122. **(A)** To qualify for the position, applicants must <u>demonstrate</u> strong communication skills.
中譯　為了符合該職位的資格，應徵者必須展示出強大的溝通能力。
說明　must 後要接原形動詞，demonstrate 表示「展現」。

123. **(D)** The new software update will <u>refine</u> the user interface, making it more intuitive and easier to navigate.
中譯　新的軟體更新將優化使用者介面，使其更加直觀且更易於導航。

> **說明** will 後要接動詞原形 refine 來表達對「用戶介面」進行改進的動作，意思是「改善」或「完善」，這與句子中「將改進」的語境相符。

124. **(C)** The company has consistently sought <u>to enhance</u> the efficiency of its production processes through innovative technology.
> **中譯** 公司一直致力於透過創新技術提升生產流程的效率。
> **說明** 這裡需要的是動詞原形，表示「提升」公司在處理客戶詢問時的效率。

125. **(A)** The board of directors will meet next week to discuss the <u>approval</u> of the proposal.
> **中譯** 董事會將於下週召開會議，討論提案的批准事宜。
> **說明** 句意為「討論提案的批准」，discuss 後面要加受詞，approval 是名詞，符合句意。

126. **(D)** The CEO's decision to <u>recalibrate</u> the company's expansion strategy has resulted in significant growth in new markets.
> **中譯** 執行長重新調整公司擴展策略的決定，已帶來新市場的顯著成長。
> **說明** 這裡需要的是動詞原形，表示「重新調整」公司的擴展策略。

127. **(C)** The team managed to complete the project on time <u>in spite of</u> the unexpected delay.
> **中譯** 儘管有意料之外的延誤，團隊還是設法按時完成了專案。
> **說明** in spite of 表示「儘管」，用於引出逆境，後面會接名詞或名詞短語，符合句意和語法規則。

128. **(B)** <u>Having finished</u> the presentation, the team gathered feedback from the audience.
> **中譯** 在完成報告後，團隊從觀眾那裡收集了意見。
> **說明** 這是分詞構句，表示在完成某事後，接著進行其他動作。

129. **(A)** The factory has increased production capacity to meet the growing <u>demand</u> for its products.
> **中譯** 工廠已提高生產能力，以因應產品需求的增長。
> **說明** demand 表示「需求」，符合文意。

130．**(D)** The manager's competence in resolving the issue demonstrated his leadership skills.

中譯　經理在解決問題上的能力展現了他的領導技巧。

說明　這裡需要的是名詞形態，表示「能力」或「勝任」，符合句子語境。

Part 6

問題 131 - 134 請參考以下的信件。

主旨：辦公室翻新通知

親愛的團隊，

我們很高興通知您，我們的辦公室將於下週一開始進行翻新。預計翻新工程將持續兩週，期間某些區域可能會暫時無法進入。為了將干擾降至最低，我們已為員工 ¹³¹**安排了替代的工作空間。** ¹³²**此項目已經過精心規劃，以確保對員工的影響降到最小。**

請注意，施工噪音有時可能會影響 ¹³³**生產率**。我們建議大家根據需要使用降噪耳機。

此外，三樓的會議室在此期間將無法使用。感謝您在我們進行這些改善工作以創造更舒適、更現代化的工作環境時，對我們的 ¹³⁴**耐心**與理解。

如有任何問題或疑慮，請隨時聯繫我們，電子郵件地址為 facility@company.com。

設施管理部敬上

131．**(A)** To minimize disruptions, we have set up alternative workspaces for employees.

中譯　為了將干擾降至最低，我們已為員工安排了替代的工作空間。

說明　set up 表示「安排」，符合文意。其他選項的意思：set off（補償）、set out（著手）、set in（開始），都不符合語境。

132. (A) We are excited to see the positive changes these renovations will bring.
(B) All employees must vacate the building during the renovation period.
(C) This project has been carefully planned to ensure minimal inconvenience to staff.
(D) Construction permits have been approved by local authorities.

中譯 (A) 我們很高興看到這些翻新將帶來的積極變化。
(B) 所有員工在翻新期間必須撤離大樓。
(C) 此項目已經過精心規劃，以確保對員工的影響降到最小。
(D) 建築許可證已經獲得當地主管機關的批准。

說明 選項 (A) 正面但過於籠統，且不符合此處強調「規劃」與「減少不便」的上下文。選項 (B) 過於嚴苛，且與前文提供替代空間的說明矛盾。選項 (C) 強調精心規劃並減少不便，與上下文完美契合。選項 (D) 與上下文無直接關聯，和段落核心主題無關。

133. **(B)** Please note that construction noise may occasionally affect productivity.

中譯 請注意，施工噪音有時可能會影響生產率。

說明 productivity 是名詞，用來指「生產率」，符合語法與句意。其他選項：productive（形容詞：富有成效的）、production（名詞：生產）、productively（副詞：有效率地）都不適用。

134. **(D)** We appreciate your patience and understanding as we make these improvements to create a more comfortable and modern workspace.

中譯 感謝您在我們進行這些改善工作以創造更舒適、更現代化的工作空間時，對我們的耐心與理解。

說明 patience 表示「耐心」，符合文意。其他選項：information（資訊）、consent（同意）、decision（決定），均與句意不符。

問題 135 - 138 請參考以下信件。

主旨：顧客滿意度調查

親愛的尊貴顧客，

感謝您最近向我們購買商品。我們致力於提供最佳服務，¹³⁵ **您的意見將用於改善我們的顧客體驗策略**。請花幾分鐘時間完成我們的線上滿意度調查。

您的回答將幫助我們找出需要改進的地方，並確保我們的產品符合您的 ¹³⁶ **期望**。調查表可在 5 分鐘內填寫完成，所有回答將 ¹³⁷ **保密處理**。

為了聊表心意，在 5 月 15 日以前完成調查表的參與者將有機會參加抽獎，獎項為 50 美元的禮品卡。請點擊 ¹³⁸ **以下**連結填寫調查表。

感謝您的時間與支持。

客服團隊敬上

---

135. (A) want to take this opportunity to tell you about our new line of products
   (B) we encourage you to be completely honest in providing feedback
   (C) your feedback will be used to improve our customer experience strategy
   (D) ask for your opinions about our latest advertising and marketing campaign

   【中譯】(A) 我們想藉此機會向您介紹我們的新產品系列
   (B) 我們鼓勵您在提供意見時完全坦誠
   (C) 您的意見將用於改善我們的顧客體驗策略
   (D) 徵求您對我們最新廣告和行銷活動的意見

   【說明】這一空格的內容應該與「顧客意見對我們的發展至關重要」相呼應。選項 (C) 強調顧客意見對改善顧客服務體驗策略的重要性，與原文前後文想表達的方向一致。

136. **(B)** Your responses will help us identify areas for improvement and ensure that our products meet your expectations.

   【中譯】您的回答將幫助我們找出需要改進的地方，並確保我們的產品符合您的期望。

説明　句意為「確保我們的產品滿足您的期望」。expectations 表示「期望」，符合文意。其他選項：exceptions（例外）、inspections（檢查）、explanations（解釋）都與句意不符。

137．**(C)** The survey should take no more than 5 minutes to complete, and all responses will remain confidential.

中譯　調查表可在 5 分鐘內填寫完成，所有回答將保密處理。

説明　confidential 表示「保密的」，符合句意。其他選項：protected（受保護的）、conditional（有條件的）、optional（非強制的）都不符。

138．**(B)** To access the survey, please click on the link below.

中譯　請點擊以下連結填寫調查表。

説明　below 表示「下方」，符合文意。其他選項：above（上方）、aside（旁邊）、near（附近）都不適用。

問題 139-141 請參考以下公告。

> 主旨：即將舉行的工作坊報名
>
> 親愛的員工：
>
> 我們很高興宣布將舉辦一場職業發展工作坊，主題是提升團隊合作與溝通技巧。工作坊將於 6 月 10 日在市中心的訓練中心舉行。名額有限，請 [139] 立即報名。
>
> 參與者將參加互動式活動和小組討論，[140] 這些環節將促進所有參與者的合作氛圍。現場將提供午餐和茶點。
>
> 若要報名，請上人力資源入口網站並填寫報名表。您的報名 [141] 確認後，將會收到一封確認郵件。
>
> 如果您有任何問題，請隨時聯繫人力資源部。我們期待在工作坊見到您，希望您覺得本活動寓教於 [142] 樂。
>
> 人力資源部敬上

139. **(B)** Space is limited, so please register immediately.
   中譯 名額有限，請立即報名。
   說明 immediately 表示「立即」，符合文意。其他選項：completely（完全地）、occasionally（偶爾）、consistently（持續地）都不合適。

140. **(A) These sessions will foster a collaborative environment for all participants.**
   (B) Teamwork is one of the core values we strive to promote within the organization.
   (C) We believe this workshop will provide valuable insights for improving group dynamics.
   (D) Workshops like this are integral to building a strong and cohesive workforce.
   中譯 **(A) 這些環節將促進所有參與者的合作氛圍。**
   (B) 團隊合作是我們努力在組織內部推廣的核心價值之一。
   (C) 我們相信這個工作坊將提供有價值的見解，幫助改善團體動態。
   (D) 像這樣的工作坊對於建立強大且團結的員工隊伍至關重要。
   說明 前面的句子需要補充「設計這些活動的目的是鼓勵合作」。選項(A)提到促進合作氛圍，符合上下文語境。

141. **(D)** A confirmation e-mail will be sent once your registration is verified.
   中譯 您的報名確認後，將會收到一封確認郵件。
   說明 verified 表示「驗證」，符合文意。其他選項：declined（被拒絕）、postponed（被延遲）、ignored（被忽略）不符。

142. **(A)** We look forward to seeing you at the workshop and hope you find it both informative and enjoyable.
   中譯 我們期待在工作坊見到您，希望您覺得本活動寓教於樂。
   說明 enjoyable 表示「有趣的」，符合文意。其他選項：convenient（便利的）、promising（有前途的）、optional（可選擇的）不適用。

問題 143 - 146 請參考以下的信件。

主旨：新員工入職培訓

親愛的新團隊成員：

歡迎加入我們的公司！我們非常高興您能成為我們的一員，並期待和您一起共事。為了幫助您起步順利，我們已安排了下週一上午 9 點在主會議室舉行的新員工入職培訓。

在入職培訓中，您將了解公司的政策、福利和流程。您還將見到團隊中的關鍵成員，他們將幫助您 [143]**適應**新的角色。

請攜帶政府頒發的身分證明和尚未 [144]**提交**給人力資源部的任何文件。[145]**這將有助於我們有效地規劃並確保所有必要的安排都已完成**。如果您無法參加培訓，請至少提前 24 小時通知我們。我們將盡力安排替代的培訓時間。

再次歡迎加入我們的團隊！我們對未來的旅程充滿期待，相信您在這裡的時光將是既有收穫又 [146]**受益匪淺**。

人力資源部敬上

---

143. **(D)** You will also meet key members of the team who will assist you in <u>adapting</u> to your new role.

中譯 您還將見到團隊中的關鍵成員，他們將幫助您適應新的角色。

說明 adapting 表示「適應」，符合句意。其他選項：changing（改變）、converting（轉換）、agreeing（同意）都不符。

144. **(B)** Please bring a government-issued ID and any documents that you have not yet <u>submitted</u> to HR.

中譯 請攜帶政府頒發的身分證明和尚未提交給人力資源部的任何文件。

說明 submitted 表示「提交」，符合文意。其他選項：permitted（允許）、returned（歸還）、notified（通知）不符。

318

145. (A) We appreciate your flexibility and understanding in scheduling this session.
(B) Timely updates help maintain a smooth and organized orientation process.
(C) Your prompt communication helps us better accommodate your onboarding needs.
(D) This will allow us to plan effectively and ensure all necessary arrangements are made.

中譯 (A) 我們感謝您在安排這次培訓時的靈活性與理解。
(B) 您的迅速溝通有助於我們更好地安排您的入職需求。
(C) 您及時的更新有助於保持入職培訓過程的順利和有條理。
(D) 這將有助於我們有效地規劃並確保所有必要的安排都已完成。

說明 此處句子應補充與「提前通知」相關的意義，且需與後文「安排替代會議」的語境一致。選項(D)符合上下文需求。

146. **(D)** We are excited about the journey ahead and are confident you will find your time here both rewarding and beneficial.

中譯 我們對未來的旅程充滿期待，相信您在這裡的時光將是既有收穫又受益匪淺。

說明 beneficial 表示「有益的」，符合句意。其他選項：substantial（重大的）、mutual（相互的）、effective（有效的）和語境不符。

Part 7

問題 147-150 請參考以下的電郵。

主旨：會議重新安排

親愛的團隊：

由於不可預見的情況，¹⁴⁷ 我們原定於星期三下午 3：00 的 ¹⁴⁸ 每週會議已更改為星期四同一時間。議程保持不變，¹⁵⁰ 我們仍將在 A 會議室召開會議。

請根據新的安排調整您的時間表，¹⁴⁹ 如無法參加，請通知我。感謝您的理解。

營運經理

¹⁴⁹ **Emily Harper 敬上**

319

147．**(D)** To announce a change of schedule
中譯　宣布會議時間變更
說明　根據第一句 "Due to unforeseen circumstances, our weekly meeting… has been moved"，此郵件的目的是通知會議時間的更改。其他選項與郵件內容不符。

148．**(B)** Thursday at 3:00 PM
中譯　星期四下午 3：00
說明　郵件提到 "… moved to Thursday at the same time"，即原定於星期三下午 3 點的會議改到星期四，時間不變。

149．**(B)** Inform Emily Harper
中譯　通知 Emily Harper
說明　郵件中提到 "notify me if you are unable to attend"，參與者需通知發信人 Emily Harper 無法出席的情況。

150．**(D)** Conference Room A
中譯　A 會議室
說明　郵件提到 "we will still meet in Conference Room A"，會議地點不變，仍在 A 會議室。

問題 151 - 155 請參考以下廣告。

---

[151]推出全新的 Aeroflex 2000 吸塵器

Aeroflex 2000 現已在所有主要零售店上架！[155]這款吸塵器設計以最佳效率和易使用性，具備強大的吸力、輕巧的結構和先進的空氣過濾技術。

主要特點：

　・[152]HEPA 過濾系統可捕捉 99.9% 的灰塵和過敏原
　・可調吸力級別，適用於不同表面
　・可拆卸手持配件，便於清潔狹小空間

[153]於 6 月 30 日前購買 Aeroflex 2000 可享有 20% 折扣。[154]欲了解更多詳情，請上官網：www.aeroflex.com

---

320

151. **(A)** To promote a new product
中譯　宣傳新產品
說明　這是一篇介紹 Aeroflex 2000 吸塵器的廣告，目的是宣傳該新產品。其他選項（如解釋清潔技術或宣布店鋪地點）與文意不符。

152. **(B)** HEPA filtration system
中譯　HEPA 過濾系統
說明　文中提到 "HEPA filtration system to capture 99.9% of dust and allergens"，即 HEPA 過濾系統能幫助減少過敏原。其他選項（如調節吸力或輕量設計）與過敏不相關。

153. **(C)** June 30
中譯　6月30日
說明　廣告提到 "Purchase the Aeroflex 2000 by June 30 to receive a 20% discount"，折扣優惠到6月30日截止。

154. **(B)** By visiting the website
中譯　上網站
說明　文中提到 "Visit www.aeroflex.com for more details"，客戶可以上官網了解更多資訊。

155. **(D)** A home appliance
中譯　家用電器
說明　選項 (A) cleaning product（清潔產品）指的是清潔劑，像是洗衣精、洗碗精等。文中介紹的 vacuum cleaner（吸塵器）為家用電器，因此選 (D)。

問題 156 - 160 請參考以下公告。

主旨：新的停車規定

親愛的員工，

[159]從 **7月1日起**，[156]將實施新的停車規定，以確保更安全、更有序的停車體驗。[157]**所**有員工必須向人力資源部門登記車輛，並在擋風玻璃上顯示有效的停車許可證。

停車位將根據部門和資歷分配。沒有有效許可證或停放在未授權區域的員工將收到警告通知。[158]**重複違規可能會導致罰款或停車特權被撤銷。**

[160]**如有任何問題或疑慮，請聯繫人力資源部門**，電子郵件地址是 hr@company.com。

感謝您的配合。
設施管理部敬上

---

156. **(B)** To ensure safety and organization
   - 中譯　確保安全和秩序
   - 說明　公告提到 "to ensure a safer and more organized parking experience"，新規定的目的是確保停車安全與秩序。

157. **(C)** Register their vehicles with HR
   - 中譯　向人力資源部門登記車輛
   - 說明　公告明確說明 "All employees must register their vehicles with the HR department"，需將車輛向人力資源部門登記。

158. **(A)** They will lose their parking privileges
   - 中譯　失去停車特權
   - 說明　公告中提到 "Repeated violations may result in fines or revocation of parking privileges"，多次違規者可能會被撤銷停車權限。

159. **(C)** July 1
   - 中譯　7月1日
   - 說明　公告提到 "Starting July 1, new parking regulations will be implemented"，新規定於7月1日生效。

160. **(D)** To the HR department
   - 中譯　人力資源部門
   - 說明　公告中提到 "For questions or concerns, please contact HR"，有問題可聯絡 HR 部門。

問題 161-165 請參考以下文章。

本地企業擴展至新市場

[161]科技專業方案，為領先的軟體服務提供商，昨日宣布將在東南亞的三個新的國家擴展業務。這一舉措是公司長期戰略的一部分，旨在滿足對數位轉型解決方案日益增長的需求。

[162]該公司計劃在越南、印尼和菲律賓[164]於年底前設立區域辦事處。[163]這些辦事處將專注於為各行業的企業提供客制化的軟體解決方案，包括零售、醫療保健和製造業。

[165]根據 CEO Michael Lee 的說法：「我們的擴展體現了我們為全球客戶提供創新解決方案的承諾。」

---

161. **(B)** A company's international expansion
   - 中譯　一家公司的國際擴展
   - 說明　文章主旨為「科技專業方案將業務擴展至三個新的國家」，內容聚焦於國際擴展，符合選項 (B)。

162. **(A)** Vietnam, Indonesia, and the Philippines
   - 中譯　越南、印尼和菲律賓
   - 說明　文中提到 "regional offices in Vietnam, Indonesia, and the Philippines"，公司將擴展至這三個國家。

163. **(B)** To offer tailored software solutions
   - 中譯　提供量身定制的軟件解決方案
   - 說明　文章提到 "focus on providing customized software solutions for businesses"，customized 為「(按顧客要求) 訂做」，新辦事處的目的是提供量身定制的軟體解決方案，選項 (B) tailored 為「特製的」符合題義。

164. **(D)** By the end of the year
   - 中譯　(D) 年底之前
   - 說明　文中提到 "by the end of the year"，表示公司計畫在年底前建立新辦事處。

323

165. **(C)** The CEO of TechPro Solutions
中譯　科技專業方案的 CEO
說明　quote 為「引用」，文中引用了 CEO Michael Lee 的話，"Our expansion reflects our commitment..."，因此引用的對象是公司 CEO。

問題 166 - 170 請參考以下公告。

> 主旨：新的健康和保健計劃
>
> 親愛的團隊：
>
> ¹⁶⁶**我們很高興地宣布，新的健康和保健計劃將於下個月啟動。**這項計劃旨在促進更健康的工作環境，並支持員工達成他們的健身和健康目標。
>
> 主要福利：
>
> - ¹⁶⁷**每週免費瑜伽**和冥想課程
> - ¹⁷⁰**本地健身房會員折扣**
> - 提供在線平台，包含健身小秘訣和健康食譜
>
> ¹⁶⁸**要參加，請**¹⁶⁹**在 3 月 20 日之前透過人力資源門戶網站註冊。**名額有限，建議儘早註冊。如有任何問題，請聯繫 wellness@company.com。
>
> 期待與您見面！
>
> 人力資源總監
> 梅根·卡特敬上

166. **(B)** To promote a health program
中譯　推廣健康計劃
說明　這封郵件是關於公司推出新的健康和保健計劃。目的是促進員工的健康，並支持他們達成健身和健康目標，因此正確答案是 (B)。

167. **(B)** Weekly yoga sessions
中譯　每週瑜伽課程
說明　公告中提到的主要福利之一是「每週的瑜伽和冥想課程」，因此 (B) 是正確答案，其他選項（如免費健身房會員等）並未在公告中提及。

324

168．**(D)** Register on the HR portal
中譯　在人力資源門戶網站註冊
說明　公告中提到，員工需要透過 "HR portal" 註冊參加這個計劃。選項 (C) 是正確的，其他選項（如直接發郵件或致電）並未提到。

169．**(D)** March 20
中譯　3月20日
說明　公告中明確指出 "To participate, please sign up through the HR portal by March 20"，因此必須在 3 月 20 日之前註冊。

170．**(C)** It includes discounts for gym memberships.
中譯　包括健身房會員折扣
說明　文中提到，健康和保健計劃提供的福利包括 "Discounts on local gym memberships"，因此選擇 (C)，其他選項和文中描述不符。

問題 171 - 175 請參考以下文章。

> [171]**城市公共圖書館推出24小時還書服務**
>
> 本市的中央公共圖書館宣布安裝了自動還書系統，該系統全天候運行，為會員提供了更大的便利。[172]**新系統位於圖書館主入口**，[175]**允許用戶在任何時間還書，即使是在正常開館時間以外。**
>
> 圖書館館長蘇珊·佩雷斯表示：「這項舉措反映了我們提升社區所有會員便利性的承諾。」她補充說，[173]**圖書館計劃在未來幾個月內在分館安裝類似的系統。**
>
> 會員需注意，[174]**逾期書籍仍將收取滯納費。**

171．**(B)** To introduce a new library service
中譯　介紹新的圖書館服務
說明　24/7 的意思為「24小時，每周七天，表示無時無刻」，文章主要介紹了市圖書館新推出的24小時自動還書服務，因此答案是 (B)。其他選項並不符合文章的主題。

172．**(B)** At the library's main entrance
中譯　圖書館的主入口
說明　文中提到，新的自動還書系統設置在圖書館的 "main entrance"，因此選項 (B) 是正確的。其他選項與位置不符。

173. **(D)** To expand the system to other branches
中譯　將系統擴展到其他分館
說明　根據報導，圖書館的計劃是將這一系統擴展到其他分館，因此答案是 (D)。其他選項（如增加書籍收藏、提供免費會員等）與文中計劃不符。

174. **(C)** They still apply to overdue books.
中譯　逾期書籍仍需支付滯納費。
說明　文章提到 "members are reminded to return books on time to avoid late fees, which will still apply if items are overdue"，這表示逾期的書籍仍會收取罰款，因此答案是 (C)。其他選項不正確。

175. **(C)** It makes returning books more convenient.
中譯　讓還書更方便。
說明　文中提到，新的自動還書系統提供 24 小時還書的服務，使得用戶可以在任何時間還書，這使得還書變得更加便利。因此選擇 (C)。

問題176-180請參考以下公告、廣告和電子郵件。

給：全體員工

主題：年度公司野餐

日期：6月5日

親愛的團隊：

¹⁷⁶**我們很高興地宣布，年度公司野餐將於6月24日（星期六）在 Riverside 公園舉行，上午10點開始**。這是員工和家人共度歡樂時光的好機會。

活動包括遊戲、燒烤午餐和現場音樂表演。¹⁷⁹ **請於6月15日前填寫已發送到您電子信箱的線上表單以回覆參加意願。**

期待見到大家！
人力資源部敬上

> **讓您的活動難忘 —— 選擇 PartyCaterers**
>
> 為您的下一次活動尋找美味的餐點嗎？PartyCaterers 提供各種餐飲選擇，適合企業活動、家庭聚會和派對。
>
> 我們的套餐包括：
>
> - 燒烤自助餐：享受新鮮燒烤的肉類和配菜。
> - 素食選項：健康且美味的佳餚。
> - 自訂菜單：根據您的需求和偏好量身打造。
>
> [177] **在 6 月 10 日之前預訂餐飲服務，可享 10％折扣！**
>
> 立即致電 555 - 1234 或造訪 www.partycaterers.com 了解更多詳情。

> 寄件人：[178] John Smith
>
> 收件人：人力資源部
>
> 主旨：公司野餐建議
>
> 人力資源團隊您好：
>
> 我對即將到來的 Riverside 公園公司野餐感到很興奮！[178] **我想建議增加幾個活動，例如團隊合作接力賽或參加者的小型抽獎活動。**
>
> 此外，[180] **燒烤午餐是否會提供素食選項？** 我知道包括我在內的幾位員工都會很感激這一點。
>
> 期待參加這次活動！
> John 敬上

176．**(B)** To provide details about a picnic

> 中譯　提供野餐的詳細資訊
>
> 說明　第一篇文章的主要目的是告知員工公司野餐的詳細資訊，包括時間、地點和活動安排，其他選項不符合公告內容的重點。

177．**(D)** A 10％ discount on packages

> 中譯　可享 10％ 的折扣優惠

> 說明　第二篇文章明確提到在 6 月 10 日前預訂可享有 10% 的折扣。其他選項如免費送餐或特殊禮物並未提及。

178．**(B)** A relay race and a raffle
> 中譯　接力賽和抽獎活動
> 說明　第三篇文章中，John 提到他建議新增接力賽和抽獎活動作為額外的活動選項。其他選項未提到或與內容不符。

179．**(C)** June 15
> 中譯　6 月 15 日
> 說明　第一篇文章中明確指出員工需要在 6 月 15 日之前登記。其他日期不符合公告中的規定。

180．**(D)** The availability of vegetarian options
> 中譯　是否提供素食選項
> 說明　John 在郵件中詢問是否有素食選項，因為他和其他員工可能需要這樣的選擇，其他選項如音樂品質或活動地點並未提到。

問題 181-185 請參考以下電子郵件、廣告和分析報告。

寄件人： 行銷經理：艾蜜莉·布朗
收件人： 產品開發團隊
主旨： 聰明環保水壺推出計畫
親愛的團隊成員：   ¹⁸¹隨著我們準備於 7 月推出全新的聰明環保水壺，我想強調一些關鍵的行銷策略：   1. 社群媒體活動：從 6 月 15 日開始，我們將與網紅合作推廣此產品。 2. 零售合作夥伴關係：我們已與綠意市場 (GreenMart) 等主要零售商達成協議。 3. 顧客意見計劃：預推出的產品測試將包括來自我們忠誠計劃的 100 名顧客。   ¹⁸³請確保在 6 月 10 日之前準備好最終的產品樣品供測試使用。如有任何問題，請隨時告訴我。   艾蜜莉敬上

推出聰明環保水壺

尋找耐用且環保的飲水解決方案嗎？聰明環保水壺由 100% 回收材料製成，並擁有創新的設計，方便日常使用。

主要特色：

- 防漏瓶蓋：確保您的包包不會漏水。
- [182] **保溫效果：可保持飲料的熱度或冷度長達 12 小時。**
- 輕巧便攜：非常適合旅行及戶外活動使用。

現在訂購，即可在 7 月 1 日前享有 15% 的早鳥折扣！

立即上 www.ecosmartbottle.com 下單購買。

2023 年環保產品趨勢

最近的研究顯示，消費者在購買時越來越重視可持續性。超過 65% 的受訪消費者偏好選擇由回收材料製成的產品，此趨勢由年輕一代引領。

關鍵見解：

- [184] 社群媒體在影響購買決策中扮演著至關重要的角色，尤其是對於環保產品。
- 與注重環保的零售商合作證明能有效提升產品的曝光度。
- 顧客重視產品對環境影響的透明度。

[185] **由於聰明環保水壺使用回收材料，並且擁有強大的線上行銷策略，它在這些趨勢中擁有優勢，能夠利用這些機會。**

---

181. **(D)** To outline marketing strategies for a new product

    中譯 概述新產品的行銷策略

    說明 Emily 的電子郵件主要討論即將推出的聰明環保水壺的行銷策略，包括社群媒體活動、零售合作和客戶回饋計畫，清楚地表明其目的是概述行銷計畫。其他選項如確認日期或設計變更並未提到。

182. **(C)** It holds temperature for 12 hours.

    中譯 保溫 12 小時

    說明 retention 表示「保持」，hold 為「保持、保留」，第二篇文章明確提到，聰明環保水壺可保持飲品 **12 小時的溫度**，這是產品的一個主要賣點。其他選項（如內建過濾器、多種尺寸）並未在文章中出現。

183. **(B)** June 10
中譯　6月10日
說明　Emily 的郵件提到，**6 月 10 日** 是完成產品樣本準備的最後期限，以便進行客戶測試。其他選項如 6 月 15 日或 7 月 1 日在文章中提到的用途不同。

184. **(C)** Social media influence
中譯　社交媒體影響力
說明　第三篇文章提到，社交媒體對消費者的購買決策（特別是對環保產品）具有關鍵影響力，這是市場分析中的一個關鍵見解。其他選項雖然可能相關，但並未在文章中被強調為關鍵因素。

185. **(A)** Focus on recycled materials and sustainability
中譯　著重於回收材料與可持續性
說明　聰明環保水壺的一大優勢是使用 100％ 回收材料製造，這與消費者對環保產品的偏好相符。其他選項（如降低生產成本或更長保固期）並未在文章中提及。

問題 186-190 請參考以下備忘錄、網站和電子郵件。

收件人：銷售團隊
寄件人：區域經理，[186] **大衛・金**
主旨：全球貿易博覽會準備工作
親愛的團隊成員： 正如大家所知，[186] **全球貿易博覽會將於 9 月 15 日至 9 月 18 日在德國法蘭克福舉行**。這是展示我們新產品線、與國際客戶建立聯繫以及尋找潛在經銷商的絕佳機會。 關鍵事項： 　1. 報告材料：請確保所有促銷手冊和樣品產品在 9 月 10 日之前運送到展會現場。 　2. [188] **會議安排：請在 8 月 25 日前確認與重要客戶的會議預約。** 　3. 文化敏感度：記得了解參展地區的風俗和禮儀。 　如有任何問題，請隨時聯繫我。讓我們共同努力，確保此次活動的成功！ 大衛敬上

歡迎來到 2023 全球貿易博覽會

全球貿易博覽會是國際企業聯繫與合作的領先平台。今年，我們很高興迎來來自 30 個國家的 500 多家參展商，並預計將有 20,000 名與會者。

活動亮點：
- 專題討論：[190]**向業界領袖學習全球貿易的最新趨勢。**
- 產品展示：親身體驗最前端的創新產品。
- 聯誼活動：在輕鬆的氛圍中建立寶貴的商業聯繫。

[187]**別錯過由創新公司執行長 Elena Morales 博士於 9 月 16 日上午 10 點在 A 展廳的專題演講。**

請上 www.globaltradeexpo.com 獲取更多詳細資訊以及報名資訊。

寄件人：物流協調員，[189]約翰・泰勒

收件人：大衛・金

主旨：博覽會運送安排

大衛你好：

我想更新一下關於全球貿易博覽會運送過程的情況。[189]**促銷手冊和產品樣品已經包裝完成，並將於 9 月 5 日透過快遞運送。預計它們會在 9 月 8 日之前到達法蘭克福，遠早於 9 月 10 日的截止日期。**

此外，我已與貨運公司聯繫，確保在運送過程中妥善處理這些材料。如果還有任何其他需要的事項，請告訴我。

約翰敬上

---

186. **(D)** To outline the objectives of attending the expo

　中譯　概述參加博覽會的目標

　說明　David Kim 的備忘錄明確指出了參加 Global Trade Expo 的主要目標，包括展示新產品、建立聯繫和尋找潛在分銷商，並提供了相關準備的細節。其他選項未被提及。

331

187. **(B)** A keynote speech will be delivered.
中譯 舉行一場專題演講。
說明 根據第二篇文章，**Dr. Elena Morales** 的主題演講將於 **9 月 16 日上午 10 點**在 Hall A 舉行。其他選項如展示會或聯誼活動未與該時間對應。

188. **(A)** August 25
中譯 8 月 25 日
說明 David 的備忘錄明確指出，與主要客戶確認約見的最後期限是 **8 月 25 日**。其他日期屬於其他事項的截止日期。

189. **(B)** September 8
中譯 9 月 8 日
說明 John 的電子郵件提到，宣傳資料將於 9 月 5 日寄出，預計 9 月 8 日抵達法蘭克福，比截止日期 9 月 10 日提早。

190. **(C)** Learning from industry leaders
中譯 向業界領袖學習
說明 第二篇文章提到活動亮點包括業界領袖的座談，這為參加者提供學習最新貿易趨勢的機會。其他選項（如貸款或優先運輸）未在文章中提及。

問題 191 - 195 請參考下列新聞報導、備忘錄和分析。

全球科技公司和創新科技宣佈合併協議

全球科技公司和創新科技方案正式宣布決定合併，將組成業界最大的科技公司之一。這筆價值 120 億美元的合併案預計將在 12 月 31 日前完成，前提是獲得監管機構的批准。

全球科技執行長羅伯特·林表示：「這次合併讓我們能夠充分利用創新科技在軟體開發方面的專業知識，同時擴大我們的全球市場覆蓋。」創新科技的執行長瑪麗亞·桑托斯補充道：「透過聯手合作，我們可以加速創新，並為客戶提供更好的解決方案。」

[191]這家新公司將命名為全球創新公司，並將在統一領導團隊下營運，[194]預計在三年內節省 15 億美元的成本。

332

收件人：財務部門

寄件人：財務長辦公室

主旨：全球科技-創新科技合併過渡計劃

親愛的團隊：

作為即將進行的合併的一部分，將會進行一些財務和操作上的變更：

1. [191]**預算整合：所有部門預算需在 11 月 15 日前調整。**
2. 員工培訓：關於新的統一財務系統的培訓課程將於 10 月 1 日開始。
3. 季度報告：合併後的 Q4 財務報告將使用更新的系統編制，並於 1 月 10 日提交。

在過渡期間，您的合作對於確保順利的整合過程至關重要。如有任何問題，請聯繫財務長辦公室。

財務長
琳達·鍾敬上

全球科技-創新科技合併的行業影響

全球科技和創新科技的合併預計將顯著改變科技行業的競爭格局。分析師預測，這家新公司全球創新將在軟體和硬體解決方案領域成為市場領導者。

主要影響：
- 競爭加劇：較小的公司可能會因為無法與兩家公司合併後的資源競爭而面臨困難。
- [195]**客戶受益：由於效率提升，合併可能會導致價格下降並改善服務。**
- 創新潛力：通過合併研發的努力，全球創新很可能會比競爭對手更快推出尖端技術。

然而，一些專家警告說，[193]**整合過程可能會帶來挑戰，例如合併企業文化和調整運營系統等問題。**

---

191. **(A)** Reduced operational costs

中譯 降低營運成本

說明 根據第一篇新聞報導，合併後的新公司全球創新預計在三年內**節省 15 億美元的成本**。這顯示出減少營運成本是合併的一大優勢，其他選項（如改善員工福利或擴大法律資源）未被提及。

192. **(B)** November 15
   中譯 11月15日
   說明 根據第二篇備忘錄，所有部門的預算必須在 **11月15日** 前整合完成，以配合合併過程的要求。其他日期對應不同的事項。

193. **(B)** Difficulty in merging corporate cultures
   中譯 合併企業文化的困難
   說明 第三篇行業分析提到，專家警告合併過程可能面臨的挑戰包括**整合企業文化**及調整營運系統，其他選項並未在文章中提及。

194. **(D)** $1.5 billion
   中譯 15億美元
   說明 第一篇新聞公告提到，新公司預計在三年內節省 15 億美元的成本。

195. **(C)** Improved services at lower prices
   中譯 以更低的價格提供更好的服務
   說明 第三篇行業分析指出，合併帶來的效率提升可能使客戶受益，包括**降低價格與改善服務**，其他選項（如延長產品保固或快速交付）未被提及。

問題 196-200 請參考以下公告和評論。

歡迎來到大地平線酒店

親愛的貴賓：

感謝您選擇入住大地平線酒店。為了確保您擁有愉快的住宿體驗，請注意以下服務與設施：

1. 免費早餐：每日提供，時間為早上 6:30 至 10 點，在一樓的海景餐廳。
2. 健身中心：24 小時開放，供所有賓客使用。請於前台索取門禁卡。
3. 接駁服務：[196]**提供免費接駁車服務**，往返市中心，每小時一班，營運時間為早上 8 點至晚上 10 點。**請至少提前 30 分鐘在禮賓櫃台預約座位。**
4. [199]**客房服務：**全天候 24 小時提供。請從房間電話撥打 #101 進行訂餐。

如有任何問題或特殊需求，請隨時聯絡我們的前台團隊，我們將全天候為您服務。

祝您住宿愉快！

管理團隊敬上

> **莎拉‧P 的評論**
>
> 我最近因公出差入住了大地平線酒店，總體來說，這次體驗是愉快的。免費早餐為我的早晨提供了良好的開始，我也很欣賞可選擇的多樣化食物。
>
> 接駁服務對於前往市中心非常方便，儘管有時我的會議會開得較晚，[197] **我希望最後一班接駁車能延後至更晚時間，**[198] **而不是只到晚上 10 點。**[200] 健身中心設備齊全，但如果能提供瑜伽墊，那會更好。
>
> 房間乾淨舒適，[198] **客房服務員反應迅速且有禮貌**。我也很喜歡前台團隊全天候 24 小時服務，隨時解答任何問題。
>
> 大致來說，我會推薦這家酒店給其他出差的商務旅客。

196. **(D)** Book their seat in advance
   中譯　提前預訂座位
   說明　根據第一篇公告，客人需提前至少 30 分鐘在禮賓櫃台預訂座位才能使用接駁車服務，其他選項（如出示房卡或支付費用）未在公告中提及。

197. **(B)** The shuttle service schedule
   中譯　接駁服務班次
   說明　Sarah 的評論提到，接駁車服務雖然便利，但她希望最後一班接駁車的時間能夠延後，因為她的會議有時會開到很晚。其他選項（如早餐不足或缺乏清潔服務）並非她提到的問題。

198. **(C)** 10:00 PM
   中譯　晚上 10:00
   說明　第一篇文章明確指出，接駁車服務的運行時間是早上 8 點到晚上 10 點，最後一班車於晚上 10 點發車。

199. **(C)** Room service
   中譯　客房服務
   說明　第一篇文章提到，房間服務 24 小時提供；Sarah 的評論也提到，房間服務的員工非常及時且禮貌。其他選項（如停車、洗衣服務或延遲退房）未在兩篇文章中提及。

200. **(D)** Providing yoga mats
   中譯　提供瑜伽墊
   說明　Sarah 提到健身中心設備齊全，但建議提供瑜伽墊會更好，其他選項（如延長開放時間或增加器材）並非她的具體建議。

335

EZ TALK

完全剖熙新制多益：聽力、閱讀、口說高效應考指南

作　　　者：申芷熙	
責 任 編 輯：潘亭軒	
審　　　訂：Judd Piggott	
封 面 設 計：兒日設計	
版型設計與排版：洪伊珊	
圖 片 出 處：https://www.shutterstock.com	
行 銷 企 劃：張爾芸	
錄 音 後 製：采漾錄音製作有限公司	
錄音員：Jacob Roth、Leah Zimmermann、James Baron、Jenny Hsu	

完全剖熙新制多益：聽力、閱讀、口說高效應考指南/申芷熙著. -- 初版. -- 臺北市：日月文化出版股份有限公司, 2025.03
　　面；　公分. -- (EZ talk)
ISBN 978-626-7641-23-1(平裝)

1.CST: 多益測驗

805.1895　　　　　　　　　　　114001010

發 行 人：洪祺祥
副 總 經 理：洪偉傑
副 總 編 輯：曹仲堯
法 律 顧 問：建大法律事務所
財 務 顧 問：高威會計事務所

出　　　版：日月文化出版股份有限公司
製　　　作：EZ 叢書館
地　　　址：臺北市信義路三段 151 號 8 樓
電　　　話：(02) 2708-5509
傳　　　真：(02) 2708-6157
客 服 信 箱：service@heliopolis.com.tw
網　　　址：www.heliopolis.com.tw
郵 撥 帳 號：19716071 日月文化出版股份有限公司

總 經 銷：聯合發行股份有限公司
電　　　話：(02) 2917-8022
傳　　　真：(02) 2915-7212
印　　　刷：中原造像股份有限公司
初　　　版：2025 年 3 月
定　　　價：380 元

No part of this publication may be reproduced, stored in a retrieval system, or transmitted by any means, electronic, mechanical, photocopying, recording or otherwise, without the prior permission of the copyright holder.

◎版權所有 翻印必究
◎本書如有缺頁、破損、裝訂錯誤，請寄回本公司更換